DANGEROUS GAMES

GILLIAN GODDEN

Boldwood

First published in Great Britain in 2022 by Boldwood Books Ltd.

Copyright © Gillian Godden, 2022

Cover Design by Colin Thomas

Cover Photography: Colin Thomas

The moral right of Gillian Godden to be identified as the author of this work has been asserted in accordance with the Copyright, Designs and Patents Act 1988.

Every effort has been made to obtain the necessary permissions with reference to copyright material, both illustrative and quoted. We apologise for any omissions in this respect and will be pleased to make the appropriate acknowledgements in any future edition.

A CIP catalogue record for this book is available from the British Library.

Paperback ISBN 978-1-80280-107-1

Large Print ISBN 978-1-80280-106-4

Hardback ISBN 978-1-80280-105-7

Ebook ISBN 978-1-80280-109-5

Kindle ISBN 978-1-80280-108-8

Audio CD ISBN 978-1-80280-100-2

MP3 CD ISBN 978-1-80280-101-9

Digital audio download ISBN 978-1-80280-102-6

Boldwood Books Ltd
23 Bowerdean Street
London SW6 3TN
www.boldwoodbooks.com

For my son, Robert. This is for your birthday.
Happy Birthday, Robert.
Mum.

1

THE RUNAWAY

'Come on, Antonias, get up. Shush now, quickly.' The bedroom was in darkness; only the moonlight shining through the blinds at the windows gave a little light to see by. Antonias yawned and rubbed his eyes.

'Mummy, where are we going?' The little boy, just five years old, looked up at his mother as she pulled back the bedclothes and began manoeuvring him out of his bed.

'Shush, Antonias, we're going to play a little game of hide and seek on Grandma and Granddad. Get up, now. Let's be as quiet as mice.'

Little Antonias was still half asleep, and bleary eyed. It was the middle of the night. He stood while his mother dressed him in a T-shirt and trousers.

Annette was already dressed. She was being as quiet as she could, so she didn't disturb the rest of the household, but even her breathing seemed to make a noise, and her heart was pounding in her ears.

Annette would be glad to see the back of this place. When she had met Marias on holiday, she'd thought this was going to be *la dolce vita*, the sweet life. But all she had got was life on a boring grape farm, owned by his parents.

She was nervous but tried to hide it; she didn't want to frighten her beautiful little boy. His mop of hair – golden, like her own – was a rarity, considering he was half-Italian, although his blue eyes were like his father's – his, and that bitch, Miriam's.

Smiling and hugging him close to her, Annette made it all seem like a little secret game they were going to play.

Antonias was still rubbing his eyes, and smiling and giggling with his mummy, when Annette picked up the holdall containing the money she had taken from the safe. Miriam, her mother-in-law, had given her a cheque, but it wasn't enough; she needed more if she was going to leave this place and start again.

Annette took Antonias's hand and crept down the dark staircase, towards the front door. She opened it carefully, then turned and took one last look around the hallway, before stepping out into the darkness of the vineyard.

She winked at Antonias and put her finger to her lips, to indicate to him to be quiet. Slowly, they started to walk the long path that led up to the main road.

Annette had to carry Antonias half of the way. Although he was excited by the game, he was tired, and the night air made him shiver.

As Annette got closer to the main road, she looked around frantically. She was nearly out of breath. What with the holdall and little Antonias to carry, she was exhausted.

She looked around again and finally spotted the truck. It was parked in a lay-by, with its headlights on low beam. Carlos got out and smiled at her, and then he saw Antonias and the smile faded.

Carlos had made life worth living again. Annette had met him at the vineyard – he'd been one of the many extra hired hands they used when the grapes were ready for picking. That was a busy time

– when all the grapes were ripe and needed to be picked and stored quickly.

Carlos was exciting and funny. Annette had first seen him when she'd heard the loud, clanging dinner bell and looked out of her bedroom window. All the workers were coming in from the fields to the tables that were laden with food for them all, but it was Carlos who caught her eye.

Normally, Annette never bothered with anything to do with the vineyard. She didn't like being away from the excitement of big cities, and the place had seemed like a prison to her, especially over the last couple of years. Her husband, Marias, worked all the hours God sent and seemed to expect her to settle down here, like his mother, Miriam, had, all those years ago.

Once Carlos was on the scene, however, Annette amazed the household with her sudden eagerness to help out, as she joined them outside and offered to pour the wine and help serve the food to the workers.

Some of the hired hands, men and women who temporarily worked at many farms, offering manual labour, were grateful just to have food in their bellies. The Lambrianus were good employers who paid good wages. They were a reputable family, and had worked hard all their lives. They knew the meaning of giving their workers a good meal in their bellies, and money to pay the rent. Some of the workers were regulars who came back year after year.

Annette had watched Carlos in the hot midday Italian sun, strutting around and flirting with the young women who were working there. He also laughed and joked with the older women. He was a charmer and everyone liked him. Annette certainly liked what she saw. Tanned from the sun, and wearing only shorts and a white vest, stained from all the red grapes he had picked, he would flex his strong, muscled arms, knowing that the women at the vineyard were watching him. He was vain and proud, but as poor as a church mouse.

Carlos had noticed Annette hanging around, her long blonde hair swinging around her shoulders making her stand out from the rest. He had watched her serving the wine and glancing in his direction.

'You English, *si*?' he had asked her one day, daring to speak to the boss's wife and at the same time breaking the ice with an innocent question.

'Yes, I'm from London,' she had said, and blushed.

He had laughed with her and the others at the tables, calling her the 'queen', because only the queen lived in London, and here she was serving the wine.

Carlos had flirted with her, and she with him, whenever possible, although she always ignored him when her husband or the foreman were around, and especially when Miriam's eyes followed her like a hawk.

Annette hated her mother-in-law and resented the way she monopolised Antonias. She had to admit that, in some respects, Miriam was a good woman who wanted the best for her family, but Annette wanted more than just to be a wife and mother, buried in the back of beyond.

She wanted to go to Naples and Rome and enjoy the clubs and the nightlife Italy had to offer. Annette had expected married life to be so different.

She had met Marias on holiday, and it had been such a whirlwind romance she had decided to stay longer. Seeing the vineyard in all its glory, and realising the wealth it carried with it, had made it seem too good an opportunity to miss.

Marias worked the vines all day, and when they were able to go out, they did, but then Antonias came along and everything changed.

Annette had been expected to drop into a family routine of looking after little Antonias, and having more children to follow him. But she had soon grown bored with it all.

It didn't matter that Marias told her that one day Antonias would be a rich man and inherit everything; Annette wanted her share now.

It was actually Miriam's vineyard, and it hadn't always been a vineyard. It had once been a farm, but during Miriam and Fredo's married life, the farm had started doing badly. They had one bad crop after another, yet the bills still had to be paid. There was a living in it, but not much of one.

Fredo made wine for a hobby, using the grapes on their land. And so, to pass the time, he made a small number of bottles for himself, plus some he shared with friends.

His friends had enjoyed the wine and praised it; it had a taste all of its own. When word spread about this local winemaker, the owner of a small nearby restaurant had come to taste 'Fredo's wine', and liked it.

He had taken half a dozen bottles on sale or return. It had surprised them both that the bottles had sold and the wine was popular.

More orders were put in, and soon Fredo was taking on extra help to pick his grapes. Eventually, they decided to give up on the farm and to grow more grapes, instead.

Fredo had found his niche and he was starting to make more money out of the wine than he ever had, living hand to mouth from the farm.

The hot Italian sun made the grapes grow full and large, and Fredo knew just when to pick them, when they were at their best.

Fredo and his best friend, Alfonso, whom he had known since childhood, picked the grapes together, after Alfonso's farm fell on hard times and drained all of his funds. Fredo moved Alfonso and his family in with them, and gave him money to help pay off some of the debts he owed.

Alfonso had spoken many times of a cousin who lived on the other side of Italy. He was starting an import and export business and wanted Alfonso and his family to join him, but they couldn't afford to go.

Alfonso was a good and trusted friend and after Fredo and Miriam had talked things through together, they felt they should help him.

Fredo had given Alfonso the equivalent of 500 pounds, a lot of money at that time, but the wine sales were taking off.

He had been sad to see his childhood friend leave, but had wished him well in his new venture.

'I will pay you back, Fredo, every penny of this, I promise, someday I will pay you back for your kindness.'

'We are friends, Alfonso, I do not want your money, only your friendship. There is no debt,' said Fredo.

They had hugged each other, Fredo knowing that he would probably never see Alfonso again.

Shortly after Alfonso had left, the owner of a large restaurant in the city had come to taste Fredo's wine and had liked it very much. They offered Fredo a regular contract but had written on the contract that they wished to purchase 'Lambrianu Vineyard wine', rather than 'Fredo's wine'.

Fredo and Miriam had both agreed that, while it would always be known as 'Fredo's wine' to them, their surname did give the wine more class, and would be easier to sell, and so 'Lambrianu Vineyard wine' was born.

Their own son, Marias, had started working with his father as a young boy, and had learnt how and when to pick the grapes. He had seen the operation grow into a sizeable business. Fredo had taken a huge loan out, using the farmland and the house as collateral, and had used the money to pay for sterilising equipment, bottles and labelling.

But it had all been worth it. The vineyard had more orders than it could cope with and Fredo bought up nearby farmland, to plant more grapevines. It was all a great success.

Marias didn't need to work the vines with his father, but they both still enjoyed it. Life was good for the Lambrianu family.

Then Marias had met Annette when she was visiting Italy, and had instantly fallen in love with her. Her pale skin and long blonde hair had bewitched him. He had taken her home to meet his parents and visit the vineyard, and when he had asked her to stay in Italy and marry him, she had agreed.

Annette had seemed to enjoy playing the lady of the manor and receiving beautiful jewellery from her husband, but then she'd had Antonias and things had started to go wrong.

Miriam was obsessed with her blond-haired, blue-eyed grandson. And Annette began to resent the way Miriam lavished money on him, when he didn't need it.

Marias was always busy with business meetings with some client. And Annette simply wasn't interested in the vineyard. She was young; she wanted to go out dancing the night away. Annette didn't like the responsibility of a child and his needs, and felt she was far too young to become burdened with motherhood.

And then she had seen Carlos, who eased the boredom. He made her smile again.

Annette had told him tales of life back in London and Big Ben, and elaborated on the truth when she boasted about how many famous people she knew. He seemed impressed, and listened intently.

After several days of talking and mild flirtation, Carlos had taken a napkin full of bread and cheese, walked away from the lunch gathering and gone into one of the nearby fields, to eat his lunch.

Annette had watched him leave and had felt sad. She'd waited for the other workers to take their food into a nearby barn for shade and, making sure she wasn't seen, she had sneaked off to find Carlos.

Carlos lay in the field, perched on his elbow, his head resting in his hand. He'd known Annette would come. He knew she was smitten, and it was time to make his move. She was a beautiful woman, and now she would be his.

Annette had sat beside him while he told her how beautiful she was. He reached up to move a wisp of hair from her face and she had felt the excitement bubbling up inside her.

Tentatively, Carlos had kissed her cheek and, noticing she didn't pull away, he moved closer to kiss her on the lips.

After that first kiss, Carlos and Annette started an illicit and dangerous affair. The stolen moments they spent in the fields became Annette's whole world. Carlos's lovemaking seemed exciting and forbidden, and when Marias reached out for her in the night, she feigned sleep.

Carlos knew Annette was now putty in his hands, and that she owned half of a vineyard. He saw the fine jewellery she wore, and she was always giving him money when he said he might have to leave the vineyard to find better-paid work.

Annette was to be his ticket out of this never-ending peasant life; she could take him to London, and he would live like a rich man.

After six weeks of passion and excitement, and all the wonderful plans Carlos had made for them – if only he had the money – things had come to a head. Fate had stepped in.

One day as they were lying in the warm Italian sun, the shrill screams of panic filled the air. Annette and Carlos looked up at the sky from where they lay. They heard the commotion, straightened their dishevelled clothing and ran towards the vineyard. The foreman was ringing the farm bell and people were running around, then suddenly Annette heard the shocking news.

'Marias has been in an accident, quick, help! Marias is injured!'

Everyone in the house ran out to see what had happened. Miriam and Fredo had recently bought an adjoining field. It was overgrown and hadn't been used in years. Marias had gone out with the farmers to oversee the chopping down of the trees. One of the tractors had got stuck, and Marias and the foreman had gone around the back of it to see what the problem was.

The handbrake of the tractor hadn't been put on properly and it had rolled backwards, over Marias; he was trapped under the wheels.

The foreman, not wanting to move him, had first secured the tractor then run back to the vineyard, to raise the alarm.

An ambulance was called. The foreman tried driving the tractor forward, to release Marias from the wheels. Marias was screaming and shouting in pain. At least he was still alive.

The workers were going to construct a makeshift stretcher to lift him, but Miriam thought it would be better not to move him until the ambulance came.

When they finally arrived, the paramedics gave Marias a hefty injection of painkillers and he slipped into a deep unconsciousness.

It was obvious to them that half of Marias's body had been crushed and they moved the unconscious man as gently as they could onto a stretcher and put him in the back of the ambulance. Miriam had gone with them to the hospital.

The worst news ever, for Miriam, was that Marias's right leg was so crushed it would have to come off to give him any chance of survival.

During his hospital stay, Annette had played the dutiful wife and sat by his side, crying and showing distress while he was in a delirium, and after he had undergone extensive surgery.

But Miriam did not believe Annette. She had always been suspicious of her motives for marrying Marias, and recent gossip about her sudden interest in the farm workers and the vineyard only fuelled her suspicions. She'd voiced her opinions to her husband many times that Annette had only married Marias for what she could get out of the union.

She turned accusing eyes to her daughter-in-law. 'Where were you, Annette?' she said. 'Playing in the fields with the hired help, again?' Miriam felt bitter. She'd had a good idea what Annette had been up to with Carlos, but had kept quiet, hoping it would run its course. Now she was disgusted; not only had she turned a blind eye, but the wife of her beloved son had been with a farm hand while Marias had been crushed under a tractor, and he was now fighting for his life.

Marias didn't wake up; he got an infection in his remaining leg, which led to gangrene, and that, too, had to be amputated. A month later, despite the doctors doing everything they could to save him, he died.

Annette was secretly pleased; she hadn't wanted to play nursemaid to her crippled husband. She knew Miriam would have forced her to look after Marias, out of guilt, if not out of love.

Annette had loved Marias in her own way, but they had just been so different in their outlook to life. Marias had enjoyed a quiet family life, which was what he was used to, whereas Annette wanted fun and excitement.

Annette decided she was not going to be a widow for the rest of her life. She started making plans with Carlos, and shortly after Marias's funeral she approached Miriam.

'I've decided to go back to my family in England, Miriam. There is nothing for me here now. I need a fresh start; this place has too many memories,' she had said, then put her hands to her face and started to cry. The tears were not for Marias, they were for herself.

Annette was wearing black again, and would be expected to visit that little church in the vineyard grounds, that Miriam loved so much, and pray for Marias. She had tried to play on Miriam's sympathy, but it wasn't working.

'I understand, Annette,' said Miriam, for the first time seeing her cold-hearted daughter-in-law for what she truly was. She had only ever wanted Marias's money, and didn't care for anyone but herself. 'While you're getting yourself sorted out back in England, why don't you leave little Antonias here?' She had just lost her son, she didn't want to lose her grandson, as well.

Annette ignored the question about Antonias; she knew he was all Miriam cared about now. 'I'll need money,' she said, 'to find us both somewhere to live. Did Marias make a will or some sort of arrangement for us?' She knew Miriam didn't give a fig about her. As far as her mother-in-law was concerned, Annette could leave without a penny. That wasn't going to happen, however, and so she persisted. 'Can I have my share of the vineyard? Surely, I am entitled to something.' She cleared her throat. 'Actually, I don't want the vineyard, just Marias's money. I am his widow, after all, and I have our son to look after. Antonias, at least, has a share in all of this.'

Annette was pushing the subject hard, now.

Miriam nodded. Now she understood. Annette was prepared to sell Antonias to her, he was her bargaining tool.

Annette knew that if she let the boy stay, should she ever need any more money, she could blackmail Miriam – all she'd have to do would be to get in touch and let her know she was going to take Antonias away from her, and she would pay. Stupid old woman.

'How much do you think you would need, Annette?' said Miriam. Her voice was calm, although she was sick to her stomach. She knew Annette's intentions were not honourable. If she had been truly grief-stricken and wanting to go home, Miriam would have understood, but she felt this was more to do with Carlos than Antonias.

Both women knew exactly what they were talking about, although neither of them would say the words: Annette would leave Antonias behind for a price.

'Fifty thousand of your English pounds, Annette, is the best I can do for you now. Later, depending on how much your home costs and what your expenses come to, we will talk again.' Miriam took out her cheque book and wrote out the cheque.

Annette was disgusted; that wasn't enough. There was Marias's share and Antonias's, too, and this old bitch thought 50,000 would cover that? More to the point, was that all she thought Antonias was worth?

Annette smiled to herself. No way, thought Annette; she would take the money *and* Antonias.

During the night, when everyone was in bed, Annette had gone into the room where the safe was kept. She had watched Marias take money out of it many times and, without him realising, she had noted the key code number. There was the equivalent of 10,000 pounds in the safe; it was the wages for the workers and the petty cash. She took it all out and stuffed everything into a holdall.

That done, she had gone into the bedroom where Antonias was sleeping, taken him from his bed and disappeared into the night.

* * *

'Take him, Carlos, he's heavy.' Annette was breathing heavily.

Carlos was not happy that the spoilt brat, Antonias, was going with them. That was certainly not what he had planned. He had tried talking Annette into leaving him behind and she'd agreed.

'Why have you brought the boy?' Carlos whispered. 'Wouldn't Miriam give you the money?'

'I got it, and more,' said Annette, trying to appease him. 'Look.' Annette opened the holdall and showed him the cash she had taken from the safe; she was pleased when she saw Carlos smile.

He laid Antonias in the back seat of the truck, kissed Annette, then they jumped in the front and drove off into the night.

Annette lay her head back on the seat and smiled. This was the beginning of her new life. She was with Carlos, who had told her many times how much he loved her, and she loved him.

She had paid that bitch Miriam back for her greed and the inconsideration shown for her needs. She was glad to see the back of the place. This was going to be a whole new adventure.

She would be back in London, where she belonged. Annette laughed to herself. She would love to be a fly on the wall when Miriam discovered that she had gone and taken Antonias with her.

* * *

Miriam was being served breakfast by one of the maids. She was surprised that little Antonias wasn't up yet. He always ate breakfast with her and Fredo, and then went to church with his nonna and sat beside her while she prayed. Little sleepyhead, where was he?

'Please go and see if Antonias is awake yet,' she said to the maid.

The maid returned after just a few minutes. She was almost too frightened to tell Miriam what she'd found.

'Well?' said Miriam, when the woman remained silent.

'He's... he's not there, Mrs Lambrianu,' she said. 'His bed has been slept in, but he's not there, and he isn't with Mistress Annette, either. Her bed is empty, too.'

Miriam and Fredo looked across the breakfast table at each

other. Fredo lowered his newspaper and watched his wife jump out of her seat and run upstairs.

The maid was right; Antonias wasn't there. Miriam opened the wardrobes; his clothes were still there, but he wasn't. She ran into Annette's bedroom. Her clothes were still there, too, but Miriam noticed that her jewellery box was empty and had been tossed aside.

Instinctively, Miriam knew exactly what Annette had done. She had gone, and she had taken Antonias with her!

Miriam went downstairs and was informed by Fredo that the safe was empty. She had taken everything.

Against Fredo's wishes, Miriam telephoned the police, desperate to find Annette and her beloved Antonias. She instructed the maid to ring the large bell outside, to gather as many of the workers as possible to search the land, just in case they were both out there, somewhere.

Although Miriam feared it was fruitless, she also reckoned anything was worth a try. She was desperate and panic-stricken. More to the point, Annette had double-crossed her!

Miriam vowed she would find Antonias and bring him home, where he belonged, no matter how long it took.

The police informed Miriam and Fredo that, apart from the money being stolen from the safe, no crime had been committed. Antonias was Annette's son, and she could do as she pleased where he was concerned. Miriam didn't tell them about the other money she had given Annette.

The police said they would look for her and arrest her for the theft of the money from the safe, but that was all they could do when they found her.

Fredo spoke up, then, and insisted he wouldn't have Annette arrested for the theft. All they wanted was to know that she and Antonias were safe.

He blamed Miriam as much as he did Annette for entering into this tug of war, fighting and using his grandson as they had. He thought that after Annette returned home, she would write to them and inform them of her and Antonias's whereabouts.

He wanted to keep the peace; any contact with his grandson was better than none, and Miriam threatening Annette with the police wasn't going to make her come back.

Miriam was hot-tempered and acted in haste, whereas Fredo was a mild-mannered man who didn't want to frighten Annette. She had just lost her husband; she wasn't thinking straight.

He assured Miriam that after Annette and Antonias had had a break from everything, they would come back. After all, they only had the money from the safe, and that wasn't going to last forever.

Fredo didn't know that Miriam had given Annette money on the understanding she would let Antonias stay with them. He would have been angry if he had known she was prepared to buy her own grandson.

For now, Miriam had to admit defeat. She checked the mail every day, in the hope that there would be some news, but none came.

A week after Annette and Antonias had disappeared, Miriam sat alone in Fredo's study; she'd had an idea. Maybe, just maybe, all of Annette's family were as greedy as her. She searched for Annette's address book and found it, which meant she had the names and addresses of all her family members.

Annette hadn't kept in touch with any of them, as far as Miriam knew, apart from the odd Christmas card, but it was better than doing nothing.

Miriam picked up her pen and started writing letter after letter to the names in the address book. She explained that Annette had been grief-stricken after Marias's death and, feeling alone in her grief, had wandered off.

Miriam wrote in her letters that she needed to know that both Annette and Antonias were with them, and safe. She expressed her concern and, more to the point, she offered a reward for any information.

Miriam felt she had done her best; all she had to do now was wait and pray. Surely one of them would take pity on her and write back?

She was riddled with guilt and felt that what had happened had perhaps been of her own doing. Maybe she should have given Annette more money.

Would she ever see or hear from little Antonias again? Where was he? Was he safe?

2

TOGETHER AT LAST

Life back in London was great. Even the rain felt different. Annette, Carlos and Antonias had booked into a five-star hotel, and spared no expense.

They were happy together; this was living! Having left without any luggage, they had spent a few days in Rome, before their flight, shopping and buying expensive clothes. Carlos had been in his element.

The hotel offered a childminding service, much to Carlos's delight, because he was sick of hearing Antonias constantly moaning about going home to see his nonna, so much so he had been forced to hit him on occasion to shut him up.

Carlos liked the casinos; he liked to flash the cash at the roulette tables. Sometimes he won, sometimes he didn't, but either way, it was exciting and thrilling. They both went out every night, drinking and dancing and having fun, leaving Antonias with a childminder.

He had talked Annette into banking the cheque immediately, just in case Miriam stopped it, and had convinced Annette to withdraw all the money from her account and close it. He said that

Miriam would be looking for her, especially as she had stolen from them and suggested that maybe the police were looking for her, too.

He insisted it was for her own protection – after all, it was Annette who had stolen the money from the safe, they weren't looking for him – and what would happen to Antonias if she went to prison? But really they needed the money to support the lavish lifestyle they were living.

Annette was frightened, after that; maybe she had been too hasty in taking Antonias away from Miriam. She knew full well that Miriam would do her best to find Antonias and she'd agreed to close her bank account and transfer the money to Carlos. That way, neither of them could be traced.

But now, the money was dwindling. Annette convinced Carlos it would be better to rent somewhere in London, and said they could get a nanny to keep Antonias busy, so the boy wouldn't get under his feet.

Carlos agreed, although insisted it had to be somewhere befitting his new status. He said he liked the sound of Chelsea. He had heard 'posh' people with money lived there.

With his fine suits and money in his pockets, Annette and her spoilt brat were beginning to get on his nerves. Especially Annette's constant nagging about when they should marry.

Now in full receipt of all her money, Carlos didn't have any more use for Annette, and he certainly wasn't going to be tied down to being Antonias's father.

He persuaded her to wait a little longer before they married. After all, it would be a legal contract between them and something Miriam would be able to trace her by. He knew if he frightened Annette enough, she would agree, and she did.

He sweetened the deal by saying he would look for a job soon, like he had promised in Italy, when they had been making plans.

That would mean they could get better settled, and then he would marry her.

That seemed to satisfy Annette for the time being, but she was starting to worry. Carlos had brought no money with him, yet demanded only the best. They would have to start putting their plans into action soon or there would be nothing left.

Annette begged Carlos not to spend so much time at the casinos, but he went anyway, without her. The money was in his name and in his bank account; he had no need to saddle himself with a nag and a five-year-old boy, forever wanting his mother's attention, and making noise when Carlos was trying to sleep off his hangover. It was time to move on, alone.

Carlos picked a day when he knew Annette would be taking Antonias to a nearby funfair. He told her he didn't feel well enough to go, but to take their time and enjoy themselves.

Carlos had withdrawn 1,000 pounds from the bank. He put it on the dining table for Annette. Then he packed his clothes, helped himself to Annette's jewellery, and left.

When Annette came back, she went to the bedroom, expecting Carlos to be asleep in there. She opened the door to see if he was awake, but he wasn't there. Surely he hasn't gone out already, without me? she thought.

Annette looked around the bedroom. She suddenly felt uneasy, and instinctively she walked to the wardrobes and opened them. All of Carlos's clothes had gone, and so had her jewellery, and anything else of value in the house.

She walked back into the dining room to see what else was missing and noticed a wad of cash on the table. She sat down at the table and wept. A thousand pounds... that was all she had left in the world, and the rent was more than that.

Carlos, the love of her life, had left her, and her son, homeless.

It crossed her mind to contact Miriam, but Carlos had filled her head with all the trouble she would be in if she was found, and so she dismissed the idea.

Poor Antonias, she had dragged him away from his home and family. He could speak some English, but his main language was Italian, as he had lived there all his young life. She was the only person he had, and she had let him down.

She knew Carlos had slapped him whenever he made a noise and had always resented him being there. Maybe that was why Carlos had left. It wasn't that he didn't love her; it was all Antonias's fault.

The only thing Annette could do now was pack up their things and move on. She still had some family in London; maybe it was time to visit them, and hopefully they would take her in for a while until she worked out a plan.

Annette took Antonias and went to see her brother and his wife. She gave them a sob story about wanting to come home after Marias's death, but that she had no money and nowhere to go.

'Do you think we could stay with you, Ben, just until I get sorted out?' Annette gave her older brother a pitiful look. Ben turned to his wife. They had two children of their own and their house was already full.

'Okay, Annette,' he said, 'but go down to the local housing office and get yourself on their list, and then put yourself on some jobseekers lists and get some benefits. You can stay, but you pay your way.'

Ben knew Annette had always wanted the easy life, and he also knew she had been in London for a while before contacting him. As usual, something had gone wrong.

His wife wasn't too pleased, but if it was only for a short while, she was prepared to put up with it. Besides, the extra cash would come in handy.

However, after a few weeks of Antonias and his mum sleeping on the sofa, Ben and his wife were getting tired of hearing the constant excuses as to why Annette hadn't found work, or somewhere for them to live. She was using the money Carlos had left to pay their way, but it wouldn't last much longer.

Ben's wife, Susan, insisted that Antonias went to school, which caused a problem for Annette. To please Susan, she had registered Antonias in the same school her own children had gone to at Antonias's age, but she had changed his name and used her maiden name.

She found some temporary factory work that paid cash in hand, no questions asked, but it was lower than the minimum wage. Ben couldn't understand why she would do it. Why not just register at the appropriate offices, get some government benefits, and a roof over her head? It all seemed crazy to him, but she wouldn't listen. She always promised to sort herself out, but never did.

Ben loved his sister, but she had never been one to be trusted, and when it came to work, she was lazy, always expecting someone else to pay her way.

Ben got in bed beside his wife one night and sighed. 'I wish I knew what Annette was up to, Susan. There's more to this than meets the eye, and I don't want any trouble at my door.'

'It's Antonias I feel sorry for. He's such a lovely, pretty boy, but he's been brought back to England after losing his father, he has no place to call home, and his mother is irresponsible. She's not fit to be a parent.'

Susan kissed her husband goodnight, then turned over. She could see he was troubled and said no more, but Susan knew a lot more about it than Ben did.

Miriam had written to them some months earlier, expressing her concern about Antonias's well-being. Now, Susan could see for herself why. Annette had no life plan, she just hopped from one idea to the next, which was okay if you were single – but Annette had a child, and she dragged him around like a rag doll.

Susan thought that Antonias might be better off with his Italian family and, apart from that, she remembered that Miriam had offered some kind of reward for any information about them both. She decided she would write to Miriam in the morning.

* * *

Annette was surprised when some post came for her at her brother's home, and stunned when she saw the Italian postmark. She ripped open the envelope; there was a letter inside from Miriam, and she had also sent some money.

In the letter, Miriam had written that there were no hard feelings. What was done was done. The money didn't matter. What mattered was that Annette and Antonias should come home, back to Italy, so she could look after them. Alternatively, if Annette preferred to stay in England, she wanted them to at least stay in touch.

Annette tore the letter up. She was angry she had been betrayed, her details handed over to Miriam, but she knew her brother wouldn't have done that to her. It had to be Susan, and Annette wondered what she was getting out of it in return. She knew Miriam only wanted Antonias back; as far as she was concerned, Annette could go to hell. And, although he was becoming a millstone around her neck lately, Annette knew this was a trap and she wasn't falling for it.

Annette rounded on Susan when she showed up. 'You evil cow,' she said, 'you've written to my mother-in-law! How could you? She's a barmy old woman who has lost her son and now thinks she can take over mine!' Without thinking, Annette walked towards Susan and slapped her face.

Susan felt the stinging blow from Annette's slap, and rubbed her face, shocked.

Ben stood up. 'Come on, girls,' he said, 'there's no need for that. Nobody has written to anybody, Annette, what are you on about?'

'You tell him, Sue! You've written to Miriam, haven't you?' Annette was shouting now.

'Yes, I have,' said Susan. 'She wrote to me a long time ago, asking about you, and I dismissed it. We didn't even know you were back in England, then, did we?'

She looked at Ben and he shook his head.

Susan turned back to her sister-in-law. 'What have you been doing all this time, Annette? Where have you been?' Her voice was rising steadily, then she shouted, 'Whatever it was, it didn't turn out too well, did it!'

The room went silent.

After a moment, Ben said, 'Annette, what's going on?' He couldn't understand why his wife had done this, or why Annette's mother-in-law was treating Annette and Antonias as missing persons. He wanted to get to the bottom of it.

'There's nothing to tell, Ben. After Marias, I just had to get out of there. That's all.'

Annette tried her usual tears, but she knew this time she was on thin ice. It was time to move on.

'Don't go, Annette, not like this,' said Ben. 'Where are you going to go to, anyway?'

Annette shook her head. 'I have to, don't you see? Even Susan thinks I'm a bad mother, and goodness knows what she's told Miriam about me.'

Ben made them all a cup of coffee to try and keep the mood calm. Antonias and his own two boys were playing outside. This was their chance to talk.

'I've said nothing bad about you, Annette,' said Susan. 'Well, nothing that she didn't know already, anyway.' Susan was still smarting from the slap Annette had given her.

Ben was softer. He always tried to see the best in people, which was why Susan loved him, but there was no way she was going to let Annette stay, now.

Maybe, if they told her to leave, she would use the huge amount of money Miriam had sent her to buy a ticket back to Italy. Susan had already received Miriam's reward: 1,000 pounds, as promised.

'Ben, help me, we're family. Miriam is trying to take Antonias from me, which is why I've been hiding away from her.' To emphasise the point, Annette started to cry again and fell into her brother's arms.

'It's okay, Annette, love, we'll sort it out. Me and Sue both know you've had a hard time, what with losing your husband and everything. Look, let me have a word with little Antonias's granny, eh? Let her know you're both okay and doing well.' Ben's calming cockney accent soothed her, until she realised what he was saying.

Oh, no! He was going to contact Miriam, and she would tell him all about Carlos and the money. Ben would go mad at her if he knew she had stolen money, and had been prepared to sell Antonias.

'No, Ben, please don't. Let me talk to her, it'll sound better coming from me. I owe her that, I just haven't been myself lately. But I will speak to her, I promise.'

Ben and Susan looked at each other and nodded; at last, they had got through to Annette. She would contact Miriam and either go back to Italy or stay here. It didn't really matter either way, at least Miriam would know she was safe. She hadn't known where Annette and Antonias had gone, and naturally she had been worried sick.

They'd have been less happy had they known that after they

went to bed that night, Annette had packed a bag with essentials for her and Antonias.

3

STREET LIFE

The next day, Annette took Antonias to school, as usual, and then went to the factory. As she worked on a daily cash-in-hand basis, she got paid after her shift. That was good, because straight after work Annette was going to collect Antonias and find them somewhere else to stay. She couldn't go back to her brother's house. Not now.

Annette had struck lucky; someone she worked with knew of a flat to let that sounded just perfect. She contacted the landlord and arranged to go to see it, as soon as her shift finished.

'Yours, if you want it, love,' he said, after she'd finished looking around. 'Come round tomorrow and we can sort out the paperwork and the money.'

'When can I move in?' she asked.

'If we get it all sorted tomorrow, you can be in by tomorrow night.'

* * *

Because of going to view the flat, Annette was late picking Antonias up from his after-school club. The teacher glared at her, but said nothing. Annette didn't care; she'd never have to see the woman again. Antonias couldn't go back to that school. Ben and Susan would be able to find them, if he did.

'Why aren't we going home, mummy?' Antonias said, when she headed into town with him.

'We're going to have an adventure,' Annette said. 'We're going to camp out like boy scouts tonight, then, tomorrow, we're going to go and live somewhere new, just us. How does that sound?'

Antonias's little face beamed with smiles. It sounded very exciting to him.

Annette had to hang on to all her money to get them into the flat, tomorrow, and to buy the things they would need. There was nothing left to pay for a room for the night. They would have to spend the night on the streets.

It's just one night, she reasoned, just one night. We'll be fine, and tomorrow, we'll be snug in our own safe, warm haven.

London's 'cardboard city' was famous for all the homeless people that lived on the streets. Each and every one of them had their own doorway to sleep in. They put up cardboard boxes and used them as tents, that was where the name came from.

The streets of London were a miserable place, when you lived on them. You watched people all the time, shopping and laughing with their friends until it was time for them to go home, back to their safe, warm havens.

Annette bought a couple of sleeping bags and some warm clothes, things that would be useful when they moved into the flat, too. Antonias was thrilled with the adventure; Annette had a way of making it sound exciting.

'Here, Antonias, isn't this fun?' she said, as they sat eating a burger on a bench. She watched a group of women in short skirts hanging around on a street corner. Every so often a car would stop, there'd be some chat and then a woman got in and was driven away.

There were random shouts and catcalls as drinkers and drunks went from pub to pub. Antonias shrank into Annette, both for warmth and reassurance. He was less sure about the big adventure, now.

Soon it was time for them to get some sleep. It was dark by then, and Annette didn't know what to expect. She put Antonias into his sleeping bag and tucked him into a doorway, then wriggled into her own. She intended to sit awake all night, watching him.

The first light of dawn woke Annette up, and she realised she must have dozed off. Antonias! She turned, in panic, to find he was still asleep. She reached for her bag, to get a cigarette, and found it had gone.

All the money she had in the world had been in her bag, and while she was asleep, it had been stolen.

Seeing someone huddled in the next doorway along, Annette shouted, 'Have you stolen my bag, you thief? I'm going to call the police!' She was angry and waving her finger at the young man, who was still half asleep.

'No, I haven't,' he shouted back, 'but it happens. You should have hid it more carefully. People on the streets usually put money in their shoes, then you can feel if someone is trying to take them off and rob you.'

The young man seemed to accept it as part of everyday life. He saw Antonias waking up. 'Here,' he said, 'get him a drink.' He threw some coins at Annette.

Annette was upset and angry, but what had she expected? Not only were you exposed to the elements, the people were as desperate as each other. There were no morals with street life; you got by whatever way you could, to survive and feed yourself for another day.

Annette went into a nearby shop and bought a drink and a chocolate bar for Antonias. That was it; that was all her money gone. There would be no flat, no safe, warm haven for them. She returned to the doorway and snuggled in again with her little boy.

* * *

The next night found them back in the same doorway.

'Mummy, it's raining on my bed,' said Antonias. He was cold, he was hungry and all the drunks and the people fighting at night frightened him.

Annette raised her head from the sleeping bag; it wasn't raining, or at least, she couldn't feel it.

Then she saw what was happening. It wasn't rain, but a gang of drunks urinating on their sleeping bags. They were laughing and joking, while relieving themselves.

Annette heard a couple of women shouting, 'Oy, you bastards, leave them alone and piss somewhere else!'

She looked up and saw them, in their short skirts and high heels, chasing off the drunken louts and shouting at them. It was obvious they were the prostitutes she had seen the previous night, gathering at their street corner waiting for trade.

'Are you okay, love? How is he doing?' The woman stood there in a low top, short black skirt and high heels. A cigarette dangled from her mouth.

'Thanks.' Annette smiled. 'He'll be okay.' She proffered her hand. 'I'm Annette,' she said, 'and this is Antonias.'

The woman leaned forward and shook her hand. 'Tilly, that's what they call me. You need to go to the public toilets over there and clean up. Everyone uses it, it's open all night.' She turned to Antonias and ruffled his hair. 'Hi, handsome,' she said, and she smiled.

They were the first kind words Antonias had heard all day.

Tilly took her cigarette out of her mouth and handed it to Annette. She looked at the young woman, who was obviously naive and new to the streets. Something must have happened, especially as she had a small child with her, but Tilly had seen it all before. Some people felt safer on the harsh cold streets of London than they did at some abusive home.

Nobody asked questions on the streets, no one used their full names, it was a golden rule. They all had hard luck stories, some better and some worse than others, but it was better not to ask.

'The Salvation Army set up mobile caravans over there.' Tilly pointed around the street corner. 'Anyone can have a tea or a coffee, and they come all the time. Then there's the soup kitchen, you can always get a hot meal when you need one.' The woman felt she had given Annette enough information to get her started.

Annette stood up, and pushed her blonde hair away from her face. 'Thank you, Tilly, I appreciate that,' she said.

* * *

Three years later, and Annette and Antonias had adapted to life on the streets. Annette knew all the tricks needed to survive, including joining Tilly on the street corner and leaving Antonias asleep, in his sleeping bag.

Antonias was eight, now, and he ran around the streets, using them as his playground. He would often stand around with the junkies and alcoholics, who would light a bonfire in an old oil drum to keep warm.

He had become a clever and cunning thief, good at stealing from the local shops. When he was caught, he would reply in Italian, as though he didn't understand what anyone was saying to him.

Annette used their Italian language as a code. She knew nobody understood them, and so when she needed him to look after her money or keep a look out while she was with a customer, she too would speak in Italian.

There were other kids who lived on the streets, so Antonias was not alone. They had run away from broken homes, and thought this life was better.

Antonias was now known as Antony, although some even called him the 'Artful Dodger'. He knew if shopkeepers caught him, he was too young to prosecute. They just slapped him around the head and threw him out.

The police were always hanging around, asking questions. Antonias kept out of their way as much as possible and Annette gave them sob stories about being evicted, or fleeing from an abusive husband. She was only known to the police as Annette, no last name; no one asked or cared. The homeless were an embarrassment to the capital of England.

Antonias was running wild; he had his own friends and his own life. One of the alcoholics had been a schoolteacher and had taught him to read – it passed the time.

A couple of the prostitutes Annette knew had been thrown out of their lodgings by their pimps, because they were getting old and weren't earning enough. They had found an old derelict house and squatted in it and invited Annette and Antonias to join them.

It was dark inside the squat; the windows were boarded up and the musty smell, from the peeling wallpaper and the damp, hit you first. The house hadn't been lived in for years, but it had a roof. It was heaven.

The rats and the cockroaches didn't bother anyone, they were used to them, and they all pooled their money and bought a paraffin heater. This was home, now.

There were times when Annette longed for the boredom of life at the vineyard, but that all seemed like a million years ago.

To drown out the past, and get through the nights of man after man using her for a few pounds, she had turned to alcohol and then to drugs. She knew the local dealers, who would hang around with them and provide them with the 'goods' in exchange for sex or money.

Antonias was always left on his own for a few days at a time when Annette and the other prostitutes moved their 'pitch' elsewhere, then got so high on drugs that they just passed out somewhere.

Annette would leave Antonias some money, tell him she was just popping out for 'mummy's medicine', and disappear into the night.

4

THE LONG, STRAIGHT ROAD

A police officer on his way home after a long night shift noticed a young blond boy removing a plank of wood from one of the derelict houses, on a local estate. He stood and watched the boy, who was smoking a cigarette and holding a bottle of wine, climb in and replace the plank of wood.

He decided to investigate, not knowing what to expect, apart from some young scallywag breaking in and using it as a place to drink and smoke, while being absent from school. He radioed it in to the police station anyway, for his own safety.

When he went inside, he couldn't believe his eyes. It was obvious people lived there. There was no sign of the young boy and so the police officer crept quietly around, shining his torch into each room. There were signs of drug abuse with needles and empty foils of heroin lying around.

Suddenly the young boy appeared from one of the rooms. When he saw the officer, he started to make a run for it. The officer tried restraining the boy and offering reassurances that he meant him no harm.

Antonias was like a wild animal, punching and shouting, even reverting to Italian to confuse the police officer. The officer radioed the station for backup. It was obvious to him that this young boy lived here, but who was looking after him?

A patrol car came and took Antonias away. The police officers hadn't got any sense out of him, all he had done was speak in Italian and shrug his shoulders.

Antonias was angry and afraid. His mother would be worried about him when she came back and found he wasn't there. He needed to find her.

He thought if he played dumb and didn't speak English, he would be safe; they would let him go, like all the others had, because he was too much trouble. But they didn't.

The police telephoned social services, and also asked for an interpreter. While they waited for them, they gave Antonias a hot meal and watched him wolf it down, using his hands.

Antonias spent what seemed like hours in a police cell, then, finally, social services and the interpreter arrived. They were doing their best not to insult him by holding their noses, because the stench of body odour, alcohol and urine coming from him was foul. They could see he was riddled with head lice and scabies.

'What's your name?' the interpreter asked, in Italian, then smiled at him.

'Antony, Antony Perry,' he replied. Antonias had no choice, but he wouldn't betray his mother; that was all they were getting. His mum would come and get him soon, he was sure of it.

The report was written by the social worker about 'Antony Perry', and where they had found him. It was slim pickings, because he wouldn't give any more information.

Even when a police search had been conducted for missing persons, his name didn't come up. No one was looking for this child, no one had reported him missing, yet they all knew he had to have come from somewhere.

The police ransacked the squat, to try to find more information about who else lived there, but all they found among the debris were old unwashed clothes and half-eaten food. They had the squat secured, this time with metal shutters at the doors and windows. A police watch was set up to wait for the people who were living there.

In the meantime, the social worker had to find a place at a local children's home for Antony. After she had telephoned around a few and found a place, she set off and took him with her, leaving the car window open slightly to let some fresh air in.

After a long struggle, they managed to get Antony into the bath. The carers at the home found him some clothing that fitted and burnt the things they had found him in. Now it was up to the nurse to cut his hair and get rid of the lice, and give him a full medical. The head lice infestation had been so bad, it turned out to be easier to shave his head and start again. Antony fought them all the way, biting and lashing out until they had to restrain him.

The next few days were a long round of constant battles, with Antony trying to escape on numerous occasions. They found out no more information; they only had his name and date of birth, and no one came forward to claim him. This boy was truly a mystery; it seemed as if he had just fallen out of the sky and landed there.

Even though they knew it would be futile, the police carried out some investigations around the area they had found him in, and spoke to the homeless people that were known to them. They drew a blank; even if these people did know anything, they wouldn't say so, in case they got into some kind of trouble themselves.

* * *

When Annette and her friends arrived back at the squat, they saw that it was impossible to get in. The place had been well secured.

Her first instinct had been panic and she had run towards the house, then she noticed the police officer nearby and decided to walk away.

She wondered where Antonias was. Was he on the streets? Was he looking for her? He'd turn up, he always did. She turned and took one last look at the house, then went to join her friends back on the street corner.

Annette hoped her son was okay and was comforted by the fact he was fully adept at life on the streets and could look after himself.

A car stopped in front of her, and a man rolled down his window and asked her, 'How much?' She told him twenty pounds, because that was the price of her next heroin packet. She was a full-blown addict, now. The man nodded, and they drove off together; business was business, after all.

What Annette didn't realise was that she would never see Antonias again. Her young son was lost to her forever.

* * *

Antonias felt confined in the room they had given him. Although he had a bed and warmth and three meals a day, he would pace his room all night, unable to sleep. He knew his mother was out there looking for him; if he could only get a message to her, she would come and take him away from all this regimental routine.

Antonias went into the day room, where there was a snooker table and a television. He had never actually seen a TV this close up before, only through shop windows, and even then there had been no sound.

There were other boys there, who obviously thought they owned the place. They circled him, laughing at him, but life on the streets had taught Antonias well. He watched them, laughing like hyenas, and when they started pushing him around, Antonias dodged them and sat down in a chair, in front of the television.

'Move out the way, baldy, that's my chair,' a boy who was older than him said. He was mean-looking and putting on an even braver front than usual, to impress his friends.

'You tell him, Stevie!' one of the other boys said, and the rest jeered.

Stevie's bravado, especially with all his friends backing him up, might have frightened some of the other boys, but it didn't frighten Antonias.

'No,' he answered sullenly, 'I'm sitting here. Find somewhere else.' He had been intimidated by bullies before and knew the only way to stop them was to get in there first and show them he wouldn't stand for it.

For the time being, he was stuck here, and he had to make his point. The older boy and his friends stood in front of him.

'You still smell like a skunk,' said Stevie. 'Now, get out of my chair!'

He grabbed Antonias by the shirt and started pulling. When Antonias refused to budge, Stevie punched him in the face, knocking Antonias to the floor. The other boys all started laughing as Antonias lay there, being kicked by the older boy.

Antonias rolled over; he wouldn't cry, he was determined not to. He saw the snooker cue, and reached out and grabbed it. With one large sweep of his arm, he hit the older boy in the stomach with the cue.

Stevie fell onto the floor, gasping for breath and holding his stomach. His friends stopped laughing. Antonias stood up and lifted the snooker cue again, and brought it down even harder across the boy's back. Stevie was now screaming in pain.

Someone ran out to get one of the carers, but they were already on their way, having heard the screams.

One of them restrained Antonias by putting his arms around him tightly.

'Drop the snooker cue, Antony,' one of the male carers said as he stood and faced him. 'Put it down, now.'

Antonias threw the cue onto the floor, and then struggled to get free from the carer who held him.

'If Danny lets you go, Antony, will you calm down and behave?' said the one who was doing the talking.

Antonias looked him in the eye and nodded his head; he knew he was beaten and there was nothing else he could do. Once he had been released, he walked back over to the chair he'd been sitting in and sat down in it again. He'd made his point; no one was going to bully him again if they knew what was good for them.

After that, whenever Antonias walked into the day room, Stevie and his gang avoided him; he wasn't worth the hassle, there were easier targets to pick on.

The other boys tended to keep their distance, too. Only one of them tried to befriend Antonias. He sauntered over to the chair Antonias was sat in while he was watching TV, one day.

'My name's Eddie, and you're one crazy bastard,' he said, then he laughed and held his hand out.

Antonias didn't raise his hand to shake Eddie's, he just raised his eyes and looked at the dark-haired boy, who was maybe one or two years older. 'Antony,' was all he said, then he continued watching the television. Eddie sat down in the chair next to him and watched the programme with him.

* * *

Antonias was biding his time, but always on the lookout for an opportunity to get away. He saw his chance when the front door was left open one day, after a delivery man came, and he ran for it. His lungs breathed in the street air, and the wind blew through him. Freedom!

Antonias ran back to his old haunts, the places he had lived with his mother. Firstly, he went to the squat and saw the metal shutters at the windows; as much as he walked around the place, he could see there was no way in.

He ran all the way to the street corner where his mother and his 'aunties' used to stand, looking for trade. He recognised a couple of the women there.

'Have you seen Tilly and Annette?' he asked them, breathing heavily. They looked at him oddly, and then one of them smiled.

'Blimey, it's you Antony, I didn't recognise you with your new haircut. How are you?'

He smiled, embarrassed by his appearance, and ran his hands over his shaved head.

'Have you seen Annette?' he said, again. He looked at the woman pleadingly, waiting for an answer.

'No, love, I think they found another squat somewhere, not sure where.' The woman opened her handbag and took out a five-pound note. 'Here, take this,' she said.

'Thanks,' said Antonias.

The woman turned around to talk to her friends again, ignoring him completely.

Antonias's next visit was to the soup kitchen. His mother usually went there with him, when trade was slow. If she'd found another squat, she would have left a message for someone to pass on to him.

He went into the old church hall and scoured the long benches, full of people he knew. He sat on the benches one by one, working his way around the hall, and enquired after his mother. But Annette had left no message.

When he walked out of the church hall, he was tired and frustrated. He felt like crying, but he held it in. Then he saw Benny the dealer, or as his mother had called him, Benny the medicine man.

He ran up to him and touched his arm. 'Benny, have you seen Annette? Has she been for her medicine?'

Benny was a tall black man, aged around thirty, and always wore a black trilby hat. He flinched when he felt Antonias grab his arm, but then he saw who it was and smiled at him.

'Antony, my mate, give me five!' He held his hand up to give Antonias a high five. 'I saw her yesterday, mate, you two lost each other?' Benny found that odd. Antony was Annette's rock. She depended on him for everything. This young kid looked after his mother, laid her down to sleep when she was drunk or off her head on drugs. He had even learnt how to use a syringe, so when her hands were shaking so much she couldn't inject herself, she could still have her medicine.

Benny liked Antony, he was a good kid, and had often dropped drugs off for him at people's doors, when Benny had been too busy.

'Tell her I'm at the children's home, in South London. Tell her to come. Promise me, Benny.' Antonias was relieved someone had seen her. As soon as she knew where he was, she would come for him.

'The children's home?' said Benny. Now he was confused. Why was Antony in a children's home? Benny had seen Annette, high on drugs, but she had never mentioned Antony was missing.

'Of course I'll tell her, my man, no problem. She's probably out there looking for you, anyway.'

Antonias breathed a sigh of relief; his mother was okay, and now she would know where he was. She would be sure to seek out Benny, he was her dealer, and sometimes he brought clients around to the squat to save her from going out.

Many a time Antonias had sat in one of the other dark, damp rooms, while his mother had entertained one of her friends on the mattress on the floor. He would hear sounds coming from the room, and then the door would open and the man would leave.

'Go to Benny on the corner, Antony,' she'd say, 'he'll be there by now. Mummy needs some medicine. While you're at it, work your magic and steal me a bottle of wine. I'll share it with you.'

Annette would hand him some of the money she had just earned and he would run down to Benny, get his mother's medicine, and then run into the local off-licence and steal a bottle of wine.

Antonias had started drinking a while ago. There wasn't any water in the squat and so, sometimes, that was all there was to drink. There was usually some left in a bottle, after his mother and the other prostitutes had had a party, and so when he'd been thirsty in the night, he had picked up that bottle and emptied it.

As Antonias was walking away from Benny, a police patrol car stopped. Antonias had been reported missing by the children's home, and they were on the lookout for him.

'Antony Perry?' an officer said, as he got out of the car. 'We've been looking for you.'

Antonias's first instinct was to run. He looked across the road to where he'd been talking to Benny, and saw the dealer had gone. The last thing Benny wanted was the police seeing him.

Antony did as he was told and got in the police car. He decided it was for the best; after all, his mother would definitely come for him now, just as soon as Benny told her where he was.

Antonias waited patiently for a month, but there was no word from his mother. The case worker who was in charge of him came regularly, to see if he was okay and whether he needed anything. Time and time again, he was tempted to ask about his mother, but he didn't. He didn't want to get her into trouble.

Antonias had to go to school, but he hated it there. More rules to abide by, and more adults taking control of his life. It stifled him.

'I've found you a foster family, Antony, it'll get you away from here,' his case worker announced one day. 'You'll be well looked after, there.' The social worker actually looked pleased, but Antonias was horrified. If he left this place, his mother wouldn't know where to find him, and he'd be back to square one.

'I don't want to go; I like it here,' he lied. He hated it, but no one ever bothered him. There was just Eddie, who often sat with Antonias and watched television with him. He had become a friend, in his own way, and would often share his chocolate bar with Antonias, when more privileges were taken away after he'd been fighting again or skipped school.

But Antonias had been forced to go and have a meeting with the foster family. His shaved blond hair had grown back now, and he looked clean and well nourished.

The man and woman had two sons of their own. They eyed him up and down and although he looked like a nice kid, that wild look in those piercing blue eyes made them feel uncomfortable.

Antonias sat there, sullen and not speaking to them. He didn't want to be there, and he didn't want to see the bedroom they had prepared for him. He listened to their plans for him, and how they would love to have him stay. But he was bored, and showed it.

Within a couple of weeks, he was taken to live with the family. He soon learned that the show of welcome they put on in front of the social worker was all a front. They wanted him to clean up after their own children.

Antonias was to be used as a slave, peeling potatoes and cleaning up, while their own sons sat and watched the television. Life on the streets was better than this.

He would go to school, wait until they had taken the register and then run for the freedom of the streets, where he'd spend the day drinking with the alcoholics he knew would be standing around their oil drum, keeping warm.

As usual, the police would come and pick him up, but this time it was to take him back to his foster home. They weren't as easygoing as at the children's home.

He was shouted at and threatened. The two brothers who lived there would hit him, for making their parents worry, and so Antonias would lash out, and hit them with whatever was at hand.

Eventually, they gave up on him and he was returned to the children's home. Antonias was glad to see the back of them.

He was also glad to be reunited with Eddie, a friendly face at last. Eddie was due to be fostered out and so Antonias told him all about his short and not-so-sweet experience.

A few months later, and still clinging on to the idea his mother would come for him, he was told he was to be fostered again.

Antonias was already on his guard when he got to the new place. This time, the foster parents were an older couple and, to be fair, they didn't make him do chores. But they didn't understand him.

When Antonias disappeared for a couple of days at a time, to live on the streets and try and find out some information about his mother, they called the police. Again and again, he was taken back until, eventually, he was returned to the children's home.

Christmas came and he had helped put up decorations, and for the first time since he was small and lived in Italy, there were presents under the tree for him.

Christmastime was when he missed his mother most.

Antonias sat alone in his room, and remembered the Christmases they had spent together, standing in Trafalgar Square looking up at the large Christmas tree and listening to the big brass band of the Salvation Army play Christmas carols.

Sometimes he had spent the day alone, if his mother had gone out and left him for a few days. Then she would come back and they would share a burger and look at the shops on Oxford Street, with all their bright Christmas decorations.

Antonias wondered what she was doing now, and if she was thinking about him. He buried his face in his pillow and cried himself to sleep.

5

NO PLACE LIKE HOME

Antonias had been in care for five years and was now thirteen. It was fair to say, there'd been some ups and downs. He had been fostered out a few more times, but the foster parents had all sent him back because of his wild behaviour and the police forever being at the door, bringing him back, sometimes drunk.

The confinement of the homes and their rules stifled him; he needed his freedom, and he still lived in hope of finding his mother... although he knew now that his mother was never going to come for him.

Following a meeting, the authorities had decided it would be better if they moved him away from his old stomping ground to another children's home, but this had just fuelled his anger.

Lisa, his social worker, came to see him one day at the home.

'Antony.' She put her briefcase down at the side of the sofa on which he was sitting. He looked up but didn't stir; probably another lecture, he thought.

'An old friend of mine, Elle, is a foster carer.'

She saw his eyes flash and held up her hand to stop his

outburst. She liked Antony, he was a good kid, but had lived rough all his life. She felt she understood him.

'Just let me finish. She has seen your file and, if you want to, she's prepared to have you go and live with her. She's already fostering a young boy, Jake, he's about your age.'

Antonias opened his mouth to protest, and again, she stopped him.

'This is your last chance at living in a home, a proper home, and having more freedom. Not a lot of people want older children.' She punched his arm and laughed. 'Especially one like you, with your track record.'

'No way, Lisa, been there, bought the T-shirt. I'm not going.' Antonias was fed up with being moved from pillar to post; all he wanted was to be left alone.

'We could go on a school day, like tomorrow, maybe? I could buy you a burger and you could come with me and take a look, see what you think?'

A day off school appealed to Antonias; he hated it there, it bored him, and he was always in detention for fighting. In fact, he spent more time in detention than he did in school.

'You promise you're going to buy me a burger?' he said. 'What if I meet her and I don't want to stay? Anyway, she's already got one kid, why does she want another?'

'Jake is being fostered because both his parents were killed in a tragic car accident. He's very shy and not as strong-willed as you. Will you come?' Lisa was smiling now; she knew she had him hooked.

The next day, at the visit, Antony sat in the lounge looking around the room, bored, while Elle and Lisa had a cup of tea and talked. Elle had already read Antony's file and had expected his disinterest, after having been rejected so many times before.

'Well, Antony, would you like to come and stay with me and Jake?' Elle asked.

Antonias shrugged his shoulders. He didn't care; he knew in a matter of a couple of weeks he would be back at the children's home, anyway, so there was no point in getting excited, was there?

'It's about choice, Antony,' said Elle. She ignored Lisa and spoke directly to Antonias, like an adult. 'It's your choice, you're nearly fourteen, you can make your own decisions.' She saw the look on his face; he was confused. For once he wasn't being talked about, he was being spoken to.

'I'm willing, if you are, makes no difference to me. But I'm not doing your cleaning, and I do as I please,' Antonias said. He glared at Elle, his chin stuck out and his blue eyes defiant.

'You put your dirty clothes in the wash basket on the landing, you go to school and you don't play your music too loud. Deal?' Elle felt this was enough to be going on with.

'You're like all the others, just want the money for letting me live in your shitty house. And who's this other kid you've got here?'

Elle knew he was trying to shock her; she'd seen it all before, and worse. She saw Lisa was going to intervene, and stopped her.

'It isn't much of a house, Antony. Can I call you Antony?'

He nodded.

'But it's home to me, and yes, I do get paid. Like any other parent, I get benefits for feeding and clothing you. As I say, it's your choice. Jake is at school.'

Antonias didn't understand this woman, she was asking permission to call him by his name, and nobody had ever done that before.

He nodded. 'Okay, I'm willing to give it a go, if you are, but I warn you, I won't take any of your crap.'

Elle smiled at him. 'Okay, then, move in when you're ready. I'll be here, in my shitty house,' she added.

Antonias wanted to laugh. He liked this woman; she was straight, and funny. Maybe he could live here. He had yet to meet this other kid, Jake. Lisa had said he was shy; well, Antonias would soon show him who was boss.

When Antonias went to the bathroom, Elle and Lisa looked at each other and smiled. 'Thank you,' Lisa mouthed, so that Antonias didn't hear her.

* * *

Jake was a boring kid. They had said he was quiet, but bloody hell, he didn't open his mouth! He stayed in his room, went to school, did his homework, and seemed to walk around all the time with his head down. Antonias had been ready for a fight, but fighting that kid would have been like kicking a puppy.

After a week in Elle's house, Antonias decided to skip school and go and see what was happening on the streets.

Elle called the police, then sat in her dressing gown, waiting for news. She knew Antony had a history of running away, and she had expected it.

He had started off okay, and even though he had dropped his dirty clothes on the floor next to the wash basket on the landing, rather than putting them in it, she felt at least he had made some effort.

The police found Antonias drinking a bottle of wine with some 'friends', in a shop doorway. They finally brought him home in the early hours of the morning. He was the worse for wear and swaying back and forth.

Elle opened the door; he was shouting what sounded like angry swear words in Italian at the police, and then at Elle.

She thanked the police officers, who had asked if she was okay and whether she would be able to cope with Antony. It made her laugh to herself that they actually knew him by name.

Elle helped Antony up the stairs; he was still shouting and waving his arms about. Then she noticed something in his jacket pocket: her purse. He had stolen her purse out of her bag.

She acknowledged that she should have been more careful, that it was her own fault for leaving her handbag lying around and her purse accessible, but she was still upset that he had stolen from her.

She lay him on the bed, in his clothes, and then suddenly he sat up and vomited all over her and the bed. He seemed to think that was funny.

'Serves you right, you money-grabbing bitch, you get paid for looking after me, you can clean it up,' he said.

Elle turned and left the room. It stabbed at her heart the way he was in some kind of self-destruction mode. She had seen it many times with other children in care. Mentally she knew there had to be a way to reach Antony and gain his trust, but he was like a wounded animal, always on the defence in case he was rejected again. She was determined she wouldn't give up on him; he was a good kid who had been dealt a bad hand and had to learn to survive. He'd suffered enough harsh words in his life and she didn't want to add to them, but, she nodded to herself, there was more than one way to skin a cat and attack wasn't always the best method. Anyway, there was no point in arguing now, he was too drunk.

The next morning, Elle shouted both down boys down for breakfast before school as normal. She ignored Antony's sheepish look as he entered the kitchen and put two paracetamol beside his cup of tea on the table. Antony looked up at her as though waiting for a lecture, but none came, which seemed to surprise him even more. This made her smile; she had beaten him at his own game.

When the school telephoned her a few days later, she let out a sigh. They asked her to come for an urgent meeting. Antony had been fighting again and had even threatened a teacher.

Elle went to see the head teacher, a woman she knew well from all her years as a foster carer. She was an older woman with stone grey hair. Many difficult children had passed through her hands, and she had always given them a second chance.

'I'm sorry, Elle,' the head said, 'but we can't have Antony here. He needs some kind of special school, for anger management. I'm afraid we're going to have to expel him.'

Elle was shocked. 'Please, Mrs Anderson,' she said, 'I know he's a little wild, but it's all he's ever known – how to fight to survive, always being on his guard. Suspend him for a week, if you like, but I'm begging you, give him another chance.'

'You know I don't give up on children easily,' the head said, 'but Antony is the most disruptive child I've ever known.'

Elle pleaded his case, explaining what he had been through and what another rejection would mean.

Finally, Mrs Anderson gave a deep sigh. 'Okay, one last chance, Elle, and only because it's you. One more step out of line and he's out. I understand boys fight, but he's lashing out at the staff, as well.'

'Thank you, Mrs Anderson, I appreciate this. He just needs to settle in, that's all, thank you.' Elle stood up and left the room before Mrs Anderson could change her mind.

God knows, thought Elle as she got back into her car, how I'm going to get through to Antony about all this. I hope I wasn't wasting my time in there.

* * *

When Jake came home from school that day, he had the beginnings of a black eye. Elle could tell he'd been crying. He dropped his backpack and ran upstairs to his bedroom.

Poor Jake, Elle thought to herself. He'd taken a back seat, lately, while she had concentrated on Antony. Jake had come to live with Elle after his parents had been killed, as there was nowhere else for him to go. He'd hardly spoken since he moved in, and had become increasingly withdrawn. He'd started to wet the bed frequently, too. She wiped her hands with a tea towel and went upstairs after him.

Jake was sitting on his bed, looking at the floor, crying. Elle put her arm around his shoulders, rested her head on his dark hair and gave him a minute.

'What's up, Jakey, love?' she said, when she sensed his tears were starting to dry up. 'Is it the big boys, again?' Elle knew he was being bullied at school and had been in a number of times to discuss it with Mrs Anderson. It had stopped for a while, but then started up again.

Jake seemed to be a prime target for bullies. Elle had thought having another boy in the house might just help him come out of his shell, but it hadn't happened since Antony had moved in. If anything, he ignored Jake.

'You promise you won't tell the teachers again? That's why they do it, Elle, because you tell on them and get them into trouble.' Jake started sobbing, and Elle held him tight.

'If that's what you want, Jakey, love, but if it gets worse, you must tell me. Okay?'

Elle knew she had to help him, but she wasn't sure how. Maybe her constantly wanting discussions with the parents of the bullies had made it worse. Time would tell.

She left him in his bedroom to cry it out and went downstairs to finish the steak pie she was making for dinner.

Elle looked at the clock. Antony hadn't come home; he was doing another one of his escape acts. This time, she didn't call the police. She decided she wasn't going to inform them and let Antony be picked up and brought home like some hero.

No, whatever was out there that he needed to see so desperately, let him get on with it, get it out of his system. Maybe, like Jake, time would tell.

Three days later, she had no choice but to telephone Lisa; Antony was still missing. She knew she would be in big trouble and that it had been the wrong thing to do, leaving his absence unreported for three days.

But no sooner had Elle put the telephone down than Antony walked through the door. He was filthy, his clothes torn and bloody; he had obviously been fighting. He stank of alcohol and tobacco, and it was blatantly obvious he had slept on the streets.

Antonias looked at her. His face had a snarl on it, as though he was just waiting for a lecture.

'I'll go and pack, shall I?' he said. He was certain she would send him back to the children's home. He started to make his way up the stairs, stomping his feet hard on each one. He looked up and saw Jake, with his black eye.

Antonias turned around and looked down the stairs towards Elle. 'What's happened to pissy-pants, here? Have you been hitting him?' He raised an eyebrow, a cocky look on his face. He pushed Jake out of the way and went into his bedroom, then took out his case and started packing.

'Antony,' shouted Elle. She wasn't going to give up this easily. 'Dinner's nearly ready, get cleaned up and come down, will you? I'm about to serve up.' She walked back into the kitchen.

Yet again, Elle had surprised Antonias; he hadn't expected this. The other foster carers had gone crazy, shouting and screaming at him for making their lives hell, then rang the social worker to take him away. Normally, they had to give twenty-eight days' notice, but in some circumstances the authorities had no choice but to remove kids immediately.

Antonias stopped packing and went into the bathroom to wash

his face and hands; he would wait for Elle's outburst later. He went down and sat at the dining table. The food looked good; he hadn't eaten properly in days.

After dinner, Jake went back upstairs and disappeared into his own world again.

Elle started stacking the dishes, intending to do the washing up. 'Are you going to help me, Antony?' she asked. She was very calm and acting as normal. She knew this reverse psychology would puzzle Antony.

Antonias picked up a tea towel and started drying the plates Elle had washed up.

'I had to tell Lisa that you were missing, today. It was your third day and I was worried. It's okay, though, I've telephoned her and told her you've come home again, but I think you and I need to talk, don't you?'

Elle carried on washing up; she didn't want to make this sound like a lecture, but more of a chat.

'What's happened to pissy-pants up there?' Antonias asked, avoiding meeting Elle's eye.

'He's being bullied at school and he doesn't have your strength to fight back. I've spoken to the teachers, but I just seem to make things worse. Maybe I should think about moving him to a different school,' she said. She knew he was avoiding the issue, but at least he was talking.

Antonias finished drying the plates and, together in silence, they put everything away. Elle then walked out of the kitchen and along the hall, past the lounge, to the front door. She opened it.

'Antony, do you see this door?' She swung it back and forth. Antonias stood in the hallway and watched her. His brow was furrowed and he wondered what she was doing. Elle then closed the door, walked into the lounge and sat down in her favourite chair. Antonias followed, and she indicated he should sit on the sofa, opposite her.

The lounge was bright and airy, and the floral curtains and comfortable suite made the lamplit room seem cosy and friendly.

'We're going to have that talk now, Antony. Don't interrupt me, because when I have had my say, you can have yours, deal?'

Antonias thought Elle looked friendly enough; she wasn't scowling or shouting, just acting very oddly. Still, he was ready for his lecture. He nodded.

'Firstly, as I have shown you, that front door opens and closes. This is not a prison. However, I would appreciate you letting me know that you are safe and not just wandering off without a word.'

Antonias's piercing blue eyes stared at her face. He looked as if he was about to speak but stopped himself.

Elle paused, and watched Antonias wring his hands, while keeping his poker face.

She began again. 'I know you stole my purse last time you went missing, and when I checked it after you had fallen asleep, twenty pounds was gone. So, let's just say you "borrowed" that twenty pounds and you intend to pay it back out of your allowance, okay?'

Antonias's face went bright red; he had been caught out and for the first time in his life he felt ashamed. He looked down at the floor, not knowing what to say; he bit his bottom lip.

'I don't know what's out there on the streets that you find so fascinating, but I'm prepared to listen. Or, maybe I should say, who is out there that you're looking for, and are prepared to risk your life to find. If that's the case and you are looking for someone, I'm prepared to drive you around the streets and maybe you could show me a thing or two, eh?'

She smiled at him; she didn't want this to seem like a scolding. She knew Antonias was a very troubled boy. She had read his file and it seemed obvious to her that he was searching for something;

no one would get themselves into all kinds of trouble like he had for no reason. She was right, she knew, because at her words, Antonias's face shot up and his eyes looked directly into hers.

I've hit the nail on the head, thought Elle, he's got a secret. Considering there was no more information on him now than there had been when he had first been picked up, it was good work.

'Lastly, please stop calling Jake "pissy-pants". We know he wets the bed on occasion, but he's having enough trouble at school without coming home to it, as well. Right, it's your turn now.'

Elle sat back in her chair. She wasn't sure if Antony would open up to her; she had a feeling he wouldn't, not yet, so she took a sip of her tea and waited.

Antonias wasn't sure where to start; no one had ever spoken to him like that before. He was even tempted to tell her about his mother, but he stopped himself. While all this was going through his mind there was a long silence between them, then he started.

'I feel free on the streets. I lived there a long time, I have mates there, I like to go and see them sometimes.' He felt that was a good enough explanation. Then he mumbled under his breath, 'Sorry about your purse. Did you report it?'

He waited for Elle's answer; she shook her head.

Antonias felt strange in Elle's company, it was as though she could see straight through him.

'I'll pay you back.' To be fair, he didn't know why he'd stolen it, either – habit, he supposed. Elle gave both boys an allowance, and although Jake put his in the school bank after buying his favourite comics, Antonias's money burnt a hole in his pocket and he spent it all at once.

Then a thought occurred to him; it was a strange one, but Elle had brought it up, so he asked.

'Would you really drive me round the streets? I could show you where we light a fire in the oil drum and stand around it getting warm.' He sounded excited about showing off. 'And, yes, I will stop calling Jake "pissy-pants".'

Elle felt this was a great triumph, and that she had made real progress. He had told her as much as he was prepared to, for now, and the rest would come in time, when he felt he could trust her more.

'When you want to go for a drive, Antony, we will all go together. I promise I won't interfere; you can stand with your friends and I'll go and have a coffee somewhere, with Jake. You just let me know when. Oh, and one last thing – you have to go to school and stay there all day. I've spoken to Mrs Anderson and she's prepared to give you another chance, even though she feels you may be better off in some special school.'

Elle thought the idea of going to some 'special school' would shock him; he wouldn't want a stigma like that attached to him, his vanity wouldn't allow it.

'What kind of special school?' He narrowed his eyes. It occurred to him then that this woman had fought his corner, done his fighting for him; yet again, this was something he wasn't used to.

'For children with learning difficulties and problems, that are better off there than in mainstream schools. They get one-to-one teaching to help them.'

The kind of school Elle was describing helped children develop their social skills and talents. They were excellent. Elle knew, because she had worked in schools like that, but she smiled to herself; no way would Antony have a one-to-one teacher keeping an eye on him.

Elle stood up; enough had been said, and she had given Antonias a lot to think about for now.

'Well, I'm going to have a bath. Or would you like to have one, first?' She looked at his dishevelled appearance. Again, she was giving him freedom of choice.

Antonias laughed. He pulled his shirt nearer to his nose and smelt it. 'Phew! I think I'd better go first,' he said, and ran up the stairs. Elle sat back and finished her tea; that hadn't been as hard as she'd feared it might be.

The next morning, Elle was surprised when Antonias came downstairs in his school uniform, but she didn't comment; it was still early days, although she was pleased he was showing willing.

During the lunch break, Antonias stood in a far corner of the playground. He could see Jake from afar and watched him as he sat on one of the wooden benches, reading his comic.

Antonias saw a gang of four or five other boys circle Jake and start mocking him, then the ringleader pulled his comic from his hands and tore it up. Jake sat there and said nothing; he didn't even raise his head.

Antonias saw them throw the torn comic into the air, then he watched as they made Jake empty his pockets and hand over what spare change he had in them. Finally, they walked away, laughing.

Antonias wasn't all that fond of pissy-pants, but he felt sorry for the boy. He walked slowly over towards the gang. They knew of Antonias's reputation, and so never gave him any grief.

'Hey, Antony.' The ringleader who had torn up Jake's comic laughed and threw some of Jake's money at him. 'Do you want some of this?'

Antonias looked at Jake; he could see he was frightened, and he thought Antonias was going to join in because he didn't like him.

Antonias bent down and picked up some of the torn comic, then scrunched it up in his hand.

'No, thanks,' he said. He was very calm and very polite. He grabbed hold of the ringleader's hair and yanked on it, hard. 'But do you want some of this?' He pulled the lad's head back and stuffed the paper into his mouth, making him gag, and then he turned around to one of the others and punched him hard in the face.

His eyes turned a darker blue and he looked at them all with a smirk on his face.

'Anyone else want some?' he said, and he pulled his fist back, ready to strike another blow to any one of them.

The ringleader pulled the paper from his mouth. Antonias had pushed it so far down his throat, he was nearly sick.

The school bell rang and they all started to back away.

'Saved by the bell,' Antonias murmured.

'What's it to you, what we do to him?' one said, as they retreated. 'I thought you didn't like him.'

'I don't.' Antonias smiled, and nodded to Jake to follow him. 'But he's my brother and I'm stuck with him.'

6

THE HARSH TRUTH

That was the start of a very strange friendship. Jake idolised Antonias and was never bullied again – apart from by Antonias, of course, but he didn't mind that.

A couple of months later, Elle had to go in front of the social services review panel. The members, alternatively flicking though the various reports they had and eyeing Antonias, all seemed to feel that he would be better off back in a children's home. Even though his behaviour had improved a little, they still thought he was too much trouble for Elle to cope with on her own.

Antonias also had to sit there while they argued over him like dogs scrapping over a bone. He was alone at one end of the long oval table they all sat at, the distance between him and Elle making it seem even larger than it was. He hung his head.

This is it, then, he thought to himself, I'm leaving Elle's house and going back to the home.

'No!' said Elle, forcefully. 'Antony can stay with me. Have I ever complained about him? He's going to school, he doesn't run away any more. Okay, he still fights at school, but that's boys for you, isn't it? Anyway, why don't you ask him what *he* wants?' She looked towards Antonias. He seemed very young all of a sudden, and vulnerable.

Antonias felt the weight of their eyes on him. The panel members hadn't actually considered what he might want.

'Antony,' said Lisa, 'what would you like to do?' She crossed her fingers under the table, hoping he would say the right thing.

'I'd like to stay with Elle and Jake, if they want me, too,' he said, sullenly. He looked up briefly, then back down at the table.

Antonias had grown quite fond of them, in his own way; he even called Jake by his name now, and talked to him. He didn't tell anyone that Elle had kept her word and driven him around 'cardboard city', where he used to live. He had shown off a little, pointing out where they'd had fires, and doorways he had slept in, and he'd even said 'hello' to the local prostitutes and alcoholics they met.

Elle hadn't been sure whether he had done that to shock her. As much as she'd been squirming inside, she hadn't shown it to Antonias. She'd smiled and laughed with him; after all, this was his home, his roots.

While the review panel left to make their decision, Elle, Lisa and Antonias were left sitting at the table alone.

No one spoke; the air in the room was tense as the three of them waited.

One by one, the members of the panel came back in and sat down. Their faces gave no indication of their decision.

The chair addressed Antonias. 'Well, Antony, Elle has fought your case well, and if she is prepared to carry on for now, we are prepared to let you stay with her. You're a very lucky young man, having someone who cares about you as much as she does. We'll review this in six months' time, unless we have cause to before that.' They all stood up to leave. They figured if this woman wanted to keep the boy, so be it. They were pushed for places, as it was.

Antonias felt like crying. It would have been so easy for Elle to send him back to the children's home, but she had fought for him to stay with her. For the first time ever, he knew what it must feel like to have a mother figure protect you.

Elle ran to him and hugged him. Antonias put his arms around her, but he couldn't speak, because of the lump in his throat. However, he had a feeling that Elle knew what he was thinking.

'Let's go home, Antony.' Elle picked up her bag, hugged Lisa and they left.

By the time they got to the car park, he felt he could speak again. 'Yeah, let's go home. Can I have fish fingers for dinner?'

'You, Antony' – Elle pointed at him – 'can have whatever you want. You're my boy, now, and we're never going to go through that again, not if I have anything to do with it.'

Elle knew there would be regular meetings with his social workers – that was part of being a foster carer – but, hopefully, he would never have to face a panel like that again. For all his faults, and believe me there were many, she loved this young man.

He was like a feral cat that didn't trust anyone, and he never let his guard down for fear of rejection. She and Jake had got through his defences, though. She vowed to herself that she and Jake would always be there for him, and she wouldn't part with either of them. And, as she was a long-term carer, she couldn't see why she would ever have to.

* * *

Over the next few months, Antonias seemed to settle down a bit. He still asked for a drive around the streets now and again, and Elle would take him, as she had promised she would. But his visits became shorter, a couple of hours at most, and didn't happen nearly as often. Clearly, whatever he had been looking for wasn't there, although Elle never asked any questions.

Antonias's birthday party seemed to come as a surprise to him. He received presents, Elle got him a cake with candles, and some friends from school came round to help him celebrate. This time he had let the tears fall, claiming he had something in his eye.

Antonias couldn't remember ever having anything like that arranged for him. He had almost forgotten he had a birthday, but Elle and Jake had made a big fuss over it.

Elle had paid a subscription at a local boxing club for Antonias and Jake. She thought it might be a way for Antonias to let out his frustration. He could punch that bag all he liked, and Jake would be at his side, as always, watching him and learning from him.

Antonias loved it. He enjoyed the discipline of boxing and learning how to fight properly. Elle had been right again; this was a vent for his anger. Instead of running off, he would pick up his bag and head for the boxing club. At least she knew where he was.

Since Elle had begged for a second chance for him from the headteacher, Antonias had made sure he attended school regularly, because he didn't want to give the social services a stick to beat him with. He liked life with Elle and Jake. As a bonus, he had discovered that girls liked him.

His first speedy rough and tumble was with a sixteen-year-old girl, at the school disco, when he was fifteen. She had come over after watching him with his friends.

'You're Antony, aren't you?' she had said. She sipped on the straw in her glass of Pepsi. 'I'm Ruby.' She took a water bottle from under her dress. 'Vodka,' she said, and poured some into his glass.

Antonias knew Ruby had a bit of a reputation around the school, but he thought she was okay. He felt a little nervous, as she stood too close to him and then danced even closer. He was starting to feel his body tense, and to experience feelings he hadn't felt before.

After a while, she led him into a cubicle in the school toilets and got her friend to keep lookout.

Fortunately, Ruby knew exactly what to do, although it was all over in seconds. Antonias felt embarrassed.

'Don't worry, Antony, you'll get better. You just need to learn to take your time,' she said, and with that she left him in the cubicle and went back outside to join her friends.

She had been right, though. Antonias saw Ruby a few times after that, and she became his girlfriend. Many a time he smuggled Ruby into Elle's house and up to his room during their lunch break, while Elle was doing volunteer work at the local charity shop.

As well as Ruby, Antonias noticed some of the other girls also showed an interest in him and so as not to disappoint them, he showed them all the interior of his bedroom, while Jake sat outside the front door, in case Elle returned. After that first time with Ruby, Antonias never looked back; he liked women and they liked him.

When Jake got a bit older, he started going out with a girl, too. He had taken her to the cinema and brought her round to meet Elle, and he did everything Antonias didn't.

As they sat in his bedroom one night, Antonias telling Jake of his latest conquest, a thought occurred to him.

'Hey, Jake, what's your girlfriend like?' he said. He was grinning, waiting for all the sordid details.

'She's really nice, you know she is, you've met her. Why?' Then the penny dropped and he realised what Antonias was asking. 'No, Antony, she's my girlfriend. You have loads to choose from, leave her alone.'

'Oh, I don't want her, she's yours, Jake. I mean, what's she like? You know, sex-wise.'

'She's not like the girls you go out with, Antony, she wants to wait.' Jake looked down at the bed.

Antonias burst out laughing; he threw his pillow at Jake and gave him a playful punch in the arm. 'You're telling me, you've spent your allowance taking her out, and she hasn't even given you a grope of her boobs?'

Again, Jake looked down, then he raised his head defiantly. 'I've kissed her loads of times,' he said.

'But you haven't...' Antonias left it hanging.

Jake shook his head.

'Well, Jake, we're going to fix that right now. You tell me which girl takes your fancy, and I'll chat up her ugly mate. All good-looking girls have ugly mates, and that's a fact!'

Jake just laughed at him. 'Anyone I want, and you can manage that?' This was a challenge for Antonias.

'You pick her, Jake, and I'll work my Italian magic on her. You're getting pretty good at Italian now. Use it mate; all the girls love it.'

Jake had shown an interest in Italian when he'd heard Antonias shouting in it, and asked him what it was. Antonias had taught him all the swear words first, and then got him into trouble with the language teacher, by getting Jake to call her a fat pig. Poor Jake thought he was asking when his homework was due in.

Antonias thought what Jake had told him about his girlfriend was the funniest thing he had ever heard; he never spent his money on any girl that wasn't a 'sure thing'.

Jake was like a brother to Antonias. He always did his home-work for him, when Antonias forgot to do it, and he'd become a pretty good fighter, too.

Antonias had set him up with a few fights at school, and although Jake had been scared to at first, he was more afraid of disappointing Antonias, and so had given it everything he had, punching and kicking, the way Antonias had shown him.

Sometimes he won, sometimes he didn't, but Antonias had been proud of him and it had boosted Jake's confidence. Jake had really come out of his shell under Antonias's guidance.

Elle hadn't been all that pleased when Jake had come home with a black eye or a cut lip, but Jake assured her he wasn't being bullied, he had just had a fight.

Elle knew Antonias was behind it, and smiled to herself; Antonias had been good for Jake.

Life with the boys was fun. They were typical teenagers, always hungry, noisy, and full of bad jokes, but they were hers – for the time being, anyway.

Antonias and Jake came home one day, threw down their bags and walked into the kitchen to see what Elle was cooking.

They were surprised to find she was in the lounge with Antonias's social worker, Lisa. Lisa looked pale and nervous, unusually so. Normally she smiled and greeted him, but not today.

'Antony, could you come in here a moment and sit down,' said Elle. 'Jake, go upstairs and change out of your uniform, please.'

Elle seemed serious.

Oh no, thought Antony, the social worker is going to tell me I can't stay here any more. His mouth went dry and his palms felt sweaty. He sat on the sofa and waited.

Lisa didn't know where to begin; she decided it was best just to blurt it all out.

'We think we've found your mother, Antony. I'm afraid she's... dead.' There, it was said.

Antonias's jaw dropped. He looked at them both; he couldn't believe what he was hearing. How many times had he wandered the streets in search of news of his mother? And here it had come to him, as he sat in Elle's lounge, on her sofa. He suddenly felt exposed, more than he ever had on the streets.

How did they know they had found his mother? How did they know he even had one? He sat stunned; he didn't know what to say. There were no words.

The social worker carried on. 'A young woman going by the

name of Annette Perry has been found. Does that ring any bells with you, Antony?' she said.

Antonias didn't answer; he watched her lips moving, but his brain couldn't take in what she was saying.

'I'm afraid she was found in a squat, not far from here. It seems she choked on her own vomit. She'd been there a while, by all accounts.'

Lisa skirted around the facts. Annette had been there for a week or so, and it was only when people complained about the smell that the police had investigated and found her.

'Your mother was clever, Antony, she had your birth certificate and a small note wrapped up with this.' She held up a gold locket. 'They were in a plastic food bag, in her boots.'

Antonias recognised it at once. He thought she had sold the locket when it went missing from her neck, but she hadn't. Not even in their hungriest of times had she sold it. For whatever reason, she had hung on to it.

The paper Lisa held was old and faded, and smelt a little, from being in his mother's boots. As far as he was aware, she had never taken them off, even when he had seen her bring clients into the squat and had heard them having sex.

Lisa opened the locket and held it towards him. Antonias reached out and took it off her.

It still smelt of his beloved mother. He looked at the photos it held. He had never seen inside it before.

There was a photo of his mother, young and clean, in a wedding dress, with a dark-haired man beside her. The other photo was of Antonias, as a young boy, with his mother.

Antonias burst into tears. He hadn't wanted to, but he was heart-broken, and these two women and God knew who else at last knew his secret. He felt like a rabbit caught in the headlights.

'You're fucking lying!' he shouted at them both, as he stood up.

'You're just making all this up.' He was in denial. His last thread of hope of seeing his mother again had gone. He had always clung on to that hope, even though, as the years passed, he knew it was false.

For the first time since he had known her, Elle shouted at him. 'Sit down, Antony,' she said. 'Lisa isn't lying. Only you know your mother's name. Now, sit down and listen to what she has to say.'

He did as he was told. Okay, he would listen, but he didn't believe them.

Lisa took a breath. 'This note has her name and date of birth, and informs us that she had a son, Antonias, who is half-Italian. That son is you. We've checked and double-checked, Antony, before I came here. The police have certain information, but then the trail goes cold. Only you know the rest.'

Both Elle and Lisa knew they had struck a chord with the mention of his name. They knew, at long last, they had solved the puzzle of who he was.

'We have traced the information given, and found that "Perry" was your mother's maiden name. She has a brother, Ben. We visited him and he confirms she took you to stay with him for a while, but then disappeared without a word. Ben has identified your mother's body.'

They could see Antony was thinking. Somewhere in the dark recesses of his brain, he was remembering Ben.

'Homeless people often write a note explaining who they are, to give them some identity if anything like this happens to them. I'm sorry, Antony, I really am, but there is more. Your full name is Antonias Lambrianu, you are half-Italian, and there may be family still in Italy, we're not sure. Your uncle Ben has asked to meet you, if you want to. There is to be a funeral, in a few days' time.'

Lisa left the note and his birth certificate on the coffee table. She also left a folder, which was full of information that they had managed to unearth about his mother.

They both watched Antony stare at it; he looked like he feared it would burn his fingers if he touched it. He didn't move.

Lisa stood up to leave.

'If you want to talk to me, Antony, any time, night or day, I'm here for you. We've known each other for a long while. I'll see you at the funeral. Elle has the details.' With that, she left. Telling children in her care that their parents were dead was one of the hardest things she had to do, but someone had to do it.

Antonias sat in silence. He looked at his mother's few possessions; they didn't amount to much, for a lifetime. He picked up his birth certificate and read it. His father was Italian, and he had been born on some vineyard somewhere. He crumpled it in his hands and threw it on the floor.

He stood up. He didn't know what to do; he ran out of the front door and slammed it behind him.

Elle didn't try to stop him; he wasn't running away from her, he was running away from the truth.

Antony slept rough on the streets again. He went into a local shop and stole a bottle of wine, even though he had the money in his pocket to buy it. He didn't care if he was arrested, he didn't care about anything, any more.

What he didn't realise was that, on the label on the bottle of the wine he had stolen, it said: Lambrianu Vineyard wines. It seemed an odd coincidence that, at a time like this, he was drinking his own family's wine.

* * *

'Do you think we should go and find him, Elle? It's been two days, the funeral's tomorrow,' said Jake. He was heartbroken. He knew how it felt to lose your parents, but in his case he had known what had happened to his mum and dad, unlike Antonias.

'You're right, Jake. We know most of his old haunts, we'll go when it's dark, when they usually gather around that bonfire he was so excited to show us.'

Although Elle and Jake searched the places they thought Antonias might be, they drew a blank. Then Elle had a thought and telephoned Lisa.

'This is strictly off the record, Lisa, but you said Antony's mother was found in a squat. Do you have the address?' It had occurred to her that maybe someone had told him where Annette had been living, and maybe he was there.

The place was dark, musty, filthy, and almost derelict. Jake managed to find a way inside. It hadn't been boarded up; there was nothing to board up. There was barely any roof, slates were missing and it had no back door. The windows were broken.

Somehow, the staircase was still standing and, underneath it, Elle saw Antony. There were a couple of bottles of wine beside of him, and some empty crisp packets. He was unconscious from drink.

Elle knelt down beside him and tried to wake him. He was bleary eyed, but at least he stirred. Jake helped Elle lift him up, and they carried him to the car. They did their best to get him into the back seat without hurting him.

Elle turned and took one last look at the derelict house; it was an awful place to die in. God alone knew what had happened, to make Antony's mother live like that. She felt a tear come to her eye.

'Rest in peace, Annette, I'll look after your son,' she murmured. Then she wiped her eyes, climbed into the car and drove off.

When Antony awoke, the next day, he wasn't sure where he was, although things looked familiar. Jake had stayed with him the whole night; he hadn't wanted to leave his side. Antony was his brother, and he knew he would do the same for him.

'Where am I?' Antony asked, rubbing his face with his hands. His head was pounding, and he was still in a drunken stupor.

On hearing his voice, Elle walked into the bedroom. 'You're home, Antony,' she said. 'Where else would you be?'

* * *

The funeral was a dismal affair. Antonias shivered; the church was cold and, at the head of it, in front of the altar, was a coffin, with his mother in it.

His uncle Ben hadn't attempted to make contact, nor did he turn up, but he had sent flowers. Elle had bought a large wreath, spelling out his mother's name.

Antonias looked around the empty church. Was this it? His mother's funeral, and she was spending her last few moments on this earth in the company of her son and three strangers – Elle, Jake and Lisa.

His mother hadn't yet turned thirty-eight; she had lived a miserable, short life.

All that was left was this pauper's funeral, followed by a cremation, that had all been arranged by social services. He would never know the truth behind how he and his mother had ended up living on the streets. As hard as he tried he couldn't remember anything, only her drug addiction.

Antonias had asked if he could see his mother, but he had been advised not to, not after the time she had lain, undiscovered, in the squat. He imagined she lay in her coffin dressed in a white nightgown, her long blonde hair now clean and brushed, gleaming like a halo. Her eyes were closed and she looked asleep.

Antonias had been half-tempted to put the large gold locket in the coffin with her, but changed his mind; it was the only thing he had left of her.

The ceremony was short and sweet. Antonias never shed a tear. It had occurred to him that they had family Annette could have left him with, so he was safe and well looked after and would never have had to live on the streets, but she had been a selfish bitch that had never cared about her son. She had never even tried looking for him. She had only thought of herself, and 'mummy's medicine'. As a child, she had left him for days at a time with no food or money, in that dark squat. He vowed there and then, he would never go back to the streets again. There was nothing to look for, not any more. He knew where his mother was and she was never coming back. That life was history now.

What had Lisa said his name was? Antonias Lambrianu.

Well, that would be his name from now on. Antony Perry was buried in that coffin, with his mother.

Long live Antonias Lambrianu! This would be a fresh start. He would make more of his life than his mother ever had of hers, he was determined he would.

After the funeral, Antonias went home. Yes, he thought, this is home, and Elle and Jake are my family now.

* * *

'Elle, show me how to spell "Lambrianu",' Antonias said, a few days after the funeral.

Elle had picked up his birth certificate, after he had crumpled it up and dropped it on the floor, and had flattened it out as best she could. She showed it to him, and wrote his name down for him.

'If that's my name, I'll use it from now on, if that's okay with you,' he said.

Elle could see that he was holding a lot of emotions inside and putting on a brave front. She nodded. 'Just one more thing, Antony; do I call you Antonias now, as well?'

She waited for his response, but he was lost in his own thoughts.

'Look,' she said, pointing to the birth certificate again, 'your mother's name was "Annette" and your father's name was "Marias". I'll bet that's where "Antonias" came from – it's both their names.' She tried making light of it, hoping this would cheer him up.

Antonias just nodded. '"Antony" will do for now,' he said.

Antonias still hadn't looked at the folder Lisa had left for him, which held as much information they had found out about his mother. Elle had put it away for safekeeping, thinking maybe one day he would want to see it.

'According to your birth certificate, Antony, you're older than we thought you were. Your birthdate is different, look – that means you're eighteen already.'

Antonias stared at the print on the birth certificate. Good God, either he had been mistaken or his mother had even lied about that. What other skeletons was he going to find in the cupboard?

'Now I'm eighteen, that means I'm no longer in care, doesn't it?' he said, looking up at Elle.

'Yes, you're a free man, Antony, you're all grown up now, you can do as you please,' Elle said. She knew something was on his mind, so she waited.

'Does that mean I'm no longer going to be fostered by you and that I have to leave?'

Elle put her arms around him; so that was what had been worrying him, the fear that, yet again, he was going to be discarded.

'No, Mr Lambrianu, this is your home. You live here for as long as you want to. You're my bundle of trouble. I love you, Antony, you and Jake are my boys and always will be.'

7

HOME LIFE

Life carried on as normal.

Antonias kept his word to Jake and, a few months later, when Jake saw a girl that he liked, Antonias flirted with and charmed her 'ugly, fat friend', Glynis.

Chatting up Glynis really was scraping the bottom of the barrel, as far as Antonias was concerned, but even he had to admit, her friend, Janice, was quite a looker; if it wasn't for brotherly loyalty, he would have gone for her, himself.

Glynis was fat, had acne and stank of all the cheese and onion crisps she ate. Antonias asked her to join him for lunch, at Elle's, on the condition she brought her friend along for Jake.

Glynis had agreed, although she was suspicious of Antony, knowing what he was like with the girls.

'You're my boyfriend, though, aren't you? Janice is for Jake, right?' She put her hand in her crisp packet, and waited.

'Of course, Glynis, love.' Antonias had given her his broadest, most charming smile and looked at her with those blue eyes of his.

The meeting was all set for lunchtime the next day, when Elle would be out. God, Antonias thought, when he saw Glynis walking towards him with her bag of cheese and onion crisps, what am I doing?

'Bloody hell, Jake,' he said, 'is that all she eats? No wonder she stinks of them. You do realise this is the first and last time I do this for you, don't you? So you had better do the business.'

Jake was watching Janice, as she approached them.

'Here, take this.' Antonias threw Jake a condom. He turned his eyes to Janice and secretly wished he was about to be entertaining her, instead of her smelly friend. She was slim and quite a looker – Jake had made a good choice.

At the house, they had a couple of beers and talked, then Antonias, who was watching the clock, suggested they all spent a little time on their own.

He pushed Jake and Janice towards the stairs; he had decided to stay downstairs, to give Jake more privacy.

'Get on with it, Jake, and make it quick, we've got half an hour before Elle gets back.' Antonias glared at him and wagged his finger in his face.

Antonias had felt sick when Glynis took her chewing gum out of her mouth and stuck it on the edge of the coffee table, then was surprised when she leapt on him, ready for action.

She locked her mouth on his and shoved her tongue down his throat; he was gagging. She forced herself on top of him and, with all her overweight body, started bouncing up and down on him. He closed his eyes and thought of England, letting Glynis take the lead. In a moment, he had finished.

Glynis was ready for another round, but Antonias had had enough. He couldn't take any more. He pulled up his trousers and ran upstairs to Jake's bedroom.

As the door swung wide open, he saw Jake, with his trousers down, on top of Janice.

'Have you finished yet? For God's sake, Jake, tell me you're finished, I can't take any more.'

Jake was startled by Antonias bursting into the bedroom, and turned to look at him. His face was flushed and Janice was trying to cover herself up.

'I bloody have now!' said Jake. He looked at Antonias's appearance; he looked like he'd had a fight with a Rottweiler. His hair was all over the place, he had a love bite on the side of his neck and his shirt was torn.

Antonias went into the bathroom; he was shattered. 'This is taking brotherly love too far!' he muttered to himself.

Later that day, Antonias and Jake looked at each other and burst out laughing. 'High five, mate,' said Jake. 'God, you looked awful. Why did you have sex with her?'

They were laughing out loud now. What a day!

'Because,' said Antonias, through his laughter, 'I had no bloody choice! You did screw that Janice bird, didn't you? Please tell me I didn't do that for nothing!'

Jake gave him the thumbs up. 'Couldn't let you down, Antony, I knew you were relying on me.' He waved his hand in front of his face. 'God, you still smell of cheese and onion crisps!'

They laughed even louder – it was hilarious – but Antonias had kept his word. He wouldn't see Glynis again, though. He was due to leave school at the end of the week, there was no point in staying on for more exams, he knew he would fail, unlike Jake. Jake was meant for learning. He was a swotter. Still, at least he could avoid Glynis.

He felt sorry for the girl, and she had been a big help in his scheme, so he decided to pass her on to a friend of theirs who was just as fat and as plain as she was. They were made for each other.

It all worked out in the end – a few years later, Antonias heard they had got married and were very happy with their two children and a truckload of crisps!

* * *

Elle knew Antony would be at a loose end once he left school, especially without Jake by his side. She already had an idea up her sleeve and felt this was the answer to both of their prayers. Apart from the boxing club, Antonias's other love was cars, and these days she knew when he disappeared for hours on end, it was because he was spending time at the garage around the corner, talking with the mechanics.

He was there that often, they had offered him a weekend job valeting the cars, which he enjoyed.

Elle knew the owner, so she seized what she saw as a golden opportunity and asked the manager, Wayne, if he would take Antonias on as an apprentice, now he was leaving school. Surprisingly, Wayne didn't seem that shocked she had asked and shrugged and smiled.

'Might as well,' he said, 'he's always here, anyway. Just so long as he goes to college and does it properly. It's up to him Elle, but, I agree with you, he seems to like tinkering about with the cars and the men like him.'

Elle almost jumped in the air and kissed Wayne at the good news. She knew this would be something Antony would enjoy and put his whole heart and soul into. After all, the devil made work for idle hands, and the last thing she wanted was for Antony to have idle hands!

Antonias, Elle thought, looks like a different person, compared with the skinny boy who first came to stay. With all his working out at the gym, he had muscled arms, he filled out his shirtsleeves, and in the summertime, when he purposely wore a tight-fitting T-shirt while working at the garage, the admiring glances from the girls made all the other mechanics call him 'the stud'.

* * *

'Antony! Antony! Over here, mate.'

Antonias was having a few beers with Jake and a few friends from college. He looked around the pub crowd, to see who was calling to him. His eyes scanned the room, and then stopped. It was Eddie, who had been in the children's home with him, all those years ago.

Antonias excused himself and went over to have a chat with Eddie, who was propping up the bar. He smiled as he walked towards his old friend.

It's good to see him after all this time, he thought. Eddie looked good, too. He was wearing a suit and tie. He had obviously done well for himself.

'Eddie, mate, how are you?' Antonias envied his well-turned-out friend. He felt underdressed, in his denim jeans and shirt.

'Doing well, Antony, can't complain. What are you up to these days? Still a crazy bastard?' He hugged Antonias. They had been through a lot together; they knew each other's past lives.

Antonias didn't want all his friends knowing he had met Eddie in a children's home, and so put him on the alert to keep quiet about it, should any of them come over.

'I'm working as an apprentice mechanic, doing well, but obviously not as well as you, by the looks of it. What are you doing?'

'Bit of this, bit of that.' Eddie winked at him. Antonias wasn't sure what he meant, and so enquired further.

He listened as Eddie filled him in on his amazing lifestyle. It sounded glamorous to Antonias, and what was more, Eddie took out his wallet and showed him the contents; it was fat with notes, a full wallet. Wow!

'Went to prison for a while, Antony. Not long, just a year, but in there, I met some guys. They work for the geezer who runs the protection racket in the East End pubs.'

Antonias was puzzled. He had never heard of anything like that before, he wasn't sure what Eddie meant.

'It's like this,' said Eddie. 'This guy promises these strip pubs and local boozers protection from any trouble, and in return they pay him. It's like insurance. On the odd occasion, he makes trouble himself. That way, they pay him more, because they're frightened, and if they don't pay, we smash the place up and give the landlord a good beating.' Eddie grinned. 'It would be money for old rope for you, you always loved a fight.'

Antonias couldn't believe what he was hearing; this was like something out of the movies.

'You get paid for collecting money and beating people up, is that what you're saying?'

Antonias found this amazing. Surely it couldn't be true that all Eddie did was collect money from local striptease clubs and start fights, and he was being paid handsomely for it.

'Sometimes, we get tooled up. Other bosses want to collect money off our turf, and we have to show them who's boss.'

'You use guns? Come on, Eddie, this is all stories. Tell me the truth, have you got some office job somewhere? This sounds like some gangster movie.'

Antonias started laughing at Eddie. He'd always been fond of farfetched stories, but this was wild.

'They call it security, Antony. I tell you what, come to that strip club tomorrow night.' Eddie took out a card with the address on and showed him. 'I'll get you in, I'm working the door tomorrow.'

With that, Eddie left the pub.

Antony couldn't stop thinking about what Eddie had said; he kept going over it in his mind. He decided to go to the club. If nothing else, it would be a different experience – he had never been in a strip club before.

The next evening, Antonias got himself dressed in a pair of black trousers and a white shirt. He didn't own a suit, like Eddie, but he wanted to look smart.

Elle presumed he had a date. He had been seeing Alison, from the bookies, lately, and seemed to like her. She had passed what Jake called the 'two-week test'; if they made it past that, they were his girlfriend.

But Antonias went to the club alone. He didn't like leaving Jake, but he wanted to do this by himself. He didn't know what to expect.

He looked for the street name that was on the card, and then he heard loud music. He looked towards the pub and, as promised, Eddie stood outside, letting people in.

'Antony, you came.' Eddie seemed pleased to see him. He shook his hand and introduced him to another guy in a suit, also acting as doorman.

Antonias felt a little bit intimidated by it all; this was a whole new world to him, and for once he didn't feel so confident and in control.

Eddie took him inside and pushed through the crowds to the bar. He ordered some drinks, and Antonias noticed he didn't pay for them. He looked at him.

'Perks of the job, Antony, and so is that.' He nodded his head towards the stage in the background. There was a woman provocatively taking her clothes off to the music.

Antonias felt a little embarrassed. He could feel his body stirring at the sight of the nearly naked woman, wearing just stockings and suspenders, rubbing herself in baby oil while the crowd of men watching her cheered.

'Steady on, mate,' said Eddie, laughing, 'you're a bit quick off the trigger.' He looked down at Antonias's erection, blatantly growing in his trousers.

Now Antonias really did feel embarrassed; he blushed and felt a fool. He had seen many a naked girl, but not like this. This was a woman, teasing and bending over in front of the crowd, wiggling her backside provocatively in front of them. Her breasts were full and round, and her legs were shapely. Antonias couldn't take his eyes off her.

Eddie was full of bravado, showing off to his friend. He introduced him to more of the guys he knew and then took him into the ladies' toilets, where there were more strippers getting ready and changing, preparing to go onto the makeshift stage.

It was tacky, but it was fun. Antonias was hooked.

Suddenly, he heard a glass smash, and Eddie told him to stay at the bar and wait for him to come back.

Antonias didn't wait; he was curious. He followed Eddie towards the front doors.

A fight had broken out. One man had a knife and was waving it about, shouting and threatening everyone. Eddie was telling the man to put the knife down. He kept repeating himself.

Antonias leapt forward. He hit the man on the chin, took the knife out of his hand, then kicked him hard, in between the legs, for good measure. He turned around and handed the knife to Eddie.

Eddie took the knife. 'It's good to see some things don't change. Still fearless, eh, Antony?' He slapped Antonias on the back and led him back into the pub, then got him a drink.

Antonias seemed to be the hero of the evening. Eddie encouraged a couple of strippers to come and meet his friend. They stood next to him at the bar, wearing only their underwear. They took out their breasts, and teased him, laughing at his instant reaction.

Damn! Antonias thought to himself. If he were to come here again, he would have to learn to control his body.

'You're a pretty boy.' One of the strippers reached up and put her hands through his thick mane of blond hair and held it.

Antonias looked behind her, where Eddie stood. Eddie winked at him and gave him the thumbs up.

Antonias had had enough of hiding his excitement. He put his hand out and started stroking the stripper's breasts. She didn't stir or try to stop him; again, he looked at Eddie.

Eddie pointed to the gents in the corner, and mouthed to him, 'In there, Antony.'

Antonias took her hand and started to lead her away from the bar. She followed him, and once inside the gents, went down on her knees and undid the zip on his trousers. She performed oral sex on him, something Antonias hadn't experienced before, and it nearly blew his head off.

Afterwards, he went back towards the bar, where Eddie was standing. The grin on his face said it all. 'That's another perk of the job,' he said.

Antonias thought this was the best place on earth, and that Eddie was a lucky sod. He would definitely be back again.

Antonias became a frequent visitor to the pub, partly to see Eddie, but most of all to see Caroline, the dancer who had shown him so much attention the first time.

Each time he went there, he would look for her, and she would eventually go over to him, after speaking to the punters who paid her wages.

Caroline always said her farewells to Antonias in a sexual way. She wasn't one of the modest schoolgirls he had dated. Caroline liked sex, and in her experienced hands he learnt an awful lot.

Antonias still dated Alison on the side, but she lacked the knowledge and the willingness to try different things.

Caroline invited him to her house one night, and he had willingly gone – and what a night it was.

She knew all kinds of different positions, she liked being tied up and knew all kinds of different games. Antonias was besotted with her, he couldn't get enough of her. He would turn up on a Saturday night, bursting with excitement, taking Caroline a bottle of her favourite perfume or some other gift he could afford. She was worth it; he had even borrowed money from Jake to buy her things.

'Where do you go every Saturday, Antony?' asked Jake, one night. 'You're always late home and you never say anything. I thought we were brothers.'

Antonias felt guilty he had kept this secret from Jake, and so he sat on the edge of the bed and told him everything, giving him details that shocked Jake. Antonias was grinning broadly; it made him feel like a man.

The more shocked Jake looked, the more Antonias boasted about his sexual rendezvous with Caroline.

'Can I come with you, Antony? I wouldn't mind seeing some of that,' Jake said.

Antonias said he would ask Eddie for next week, and maybe he would set Jake up with someone.

When Antonias next got to the club and tried to have a word with Eddie, he found his friend was preoccupied.

'You'd better leave, Antony, there's going to be big trouble tonight, we're expecting things to kick off.' Eddie looked up and down the street.

Antonias was puzzled; Eddie looked nervous and agitated, which wasn't like him. Even so, Antonias had waited a week to see Caroline, and he wasn't going home now.

'What's going on, Eddie? Can I help?' Antonias was desperate to get through the doors; Eddie was standing outside with one of the other security men, and they both seemed on the lookout.

'Bossman's turf is the East End. All the bosses have their own turf, but our boss has been scamming some of the South London lot and they're not happy about it. In short, there's going to be a turf war, and I don't want you getting hurt. At least we've got protection.'

Eddie put his arm into his jacket and pulled out a gun. Antonias was shocked, he had never seen one this close up before; in fact, he'd only ever seen one on TV or in the movies.

'I'm staying with you,' Antonias said. 'You're my mate, and you never know, maybe I can help.'

Eddie stared at him. Antony had always been a crazy bastard; maybe he was right. He nodded.

'On your head be it. Just remember, I never asked you to stay.'

Antonias was prepared to take his chances; at least if he stuck around, he might be able to get in to see Caroline. Surely, she would be wondering where he was by now; he was never late.

Antonias was not prepared for what happened next. He'd thought Eddie was exaggerating, with all his talk about turf wars, but he wasn't.

Two cars sped towards them, driving up onto the pavement and screeching to a halt. Three tall black men carrying baseball bats jumped out of the cars. They weren't shouting or arguing, they looked like they meant business.

Antonias saw Eddie reach into his pocket and knew he was getting ready for the fight, getting ready to take out his gun.

The three men told Eddie and the other security guy to get out of their way, and tried to push them aside, so they could get into the pub. Antonias could see that, for all Eddie's bravado, he was scared, and who wouldn't be?

Eddie took out his gun and pointed it at one of the men. 'Just fuck off or I'll use this,' he shouted.

The music blaring out from the inside was drowning out the argument taking place outside. The three black men laughed at Eddie and his friend. 'You amateurs make me sick!' said one of them. 'Get out of my way and go home to Mummy.'

Eddie fired the gun, but the man moved out of the way and Eddie missed. Antonias reckoned he was such a crap shot; he would probably have missed anyway.

The man took hold of his baseball bat and raised it. He was just about to bring it down hard, on Eddie, when Antonias leapt forward. He grabbed the man's wrist and held it tight, shaking his arm so he dropped the bat.

The other men started hitting the other security guy; blow after blow they rained down on him with their bats. Eddie seemed to freeze; he looked at his friend on the ground, covered in blood, and then at Antonias.

Antonias pulled back his arm and slammed his fist into the face of the man he was holding by the arm. Again and again, he punched him, until he fell to the ground, then Antonias started kicking him.

Eddie held his gun out and shot at one of the two men who were hitting his friend. The man fell to the ground. He was covered in blood; Eddie had shot him in the stomach and it was obvious he was dying.

The other black man stopped beating the security guy on the ground and turned to see who had shot his friend. Eddie hit him, and the man headbutted Eddie in return. Eddie had his hands to his face. The man grabbed hold of Antonias's shirt, ripping it. He pulled Antonias towards him, and punched him hard in the face.

Antonias saw stars for a moment and felt blood dripping from his nose. He wiped it with his sleeve.

'Here, Antony!' Eddie threw a baseball bat towards him.

Antonias caught it and swung it through the air, bringing it down hard on his assailant's head and neck. He watched as the man staggered back and fell to the ground. Antonias saw him hold up his hands; he was screaming in pain, and begging Antonias to stop.

Antonias held up the bat to take another swing. 'Now who are the fucking amateurs?' he shouted at the man on the ground.

Suddenly, Antonias felt arms grab him from behind and hold him back. Someone was pulling him away.

He heard men's voices behind him. 'Enough!' someone said. 'Enough, do you hear me? Stop it, now.'

Breathing heavily, Antonias dropped the bat, then looked at Eddie, who had his hand up, indicating he should stop.

Antonias didn't want to stop. He was angry and all fired up, and then suddenly he felt the cold metal of a gun barrel at his temple.

'I said, enough, calm down. I'm going to lower the gun now and if you turn to hit me, I'll shoot you. No questions asked, okay?'

Antonias nodded. He knew on this occasion he was beaten, but he was also confused: why weren't the men behind him hitting him?

Antonias controlled his breathing. He looked up at Eddie, and saw a short stocky man, dressed in a suit and tie, standing beside him. He looked around fifty, maybe more. The man was smoking a cigarette and looking at Antonias.

The man turned towards Eddie. 'Put the dead one in the back of the car, and drive them all over to the south side where they belong, then clean this mess up.' He dropped his cigarette and ground it out with his foot, then looked back at Antonias. 'You, come and see me when you've cleaned up.' With that, he turned and walked back into the pub.

The other security guy was just about beaten to death, but he was breathing.

Antonias and Eddie put the dead guy into the boot of the car, along with the other two. They were covered in blood, and only half conscious.

Before he closed the boot, Antonias lowered his head to the ear of the man he had just hit with the baseball bat.

'Tell whoever your friends are, no one fucks with Antony Lambrianu, got it?' Antonias raised his head and waited for some acknowledgement, to show the man had heard him.

The man, his face bloodied, nodded at Antonias and then passed out.

A couple of the bar staff came out. They were holding buckets of soapy water, and threw them on the pavement to wash away some of the blood.

Antonias saw Eddie's gun lying discarded on the ground. He looked around to see if anyone was watching him, then quickly picked it up and put it into the waistband of his trousers.

'Phew, thanks for your help, Antony,' said Eddie. He looked around, in a daze. 'I can't believe I killed that guy.' Eddie was visibly shaking. His face was white, and Antonias watched him as he turned to the wall and vomited. Eddie wiped his mouth with his sleeve and turned to Antonias. 'Come on, I need a large drink, and you need to clean up before you meet the boss.'

Antonias, who had just been about to push the pub doors open, stopped and turned to Eddie. 'The boss? What are you talking about?'

'The boss, Antony, the guy who told you to clean up and go and see him. Get a move on, he doesn't like to be kept waiting.'

Antonias was gutted. He had bloodstains all over him and his shirt was ripped. His fist was swelling up as a result of the punches he had thrown, and his nose was bleeding. He would have to clean up quick, if he was going to meet Caroline. Eddie's boss could wait.

Eddie walked to the bar and Antonias headed into the gents. He stood in front of one of the washbasins and started running the cold-water tap. He put his hands into the cool water, scooped some up and threw it on his face. The water turned red. Antonias wiped his nose, and carefully felt it with his fingers; at least it wasn't broken. He ripped off some pieces of paper towel and plugged his nostrils.

Blood seemed to be everywhere – even in his blond hair. In the end he put his head under the tap and rinsed it all out.

Antonias pulled out some more paper towels and started to dry himself off. He could hear noises in the cubicle behind him. He put his head under the hand dryer and used it to dry his hair. It had the added advantage of drowning out the sounds of people having sex.

He removed the plugs from his nostrils and was relieved to find the bleeding had stopped. He finger-combed his hair, then stood back and looked in the mirror. It wasn't great, but he looked better than he had when he'd walked in. His shirt was wet, but that couldn't be helped.

Antonias took the gun out of his waistband, looked at it and grinned, then put it back again. It was hidden under his shirt, and when he put his jacket on, it couldn't be seen at all.

The cubicle door behind him opened. Antonias looked into the mirror above the sink to see who it was, and was stunned. It was Caroline, with some fat old grey-haired man. He couldn't believe his eyes; now he felt sick.

When she saw Antonias, Caroline stopped and stared at him. Then she composed herself, kissed the man she was with on the cheek and smiled at him.

Antonias stared into the mirror, looking at the scene behind him. Caroline was holding money in her hand. He felt his face burning; she was a prostitute, and she had been having sex with that old man in the toilet cubicle.

Antonias had waited all week to see her, he had fantasised about how beautiful she was, he had even boasted about her to Jake! What a fool he'd been.

The old man exited the toilets and Caroline walked up to where Antonias was standing at the sink.

Antonias looked at her; those beautiful lips, with their red lipstick, had kissed him and he had kissed them. Now they looked dirty and horrible. It was obvious she had just had oral sex with the man, as well as letting him screw her, because she swilled her mouth out under the tap, and then lifted her dress, to put her knickers back on.

Antonias said nothing. He felt like crying but didn't know why. He had thought Caroline was his girl, and their times together had been special.

'How is my beautiful pretty boy tonight?' Caroline said. She held up her arm to run her hand through his hair, but he stopped her. She looked at him, puzzled by his reaction.

'Why, Caroline? Why him?' Antonias couldn't understand it. She knew he was coming tonight but had still cheated on him.

'Why do you think, Antony? Because he has more money than you. I get tired of screwing around with these old guys and I look forward to some fun with you. Is that a problem?'

Caroline really didn't understand. He couldn't believe she was treating what he had just witnessed so nonchalantly. Because the old guy had more money... what the hell did that even mean?

'You've never asked me for money. How do you know I don't have any?' he said.

'Come on, Antony, you buy a couple of bottles of cheap perfume, you're a trainee mechanic who has fixed my car up, and I appreciate that, but I have needs, too... like paying the rent, you know? Stripping is good money, but it's the extras that boost your wages, especially as the owner takes a commission.

'I like you, Antony, I really do. You're not limp, like the others, I don't have to work hard to give you an erection, you're always ready, night and day, and more than once. And you have fun, too, don't you? So, what's the problem? We can carry on, can't we?'

Antonias couldn't believe his ears. She wanted to carry on

having sex with him, after he'd just seen her with that old, fat man. There was no way. He had put her on a pedestal, infatuated and besotted. He had even, at times, thought he loved her. How wrong he could be.

'No thanks, Caroline, I think I'll buy someone else my cheap bottles of perfume.' Antonias took out his wallet, pulled out twenty pounds, and pushed it down her cleavage.

'Here, put that towards your rent.' With that, he walked out of the toilets. Stupidly, he felt hurt and a little heartbroken. Maybe she had been his first true love, but he would make damn sure he wouldn't trust a woman again. She would be his last love, too. He should have learned his lesson from the way his mother had treated him.

Eddie was waiting for him when he went out. He handed Antonias a large whisky.

'Here, mate, you've earned it. Where have you been? With that Caroline bird? Come on, the bossman's waiting.'

Antonias stopped Eddie. 'Why didn't you tell me Caroline turned tricks? You knew I liked her.'

'I thought you knew, mate. Everybody likes Caroline, even me. The girls all do it, then they pay the bossman commission. Their striptease is just a warm up, to get the guys interested. Come on.'

Now Antonias really did feel stupid; even Eddie had been there. How could he have been so blind? What was it that Elle said? 'There's none as blind as them that won't see.' She was right. He had thought he was special, and he wasn't, he was just another punter. He downed the whisky in one and put the glass on the bar.

Eddie knocked on the back-room door. The stocky man Antonias had seen outside was sitting at a table in a grubby makeshift office, smoking a cigarette. He was on the telephone, and made them wait until he had finished his call.

'You took your time,' he said. He was trying to intimidate Antonias. As far as Antonias was concerned, bigger and harder men than him had tried and failed, and so he just shrugged and said nothing. It was Eddie who did all the talking.

'He's been cleaning up, boss, making himself more respectable for you. This is my friend, Antony.'

Antonias turned and looked at Eddie. He was nervous and sucking up to this guy and Antonias was appalled.

'You have a bad attitude, son, but you are handy with your fists, I'll give you that. I can always use a man like you. Do you want a job working the doors, on some old club I've got in the West End? It's a shithole, but I do business there. Just weekends, if you're interested.'

Antonias looked around the room, and then back at the man; extra cash was always welcome.

'How much you paying?' said Antonias. He looked the man squarely in the eye.

Smiling, the man took another draw on his cigarette and blew the smoke into the air.

'You're a cocky bastard, aren't you? I pay more than the minimum wage, if you're worth it.'

Antonias was disgusted. This so called boss had let his cigarette ash fall onto his jacket and just brushed it off. This was no way for some gangster boss to act; he was low-life scum.

'I always work with my brother, he's my wingman.' Antonias knew Jake would agree. He saw Eddie turn and look at him, out of the corner of his eye. Eddie didn't know he had a brother.

'Okay, but you're responsible for him. Now, get out there and earn me some money.'

8

BROTHERS IN ARMS

Enrolling at college for the mechanics course and working at the garage as an apprentice was like a dream come true for Antony. He enjoyed it, and it kept Elle happy. He was learning a good trade, and had even had the chance to pick up an old car and do it up for himself. It wasn't much, but it was a start.

At weekends, both he and Jake worked the doors at the worst, shittiest club in the West End. It was a run-down place set right in the heart of London, within arm's reach of all the big-name theatres. What a waste, thought Antonias, when he first saw it.

The bossman, as they now knew him, had interrogated Jake about his age and ability to fight, and Jake had followed Antonias's speech word for word. The bossman hadn't been happy enough with that; he knew Antonias had prompted his brother, and so called for one of his security men to come in.

'Prove yourself, sonny. Mike, hit him,' he said.

Mike, the security man, did as he was told and threw a punch at Jake, hitting him square in the face. Antonias hadn't expected that. Poor Jake.

Thankfully, all those years at the boxing club had paid off, and

Jake flew into Mike and punched him a few times, making him stagger back.

'Stop!' shouted the bossman. 'So,' he said to Jake, 'you're the boxer and he's the psychopath, fair enough.'

Jake was rubbing his chin. He looked at Antonias, who avoided his stare.

The club was mainly a drug-dealing shop. It also fronted as a rave club for every dropout around. It stank of glue, because of all the glue-sniffers who came in, got high and then danced the night away. Obviously, it was full of prostitutes too. His boss, Antonias decided, was just a pimp.

Antonias steered clear of all the prostitutes; he wouldn't make that mistake again. Even though they fussed over him and told him how handsome he was, he stayed professional.

Jake had a few experiences, but at least he was warned by Antonias not to get involved and always to wear a condom, for his own safety.

The money, Antonias had to admit, was good. He was earning 200 pounds for a weekend's work, as was Jake, but they had to fight every weekend, too. There was always some 'hard man' wanting a scrap.

Elle would complain and fuss and clean them up with ointments, each time they woke up in the mornings with black eyes and scraped knuckles. She knew they weren't just club bouncers, there was more to it than they were telling her, but at least they had each other. God help them.

Elle knew by the money they made that it wasn't all above board. Antonias and Jake had gone shopping and bought suits and shirts from well-known shops, things they couldn't have afforded on regular wages. For the time being she decided to stay silent.

The bossman seemed satisfied with their work, and soon he decided not to waste his two best fighters as doormen. He wanted them to do some collecting from the pubs he offered protection to. He thought the two brothers were scary, evil bastards, especially the blond one. He didn't trust Antonias, he reckoned he was crazy.

As far as Antonias was concerned, this was a promotion, and he was happy to be moving around. Jake wasn't so sure.

'Come on, Jake,' Antonias said, 'we walk in, see the governor of the pub, collect our money and leave. What's so wrong with that?'

'If that's what you think, Antony, that's your mistake. What about when these landlords see two new young guys they don't know, and don't want to pay? Have you thought of that?'

Jake was cautious. He knew the boss used them, but didn't particularly like them. Antony didn't grovel enough, and wasn't scared of him. Jake felt that was a big mistake; this bossman hadn't got where he was by having people unafraid of him. His brother should have pretended to be a bit scared, at least.

'If that's the case,' Antonias said, 'we'll kick their arses till they do pay. Nothing new there, that's what we do.'

He was looking in the mirror and combing his golden locks. He was vain, mainly because he looked like a somebody, these days, not just Antony.

Jake was amazed when he found out that this collecting the boss wanted them to do was more of a shopping list. It wasn't just a few places; there were pubs all around the East End, some he had never even heard of.

The first one they went into was pretty easy; all they had to do was tell the landlord who'd sent them, and he handed over a banker's cloth bag full of money.

'Who are you two?' the landlord said. 'Never seen you before.' He seemed friendly enough, but Antonias didn't answer his question; he just picked up the money and walked out.

The first half a dozen pubs were the same, but Jake was still wary.

'I don't like it, Antony,' he said. 'Somebody out there knows by now that we have a shitload of money on us. We're sitting targets.'

Antonias knew Jake was right; they had no protection, other than themselves. People would soon know they were the bossman's collectors. Today, though, he felt they were safe because nobody knew them yet, nobody was expecting him and Jake. Besides, even though they were both in suits, they weren't exactly driving around in a first-class car. Anyone who saw them would probably think they were office workers or something. For now, at least.

After a long day driving around, going into pubs and snooker halls, they had been to every place on the list. They went back to the boss and handed over the money.

The boss took it out and spread it all out on the table, then made them both stand there while he counted it out.

'It's all there, boys. Mind you keep it that way, don't get greedy and start helping yourselves. Got it?'

They left the office. Antonias felt insulted by the boss for assuming they would steal from him.

'Fuck's sake, did you see all that cash?' said Jake. He had been completely blown away by all the money on the boss's table.

'I did, Jake.'

They had watched him bundle it all into his safe. He had given them an extra fifty pounds each as a bonus on top of their wages.

'Jeez, Antony, all that money for sitting on his fat arse, without taking a risk.'

Antonias looked at the fifty pounds in his hand. 'Is that all he thinks we're worth? Fifty bloody quid. He needs to learn to look after his workers more, and while he's at it, he could spend some of that stash getting that filthy suit of his dry cleaned.'

'You're never satisfied, are you,' Jake said, as they were getting in the car. 'What do you want?'

'I want his job; I could do it better and with more style. You've seen the state of him, who the hell is going to respect that? But, firstly, Jake, my man, let's go for a drink, find some willing women and get laid.' He grinned at Jake and playfully nudged him in the ribs, then he started the car and drove off, heading for a nearby nightclub.

Jake was laughing. 'For God's sake, Antony, is sex all you ever think about? That, and money?'

Antonias was grinning and nodding his head, as they pulled up outside the club.

Antonias and Jake stood at the bar having a drink. They knew the local bouncers, now, and they would come and talk to them. Life seemed good, and Antonias knew, with his looks and some money in his pocket, he wouldn't be without female company for long.

He had just finished his drink and was about to order another round, when two women came and stood beside him at the bar. When their drinks came, Antonias held out his money and paid for them. They gushed their thank yous and started talking to him and Jake. He felt it was as easy as that. By the end of the night, they were all parked around some dark corner, having sex in the car.

Antonias dropped the women off at home, then drove back to Elle's.

'Bloody hell, Antony,' said Jake, 'how come I always get the front seat? I always get the handbrake stuck in the way. Next time, you can do it in the front.'

'Because, Jake, it's my car and I get first choice. But okay, if you feel like that, I'll go in the front tomorrow.' They both started laughing at each other.

Elle always left the porch light on for them and they both knew, even though she was in bed, she didn't really go to sleep until they were both home, safe and sound.

When they got upstairs, they tapped on Elle's door and went in.

'Night, Elle,' said Antonias.

'Night, Elle,' echoed Jake.

They watched her go through the same routine she always did.

She switched on the bedside lamp and said, 'Oh, is that the time? Sorry, boys, I was asleep. Did you lock up?'

Jake nodded.

'Are you both okay? Did you have a good time? Do you want a drink or something?' Elle was getting ready to pull back the covers to get up and make them something to eat and drink.

They turned and smiled at each other, then looked back at Elle. They each put a hand up to stop her getting out of bed. 'No, we're fine Elle,' said Antonias. 'You get some sleep, we're going to bed, now.'

They both knew they were lucky to have her; she loved them and would do anything for them.

'You know what, Jake? I think we're too old to live at home,' said Antonias, quietly. 'We should get our own place, and then you wouldn't get stuck on the handbrake. We'd have somewhere to take girls.'

'We couldn't leave Elle, she'd be devastated. No, give it a while longer, let's get some more money together, first.' Jake didn't like the idea of leaving Elle on her own, she'd been so good to them both.

'We wouldn't be leaving her. She does expect us to grow up and move on, you know. Anyway, someone's got to do the washing and cook us a decent meal every now and again.'

Jake shook his head. 'She's not the bloody housekeeper, she's our mum, and you're a cheeky bugger.'

Antonias lay in bed that night, thinking. Even though he was tired, he thought about what Jake had said. He'd lived with Elle for years and not thought of her like that, even though she had always been there for him. Yes, she was 'our mum', or the closest they would ever get to one.

* * *

As the months passed, Jake and Antonias carried on collecting. They ran into a few arguments along the way, but nothing they couldn't handle. Antonias had used his head and bought a large safety box with a lock and key, to put in the boot of his car. While he was working at the garage, one day, he had screwed the safe in place, under the spare wheel. He also decided to start carrying the gun he had picked up after the big fight at the strip club, just in case.

Antonias was doing well at college and had nearly finished his course.

Jake was more studious. He had wanted to go into teaching, but then thought better of it and decided to try bookkeeping, instead.

Alongside all this, they worked for the bossman; the money was rolling in.

But things turned nasty, one day, when they went to collect from a pub they had been in many times before. Antonias suddenly felt uneasy. He looked at Jake and frowned.

They walked up to the bar as normal, but all the while, Antonias was looking around at the few men in there, having a drink. Something was definitely wrong; you could feel it in the air.

Antonias's eyes stopped on one man. He was sitting at a table with a friend, and Antonias recognised him instantly.

It was the man he had given his name to, on the night he had put him in the boot of the car, when he had been in the fight with Eddie.

Antonias looked at Jake and discreetly pointed his thumb behind them, to the black man.

They were now on their guard. They stood and watched as the two men walked up to the bar and stood beside them. The landlord seemed to be taking longer than ever to get his money together.

The landlord put the money bag on the bar, then cast a glance at the two men. One reached out and put his hand on the bag.

'Not so fast, pretty boy, that's mine.' He pulled out a knife and, with his other hand, held it to Antonias's throat. The second man stood behind Jake; he had a knife pressed against his back.

The other drinkers saw what was going on and hurried out.

Antonias looked calmly at the landlord. He seemed to be smiling at the scene before him, as though he was glad he and Jake were getting their comeuppance.

'Take it,' said Antonias, 'it's yours, if you want it that badly. I'm only the collector.'

Recognition sparked in the man's eyes. 'Wait a minute, I know you, pretty boy, don't I? You're that Lambrianu bloke who shut me in the boot of a car, and parked it outside of my boss's house, you bastard.' The man's voice was getting louder as his anger built, the memory of his humiliation still a festering sore. 'Not so brave now, without your mates, are you?' He was spitting as he spoke, his face a snarling mask of hatred.

He picked up the money bag and, still with the knife pressed at Antonias's throat, gave it a little jab, just enough to make it bleed.

Antonias raised his knee and hit the man in the groin, then grabbed hold of the arm holding the knife and shook it, until the weapon dropped on the floor. The man was howling and holding his groin.

Jake pushed his elbow back into the ribs of the man standing behind him, then turned and punched him in the face. The man staggered back and fell. Jake walked up to him and kicked him in the face, then kicked the knife clear. It skittered across the floor and ended up under a table. He turned to look at Antonias. Jake's jaw nearly dropped when he saw what he was doing.

Antonias had his guy lying on his stomach on the floor. He had the knife in his hand and was using it to carve 'Lambrianu' into the man's back. The man was howling and begging for mercy; the floor was covered in blood.

Antonias shouted, trying to be heard above the screaming, 'You won't forget my fucking name again, will you? Show your boss that, arsehole.' He straightened up and looked across at Jake. 'All done,' he said. He walked over to where the second man lay on the floor. The man was winded, his face a mess, and Jake had his foot on his chest. 'You have to finish the job, Jake,' said Antonias. He took hold of the man's arm and broke it. An audible snap was followed by a howl of pain.

Jake said nothing; he had always known Antonias had a foul temper, but this was pure horror, and it frightened him. He looked at Antonias's blue eyes: they were dark blue, almost black. Gone were the charming sea-blue eyes, with the sparkle in them. They were Jekyll; this was Hyde.

Antonias picked up the money bag and turned his eyes on the landlord. 'You, in the back, now.'

The landlord had wet himself; he hadn't expected this kind of massacre in his pub. He did as he was told and went into the back room.

'This is the bag of money for the bossman; is it all there?' Antonias asked. He was strangely calm.

The man nodded at him.

'Good. Now I want another 500, as compensation for this.'

Antonias could see the man was stunned. His mouth flapped, and then he started making up all kinds of excuses about how he couldn't afford it. Antonias ignored him; he took out his gun and pointed it at the man.

'Five hundred, you snivelling bastard. You set us up, and you will never do it again, do you hear me?'

The landlord opened the safe, counted out the money and handed it to Antonias.

'I'll be telling the bossman about this. You're stealing off him, as well, you know.'

Antonias stayed very calm, he was almost charming, but his eyes were still dark and his face was flushed. He held up the money bag with the bossman's money in. 'This is for him,' he said, then he picked up the 500 pounds and added, 'and this is for me.' With that, he put his gun away, turned, and walked back into the pub, where Jake was waiting.

Antonias saw that the pub was empty; the two men they had fought had gone. He looked directly at Jake.

'Some guys came and took them away,' Jake said. He saw Antony was carrying a wad of cash, as well as the bank bag.

Antonias was covered in blood, and Jake had some on his hands and shoes, too. They couldn't go anywhere like that, they would be seen and probably reported to the police.

'Come on.' Antonias remembered the twenty-four-hour toilets that all the homeless and dropouts used to wash themselves; he had washed there many times, himself. He knew they would be safe to clean themselves up there, because on the streets, no one saw or heard anything; it was the code.

Jake held his nose as he walked down the steps to go inside the toilets, the smell of urine filling the air.

'For God's sake, Antony, this place stinks, and it's filthy. Look – there's a sleeping bag down there, somebody lives here. Jesus Christ, it's a hovel, not fit for pigs.'

Antonias turned the rusty, mouldy taps and waited for the water to run clear, then started to wash.

Jake didn't have all that much blood on him and he cleaned up quickly.

Antonias was drenched in it. He turned to Jake. 'There's a shop on the corner, go and buy us a shirt and a pair of tracksuit bottoms, will you?'

Jake was grateful to leave. The place was a hellhole, it looked like the toilets hadn't been flushed in years and there were no doors on the cubicles.

Antonias washed his hands and face and rinsed the knife under the tap. Someone came in and went to use the toilet. They didn't acknowledge each other. Antonias looked around at the mouldy, cracked tiles on the walls. Many a time he had felt safe, there. He had gone there to wash, and to sleep, when it was blowing a blizzard outside. This had been his home.

Jake came back holding a shirt and tracksuit bottoms. 'This was all I could get,' he said. He handed Antonias his new clothes, then waited in silence as he got changed.

It was then Jake noticed there was a man sitting down in the cubicle, going to the toilet.

'For God's sake, Antony, let's get out of here, this place is freaking me out, come on.'

Jake ran up the steps, back to the fresh air of the streets. He turned to see if Antonias was following and saw him take out twenty pounds and hand it to the man in the cubicle before he, too, left the place.

They walked to the corner of the next street. Antonias was holding the bundle of bloodstained clothes in one hand and he threw them into an old oil drum that had ashes in it, where someone had clearly had a fire, then put a match to them.

Suddenly, it dawned on Jake that he had been there before. When Elle had driven Antonias around the streets, he had seen that old oil drum, with a bonfire burning in it. The homeless people used to stand around it to keep warm. Damn! Him and his big mouth. No wonder Antonias knew where to come to wash and clean up, without being noticed.

Back in the car, Antonias started the engine, and was about to drive on, when Jake touched his arm.

'You frightened me in there, Antony, you were crazy. That poor guy's going to be scarred forever. Oh, and I'm sorry about what I said about those toilets. Maybe when we get some real money behind us, we could get the council or someone to fix the place up a bit, make it more hygienic, like.'

Antonias looked at Jake and smiled; he was his usual self again. 'It's a shame I don't have a shorter surname,' he joked, then he turned serious. 'Jake, you have to realise those guys were going to do the same to us, if not worse. They could have killed us.' He put his hand to his throat; the bleeding had stopped, but the gesture wasn't wasted; his throat could easily have been slashed open. 'The toilets, maybe you're right, maybe we could do something. You see, I always need my level-headed brother with me.'

They drove back to the bossman's club in the West End and gave him his money.

'You look like there was a bit of trouble boys; everything okay?' the bossman said.

Antonias nodded and they waited, as usual, while he checked the money.

When they were outside of the grubby little office, he said, 'To me, Jake, that place makes those toilets look cleaner. Never forget, he chooses to live like that.'

9

FAME AT LAST

A couple of years passed, by which time Antonias had become a qualified mechanic and Jake an apprentice bookkeeper – an accountant, as he liked to put it. Although he was still at college, he was doing a bit of work here and there as work experience. Elle was proud of them both; they had done so well and had turned their lives around.

They were renting a small flat above a shop. It wasn't much, but Elle had insisted on working her magic and had cleaned it from top to bottom for them. By the time she had finished, it looked great.

She made sure their fridge was full and, as Antonias had predicted, she did their washing and ironing.

Antonias was in his element; this was 'his' place, somewhere to all his own, plus, it was great to be able to take home the women they met, and not have to hurry up in the back of a car or wait until Elle was out.

This was freedom, and he and Jake often took a couple of women back with them and had a party. They would swap and change women, get drunk, and have great fun.

They were still working for the bossman. When he had heard

that Antonias was good with cars, he had offered him a little side-line.

'Sometimes, I deal in cars, Antony. We find them, give them a makeover and sell them on. Are you interested?'

Antonias knew exactly what he meant. He meant he stole them, changed the plates, and then sold them; that was his offer.

They agreed on a price and, as usual, Antonias brought Jake in on the deal – he never did anything without him. Even now, when he was charging the pubs a little extra, he split it with Jake.

Jake refused at first. To him, it seemed Antonias did all the thinking and most of the work, and he didn't want Antonias to feel he had to cut Jake in.

'Don't insult me, Jake,' Antonias had said. Jake could see he had upset him – his eyes were changing colour. 'You're my brother; we live together, fuck women together and we'll probably die together – got it?'

'Enough said,' said Jake. It might not be the nicest way of putting it, but that was the best he was going to get.

As it was, the car scam turned out to be pretty easy. The bossman gave them a list of the cars he wanted, and then Antonias would hot-wire them and drive them away to some old warehouse the boss had.

Antonias, along with Jake, would change the number plates and chassis numbers, and once they were all done, the motors were ready to sell.

The bossman paid well for this, but Antonias wasn't happy; he begrudged handing over the cars for his boss to sell. 'Why the hell are we doing all this and giving it all away to him, Jake? We could do this ourselves and take the lot,' he said.

'Shut up, Antony, someone will hear you. We don't have the parts, or the contacts to sell them on to, that's why.'

Antonias looked at Jake and raised his right eyebrow. Jake had a point. Where did they go? Who actually bought these cars? Antonias was going to make damn sure he found out. For now, he settled on changing the subject.

'How's your girlfriend working out?' he said. 'You getting any, lately?'

Jake had met a woman at college, while he was studying accountancy. Sharon was much cleverer than him, and she was pretty. He had been having trouble with some calculations, and she had offered to help him.

Their friendship had started slowly and they would sometimes just go for a coffee. She was funny, she made him laugh and although Antonias had told him to get on with it many times, Sharon had given no indication to Jake that she wanted anything more from him than friendship.

Up until then, Jake's affairs had been very short – some lasted just long enough for him to pull his trousers up – but Sharon was different. Or she would be, if he could only move things on from them being 'just good friends.'

Jake gave Antonias a wry smile; no, he wasn't getting anything from Sharon, he wasn't even sure Sharon liked him – not like that, anyway.

Jake hadn't wanted to introduce her to Antonias, knowing that with his looks and charm, he could sweep her off her feet and he would lose her forever.

Antonias, however, had made it his business to see this woman of Jake's who kept popping up in their conversations. He purposely popped into a local coffee shop, which always seemed to be mentioned when Jake talked about meeting up with Sharon, one night to meet Jake and there he was, looking almost coy, talking to a smartly-dressed pretty woman. Her curves, Antonias noticed, were all in the right places. Very nice, indeed.

He walked over and said hello to Jake, then looked at Sharon and smiled. 'Hi, I'm Antony,' he said, and held out his hand to her.

'Sharon,' she said, and they shook hands. He could see Jake felt uneasy.

'I was just passing, mate, wondered if you fancied a drink,' he said. Again, Jake looked uneasy. Antonias's calculations had been wrong. Jake obviously liked this woman more than he had let on and wanted to be alone with her. 'Actually, Jake,' Antonias said, as he looked at his watch, 'I've just realised I have to be somewhere. Sorry, got to go.'

Antonias made a hasty exit. He had been curious about Sharon, but he could see Jake had felt a little intimidated by his presence. He wouldn't do that to Jake, he was his brother. What was it they said? 'Mates before dates.' Well, that was how he felt; he'd apologise to Jake later, for gate crashing.

* * *

The next day, they had both gone to the bossman. They'd had keys made for the cars they had renovated and handed them over.

They were both making a lot of money, and life was hectic.

'Take these over to my wife,' the bossman said. 'Here's the address, hopefully it'll shut the moaning cow up.' He handed over a scrap of paper with his address on, plus the keys to an old Jaguar they'd done up and resprayed. The car was a death trap.

'Is that all he thinks his wife is worth?' Antonias said to Jake. 'The amount of money he's making and this is the best she gets. What a tight-fisted bastard!'

'Yeah, right, it's because he spends all his money paying prostitutes and on that mistress of his. I bet she's got a brand new car.'

Antonias drove the Jag and Jake followed behind in his car, so that he could drive them both back home after the motor had been delivered.

The bossman's house turned out to be a decent detached house, with bay windows and a drive. Nice enough, but nothing special. They knocked at the door and waited.

A woman in her thirties answered. She wasn't bad looking and had an ample bosom. Antonias and Jake looked at each other; they hadn't expected the wife to look like this. They had expected some old woman, the same age as the boss.

Antonias checked who she was, just in case this wasn't the bossman's wife; after all, he didn't know her.

It was the middle of the day, and she was dressed in a silk camisole and dressing gown. She had all her make-up on, and she was sipping a clear drink from a cocktail glass.

'Come in, boys, what does the old fart want now? Why has he sent you?'

It was obvious to them both that she'd had more than one cocktail, when she waved her arm and spilt her drink.

They both stepped through the door and followed her, as she walked into the lounge.

'We've brought you these,' Jake said, shaking the car keys. 'The boss thought you might like a present.'

'Another stolen car, whoopee!' she shouted, and she went over to the coffee table, picked up a glass jug filled with some of the cocktail she had made up earlier, and poured it in her glass.

'Leave them on the side,' she said and pointed to a wall unit near the door.

Then she looked at Antonias, walked up to him and stroked his face.

'Well, aren't you the handsome one.' She turned to Jake, and stroked his face, too. She stood in front of Antonias and adjusted her camisole, so that it showed more of her ample bosom. Antonias looked at Jake and smiled.

'We'd better be going, then,' said Antonias. He winked at Jake and walked very slowly out of the room. He knew what was coming; this bored housewife was ignored, taken for granted and cheated on regularly... no wonder she drank. She was lonely, and more to the point, she was frustrated.

'Must you go, so soon?' she said, and pouted.

There is no way, thought Antonias, the boss is making time for her. He was far too busy hanging around with his mistress, and anyone else that came along.

The bossman used the club in the West End as his own private knocking shop; it was no wonder it never made any money. The only time it did was when the junkies went in to buy their drugs off him.

'Why don't you two boys stay a while and keep me company.' She went and got another two glasses and started pouring the cocktail mixture into them.

'Vodka martini; you don't mind that, do you?' She walked over to them and handed them a glass each. 'I'm Carrie, by the way.'

Antonias took a sip. 'It's nice,' he said. He looked at Jake, then took another gulp of his drink and finished it.

'But why waste a perfectly good afternoon drinking, when we could be doing something else?' Antonias reached out and pushed the silky dressing gown from her shoulders. It dropped to the floor.

He grabbed hold of her and pulled her towards him, letting the straps of her camisole drop, leaving her naked. 'Where's the bedroom?' he asked.

Carrie pointed up the stairs and started walking towards them.

'Have you got enough for two?' Antonias nodded towards Jake.

Carrie looked at them both, wet her lips and nodded; she walked up the stairs and they both followed.

After a few hours, they both got back in the car and made their way back to the bossman.

'Bloody hell, Antony, that woman's insatiable. I thought she was never going to stop.' Jake put his head back on the car seat and yawned.

Antonias was grinning. 'I think we satisfied her needs, but you're right, she's sex-starved, and we're going to see to it that she never goes hungry again. What a way to spend an afternoon, eh?'

Visits to Carrie became a regular occurrence for Antonias. Jake sometimes went with him, but he had finally got together with Sharon, and didn't want to spoil things with her. He still liked the odd afternoon with Carrie and Antonias, though. It was fun. It was just the way Antonias liked it – there were no strings, no commitments and no promises.

It wasn't some lovestruck young woman telling him she loved him and planning their future together, it was what it was: just sex and nothing more.

Carrie did have her other uses, though; she bought Antonias a gold cigarette case and lighter, an expensive suit, and silk ties. Sometimes, she had her friend visit and she was just as willing as Carrie, and afterwards, she would hand him some cash and tell him to buy himself something nice.

'You're playing with fire, Antony, having sex with the boss's wife, for God's sake. How much longer do you think you can get away with it?' said Jake.

'It's just a bit of fun, where's the harm in it?' He grinned. 'Do you like the suit?' Antonias was showing off, twirling around in front of the mirror, admiring the expensive suit he was wearing.

'Antony, you're acting like some male prostitute. Carrie and her friend are paying you... what happens when you don't want to do it any more? She thinks she's bought you, lock, stock and barrel.'

Antonias had never thought of it like that before. Between jobs, when he knew the boss was busy, he would slip off to see Carrie. He had tried to make it the same regular days, and they'd had some wild afternoons. Afterwards, she always stopped him before he left and said she had bought him something.

He realised Jake was right; he was acting like some male prostitute, but it was addictive. Carrie didn't mind how many times Antonias was ready for sex; as far as she was concerned, the more times the merrier. Her friend was the same. Antonias had a high libido, he was always ready for sex.

Antonias decided to heed Jake's warning; he'd had his fun, now was the time to stop, before it got out of control.

The next week, he didn't turn up at Carrie's house on their usual day, or the day after that; he presumed she would get the message.

Antonias went to a local nightclub one night with Jake. He knew Tommy, the man on the door, and waved to him as he walked in.

Tommy called him over. 'Antony, have you been messing with the boss's wife?' Tommy asked him directly.

Antonias was taken aback. 'Why do you ask that, Tommy, mate? That's a strange thing to say.'

'You're a good mate, and I think I should warn you, the boss knows somebody has put the smile back on her face. Let's be honest, you're not discreet about that dick of yours, are you?'

Antonias felt his face flush; he didn't know what to say. Trouble was definitely brewing and he had no one else to blame but himself.

'Watch your back, Antony, she'll point the finger at you, if she has to. Be careful.'

Antonias decided not to go into the nightclub; he turned and went home, instead. Just how much did the boss know? Damn it, his stupid sex drive was going to lose him his income; more than that, possibly his life.

He avoided Carrie and made no contact, hoping that would be

the end of it and she would soon find someone to fill his place. After all, she was a grown woman, she had known the score.

A couple of weeks later, Antonias bumped into Sharon in the street. They'd stopped to speak, then decided to go for a coffee. They were friends now. It was purely platonic, not least because it was pretty obvious that she had eyes only for Jake, and that pleased him. Apart from Elle, he had never had a woman as a friend before, so this was a whole new experience.

Afterwards, Antonias went back to the warehouse, where he was fixing up the cars and changing their identity. He was busy with a Merc when, suddenly, the doors burst open and the police walked in. There was nothing Antonias could do. He had been caught red-handed; all the evidence of the stolen cars stood around him.

Thank God Jake had been doing some bookkeeping for a local shopkeeper. The last thing Antonias wanted was for Jake to be dragged into all of this.

The police put his hands behind his back and handcuffed him; there was nothing he could do but get into the car with them.

He was charged with car theft, and selling stolen vehicles. The police had received numerous reports of people's cars being stolen, and now they had their man.

What Antonias hadn't known was that, while he had been sitting in the café having a coffee with Sharon, Carrie had driven past and seen them laughing and joking through the windows. She was jealous and angry; she thought she now knew why Antonias hadn't been to see her. He had traded her in for a younger model.

She told her husband, the bossman, that she didn't want Antonias going to the house any more, because he had frightened her, and he had tried forcing himself upon her. She had almost accused him of rape, and cried on the bossman's shoulders, telling him all about that awful Antony.

The bossman, while not 100 per cent sure whether to believe

her, knew someone had been messing around with his wife. There was gossip going around and he had to do something about it, to save his reputation. He decided to teach that cocky Italian who was boss.

He told Antonias that he needed some expensive 'hot' cars dealing with straight away, and Antonias had walked right into his trap.

No sooner had Antonias started stripping the cars down than the police had been tipped off about who was stealing and dealing in the cars. Little did anyone know, but the boss was a known informer to the police, so they knew he wasn't lying.

No matter what the legal aid lawyer tried to say in Antonias's defence, he really didn't have a leg to stand on; he had been caught red-handed. The police had questioned him about who was dealing in the stolen cars with him. The fact was, they already knew, but they wanted to know if he would rat out the boss to save his own skin.

Antonias said nothing; he took all the blame and held his hands up, much to the annoyance of his lawyer, who had tried and failed to persuade him to talk.

He had been allowed his one telephone call and used it to ring Jake, to tell him what had happened.

When he appeared in court to hear the charges against him, Jake and Elle were there, and were surprised he wasn't allowed out on bail. Apparently, the police had told the judge they feared he might make a run for it, and not turn up for his court case.

Elle and Jake visited him while he was in custody. They sat on opposite sides of a small table, and Elle cried the whole time. Antonias was sorry about that; he had never meant to upset her.

'Who did this, Antony?' Jake asked. He was determined to find the culprit.

'I did, Jake. You keep out of it, promise me that. I've only got myself to blame. Anyway, it won't be so bad in here. I get three meals a day, and it's not the first institution I've been in, is it, Elle?'

He was trying to make light of the situation, for her sake. He told her he didn't want her to visit him again; this wasn't the place for her, surrounded by all kinds of criminals, but she wouldn't hear a word of it. She wagged her finger in his face in a motherly fashion and told him to send the visiting orders.

When it was time to go back to his cell, Antonias got a lump in his throat. Elle and Jake were going home without him, Elle to her cosy home and Jake to their party flat. He was alone again.

The prison was a grim place, and God knew how long he would end up in there for; that, he would soon find out when he went to court. He was sharing a cell with an old guy called 'Badger', mainly because he had black hair at the sides, and was going grey in the middle.

'I'm on the top bunk,' he'd said to Antonias, when he'd turned up on his first day. 'What's your name?'

'Antony,' was all he said. He lay on the bottom bunk and sighed; after all his bravado, this is what he'd come to, he'd gone right round in a circle, back again to an institution, with rules and regulations.

Still, he thought to himself, considering the things I've done in the past, this is a small price to pay. As far as he was concerned, he had got off easy.

At least he was a fighter and could hold his own; he knew it would be one constant battle in prison until he had proved himself.

Antonias kept himself to himself and didn't make a point of leaving his cell during recreation time.

He was reading the newspaper, one afternoon, when three men

walked in. The cell doors were always open during the day; there was no privacy.

'Well, well, aren't you the pretty boy.' One of them walked up to Antonias and put his hand on his shoulder. Antonias carried on reading his newspaper.

'We don't get many blue-eyed blonds, fresh for the picking, in here.' They all smiled at each other.

It had already crossed Antonias's mind that he would be a target inside prison and now, he knew he was right.

These perverts didn't care who they bullied and raped, just as long as they could relieve themselves somewhere.

One of the others closed the cell door; the guards were walking the far side of the landing, so they had time and opportunity to do what they intended to do. Antonias looked up and saw that Badger had been about to walk in, but when he saw the three large men with Antonias, he decided to turn around and leave.

'You keep watch, I'm going first,' one of the men said, and started undoing the zip on his trousers.

'You' – he pointed to the other inmate – 'hold him down and gag him. I don't want any noise.'

Antonias looked at the man; he could see the excited expectation of what was to come in his eyes.

'Okay, guys, there's no need for that,' said Antonias. 'Let's just keep it friendly, eh?'

The three of them all looked at each other and smiled; this was going to be easier than they'd thought. Maybe this pretty boy liked this kind of thing and was used to it. Well, they would show him.

The man who had decided he was going to be first had already taken out his penis; it was erect and ready for action.

Antonias smiled and held out his hand towards it; the man closed his eyes, in anticipation. Antonias grabbed it and yanked it with force, making the man yowl with pain and surprise as he dropped to his knees. The other two stepped in front of Antonias; they knew what they had come for and they were going to get it.

One of them reached out to hold Antonias's arms, and Antonias head-butted him, then he turned to the other one, kicked him in the groin, and punched him.

They hadn't expected this young pretty boy, as they called him, to put up such a fight. Normally their victims struggled a bit, but once they were held down, they had no choice but to submit.

Antonias grabbed the rickety wooden chair in the cell, raised it and hit the man on the floor with it. He raised it again, but the man, half conscious, held his arm out for him to stop.

The other two came rushing forward. One had produced a knife, which made Antonias smile; it wasn't the first time someone had held a knife to him.

'Go on, then, you pervert, use it. Cut my throat, stab me, go on, you worthless piece of shit!'

Both men stood and stared at him; the one with the knife plunged it towards Antonias and stabbed him in the arm.

Antonias's eyes grew dark. The pain was excruciating and he saw the blood start seeping through his prison-issue sweatshirt, but he knew he couldn't give up now and let them win.

Antonias grabbed the man's arm and, with his other hand – now with blood trickling down it – grabbed the knife off him and stabbed it in his eye. The man was holding his face and screaming in pain.

Suddenly, the door flew open and two prison warders ran in. They saw the knife in Antonias's hand, and the chaos with the three other men in the cell.

'Drop it, son,' one of the guards shouted. Another prison guard took out his baton and hit Antonias in the guts with it, winding him and making him drop to his knees.

They dragged him out on to the landing. The other prisoners

gawped at the commotion. Some had seen the three well-known bullies entering Antonias's cell, and Badger had told the rest what was happening in there, but they were all wrong.

More guards came. Antonias was dragged across the landing, scraping his stomach and knees. The blood from the stab wound in his arm left a trail on the floor.

The other prisoners watched as the three would-be assailants were dragged out, and what a state they were in. It was a bloodbath.

'Go and call an ambulance, and tell the prison governor what the hell has happened here,' one of the prison officers said to a colleague.

It was chaos. Antonias was dragged away and pushed into a cell on his own. He was losing a lot of blood and was exhausted. He leaned his head against the cell wall and passed out.

* * *

When Antonias woke up, he was in the prison hospital and his arm was bandaged. It was throbbing, but at least he was okay.

'Morning, how are we today?'

Antonias looked up; he presumed he was dealing with the doctor, because the man was wearing a white coat.

The doctor told Antonias that he was lucky; it was just a flesh wound, but the knife was old and rusty and so they had given him a course of antibiotics, in case of infection.

The food was better in the hospital, Antonias thought, not like the usual slop they served up.

The prison governor came later that day with two of the prison officers; he wasn't happy.

'What happened?' he said. 'Why did you stab that man in the eye? He's in hospital and he's actually lost his eye, thanks to you. So, come on then, let's have your excuses.'

Antonias knew he had to answer, but he wasn't going to tell him the truth.

'I don't know what happened, sir, I must have stabbed myself in the arm and then fallen on that other fellow and poked him in the eye.'

'And the rest? What about the two other men in your cell? I have to explain all of this, you know.'

'What did they tell you?' asked Antonias. 'Did they tell you why they were in my cell, all three of them?'

The prisoner governor knew what these men were like, and he knew exactly what Antonias was saying. He turned towards one of the senior warders.

'Well? What did they tell you? And how did that knife go unnoticed?'

Now the prison governor needed someone to blame, and he'd decided it had to be the warders' fault for not keeping their eyes open and not noticing an illegal weapon.

The warder gave his excuse about being on one of the other landings. As for the knife, well, these criminals always found some way of smuggling things in. He looked at Antonias for confirmation, because he was in just as much trouble.

'You'll be put into solitary confinement, you'll have no privileges, and if those men wish to press charges against you, so be it,' said the prison governor. He was more concerned about news of the attack getting out to the newspapers. Inmates had fights all the time, but a man had lost an eye and had been taken to the hospital.

'What about me?' said Antonias. 'Don't I get the opportunity to press charges for this?'

'Shut up and show some respect to the governor,' the warder shouted at him. He gave Antonias a stern look.

'Well, yes, I suppose you could, if you wanted to.' The governor nodded. He wanted to keep this incident isolated. 'The other men are just claiming it was a game that got out of hand. Some bloody game!'

'Well, that's what happened, then, sir.' Antonias knew the governor really wanted to know what he was going to do about it, and this seemed to satisfy him.

The governor glared at him. 'You do realise this will go on your record, and when you go to court, time will be added on for this actual bodily harm incident.'

Antonias knew he was testing him; he nodded respectfully, and apologised.

Again, this seemed to satisfy the governor, and with that, he left the prison hospital.

'You did well, there, lad,' said the warder. 'I thought you might be one of those moaning lot, ready to cause trouble, wanting to see your lawyer and stuff.'

Antonias looked up at him. 'Looks can be deceiving, sir.'

* * *

Badger came to the hospital to visit Antonias. He was a helper in the prison library, if you could call it that, and often walked around with a dozen well-read, tattered books on a trolley.

'Here, Tony, lad, sorry I left you alone, but you understand, don't you? I'm an old man.' He slipped a small bar of chocolate under Antonias's pillow.

'It's Antony,' he said, but he nodded and smiled. Badger meant no harm. In prison, you had to put yourself first every time, and everyone knew that. Badger handed him a book, then wheeled his trolley out.

Badger's chocolate was precious to him; that and cigarettes were like gold dust in prison. Giving a bar of chocolate to Antonias was, to Badger, worth more than just an apology.

Antonias learnt, as the days went on, that the other three men had all been moved to different prisons. Badger had all the gossip; he was much better than those well-fingered books.

Antonias was put into solitary confinement. It was a bare cell with a bucket and an iron bed. He didn't mind it, though, he preferred his own company, and he was let out in the yard for some fresh air, on his own, for an hour every day. He wasn't allowed any visitors, though; that was a privilege.

A month passed and he was finally due to appear in court. Antonias looked across the courtroom and saw Elle and Jake sitting there; he also noticed Carrie was sitting at the back, watching. As he stood in the dock, telling the judge what he had done with the cars and apologising for his misdemeanours, he noticed she had a smug grin on her face. So, Antonias thought, she set me up; a woman scorned, eh?

'A custodial sentence of two years is to be served,' the judge had said.

That was it, then; Antonias was going to serve two years in that hellhole, and all for a few afternoons of sex with the boss's wife. How ridiculous was that!

Elle was in tears, when she was allowed to see him after the trial. She talked of the injustice of it all, and was holding on to Jake's arm, because she wasn't allowed to touch Antonias.

'I saw that bitch in court,' said Jake. He was angry and worried. Two bloody years for stealing a few cars; some people didn't get that for selling drugs on the street to kids, or robbery. Antonias had been well stitched up.

Antonias looked at Jake and shook his head; he didn't want to discuss this in front of Elle. She was upset, and he felt depressed at the thought of the days ahead, in prison.

* * *

Antonias didn't smoke, but took his weekly allowance and sold them on to the other inmates for things he did like, including decent magazines, extra portions at dinner, and chocolate.

He was never bothered again by any of the prisoners. Apart from them thinking he was an okay guy, sharing his cigarette ration, they also knew he was not a man to be trifled with and was as hard as nails.

He used the gymnasium every day, to work out and keep fit and to keep his mind busy. Then one of the tutors that came in on a regular basis asked to see him. He explained that there were all sorts of courses that people could take – English and maths, wood-work, and, of course, drug rehabilitation.

Life in prison is funny, Antonias thought. It has you locked up twenty-four hours a day, and yet they spend all their time trying to rehabilitate everyone for the outside.

'I run the mechanics class,' the tutor said, 'and I hear you're good with cars, Tony. Badger and some of the others have mentioned it.'

Antonias opened his mouth to speak.

'No, they haven't gone into any detail – after all, everyone in prison is innocent, we all know that.' He smiled at Antonias.

He was right, of course. No one spoke of their crime, but they all swore their innocence.

'What's your class got to do with me? I do know a bit about cars, I'm a trained mechanic. What of it?'

'Well, I've spoken to Mr Edwards, the governor, and he's prepared to give you a probationary trial if you help me in my classes. What do you think? I could do with the help.'

Antonias felt this was the governor's way of appreciating that he had kept his mouth shut.

'Yes, okay, I'll give it a go.' Antonias shrugged his shoulders; it was something to do to pass the time.

Antonias liked the classes; he enjoyed showing the men how to put bits of cars together and how engines worked but, again and again, he found they kept calling him Tony. No matter how many times he corrected them, they would shout 'Tony' when they wanted him. In the end he gave up telling them, and accepted it.

Jake had been to see him and told him that he had also given up working for the bossman; he wouldn't do it without Antonias.

'It's money, Jake, don't throw it away for my sake,' Antonias said. Now he felt guilty; Jake had lost his job, too.

'Hey, Tony, mate, over here!' Badger shouted. 'This is the wife, and my daughter.' Badger had often mentioned them, and now he had the chance to introduce them.

'Tony?' said Jake. He had a puzzled look on his face. 'Since when have you been "Tony"?'

'Some of them find Antony too long to say and it's just stuck; you don't really think his name is "Badger", do you?' He burst out laughing.

'I like it,' said Jake. 'You know, it suits you: Tony Lambrianu. Yes, mate, it has a ring to it.' Jake was nodding and repeating it to himself. 'Yes. Tony, it is.'

'Might as well; they all call me it, anyway. You could have a point, though, maybe I should have a new name and a fresh start. Yes, Tony Lambrianu it is, then,' said Tony, nodding.

'For God's sake, Tony, you have more disguises than a chameleon, and more fresh starts.' Jake laughed.

Jake continued to fill Tony in about Elle and Sharon. He was doing some more bookkeeping, and at least they both had a lot of savings, to get them through. Tony told Jake that if he got short of money, he was to use his.

'I'm okay, mate,' said Jake. 'Anyway, you're going to need every penny when you get out.'

The visit ended all too soon. Tony hated visiting times; he

looked forward to seeing Elle and Jake, but after they'd gone, it made him feel depressed. All the prisoners felt the same; there was always a subdued silence afterwards.

* * *

Days turned into weeks and then months. Tony had now served a year, and was informed that, because of his good behaviour, and for being so helpful, he was due for parole. He would have to wear an ankle tag, observe a curfew and report to a probation officer on a weekly basis, until he had finished his time. Of course, if he were to do anything illegal on the outside, not only would he get sentenced for that, he would get the year added on, too.

Tony couldn't believe his ears; all he had to do was keep his head down and behave for a year and he'd be free and clear – and he would be on the outside. Freedom, at last. It had been a long, hard year. Even though he'd had a job in the mechanics' workshop, doing what he liked, and nobody had bothered him, it still had been hard.

Jake was waiting outside for him. It was early morning, and he was walking out the gates a free man; he vowed he would never go back there again.

'Come on, Tony.' Jake had got used to calling him that and so had Elle; it was second nature, now.

Tony expected them to go to Elle's house. He knew Jake had given up the flat above the shop, because he didn't see the point in keeping it on his own. Jake spent the odd night at Sharon's bedsit, and the rest of the time he lived with Elle, to look after her. She was so worried about Tony, wondering if he was okay. Jake often wondered which of them, Elle or Tony, was actually in prison. Jake surprised him by driving to a block of flats, instead.

'Isn't this where Eddie lives?' said Tony, looking at the flats.

'Yes,' said Jake. He was beaming; the smile on his face couldn't have been bigger. 'He's letting me borrow it for the day, while he's out.'

Tony got out of the car and followed Jake to the door; he wasn't sure what his brother was up to.

'Hey, Jake, I've been out of prison for an hour. I'm not getting into trouble, so whatever scheme you have up your sleeve, leave me out of it.'

Jake unlocked the door. 'Come on,' he said, like he had some great secret. Tony gave a deep sigh and followed him.

In the bedroom, three scantily dressed young women lay on the bed, waiting for them.

'Welcome home, Tony,' said Jake.' I figured you might like this before going back to Elle's; it's been a long time.'

Tony grinned broadly. Yes, he had definitely missed this, and Jake was the best brother in the world. The women were smiling and beckoning to him. What a great sight to behold, after a year. It was party time.

'Ladies, I'm all yours,' Tony said, grinning. He ripped his shirt open, sending the buttons flying across the room, and jumped on the bed.

* * *

After a fantastic homecoming, it was time for the girls to leave. Tony felt it was just as well, because he was out of practice.

They drove back to Elle's house. Eddie had been a good friend, lending Jake his flat, and they owed him one.

Elle had prepared a large steak pie, with all the trimmings. She had been watching the clock and wondering what had happened to them; she was worried in case the prison had changed their mind.

'Sorry, Elle,' said Jake. 'I took Tony for a quick drink before coming home.' He kissed her cheek.

She patted Jake on the arm then turned to Tony and opened her arms wide. 'Tony, my love, come here,' she said. Tears were streaming down her face.

Tony walked into her embrace and let her squeeze the life out of him, while she kissed his face and stroked his hair. Tony actually felt guilty for coming back so late, but Elle wasn't stupid, nobody went to the pub at nine in the morning.

Tony was soon sitting at the table with the two people he loved most in the world and enjoying Elle's home cooking. It was great to be home. Next was a long soak in the bath, full of hot water, and without someone watching his every move. Privacy was worth its weight in gold.

* * *

Jake had been seeing Sharon for over a year, now, and it seemed they were serious about each other. Now and again, Jake had mentioned that he was thinking of settling down with Sharon and Tony reckoned it was just a matter of time before they got married.

One night, a few weeks after he'd got out, Tony was sitting in his old bedroom at Elle's; he felt he had fallen a long way down. He was back to where he had started, but he had learnt a lot of lessons while sitting on his bunk bed in his dark cell, with Badger snoring his head off.

Tony had had time to think in prison. He didn't know what he was going to do next. He had lost his job at the garage, and having a conviction didn't improve his job prospects much.

As the weeks passed, he felt like a hamster in a cage, going around and around on his wheel. He would get up, go to the boxing club, have a drink with Jake and Eddie, and then he had to go home, because of the tag on his ankle.

His probation officer tried setting him up for interviews at supermarkets, but he wasn't interested. He made a point of telling them he was just out of prison, even though he knew they already knew that.

Tony was at an all-time low. He didn't know what to do with himself and felt completely at a loss.

Elle had said it was post-prison depression.

Then Jake rushed in from work one day. 'Come on, Tony,' he said, 'I've got you a job. It's legal and you'll like it.'

Jake had been doing some bookkeeping at a local bookies, that was part of a bigger chain. Jake had overheard them saying they were short staffed and had mentioned Tony. He knew the boss well, by then, and told him the truth: Tony was just out of prison, but he was honest and he knew a bit about gambling.

The boss had agreed to give Tony a three-month trial, to see how things worked out. In truth, he was doing it more for Jake than the unknown convict, but it turned out Tony was good at the job.

Tony had always enjoyed betting, and knew how to work out the odds. The boss liked him, and so did the punters. He knew Jake had put his reputation on the line for him, and so for Jake alone, Tony gave it his best shot.

A few months later, Jake finally announced he had asked Sharon to marry him, and she had said yes. They were going to rent a small flat together. They all had a lunchtime drink at the local pub to celebrate. They couldn't go to a club, because of Tony's curfew. He told Jake and Sharon to go out for a meal, on him, and gave them the money to do so.

The wedding was set for two months' time. It was going to be a small affair. Jake had some savings left from the money he and Tony had earnt collecting, and from the car scam, and Sharon's parents were keen to contribute, but Jake and Sharon felt the money would be better spent on practical things, such as some furniture for their flat, rather than a big, fancy do. Eventually, they could perhaps put down a deposit on a house.

The wedding was a small ceremony, but a nice one, at the local register office. Tony was, of course, the best man. Sharon's parents and siblings were there, and Elle wept all the way through it all.

After the ceremony, the bride and groom and their guests all went to a local restaurant and had a slap-up meal, with champagne, to celebrate. Everyone wished Jake and Sharon well; they made a good couple.

They moved into a rented flat and turned it into their own home, and for the first time, Tony felt envious of Jake. He felt trapped, and yet here was Jake with a wife, a home, even a career. He was pleased for him, but he couldn't wait for the chains that bound him to be loosened, for the year to be up, so he could do as he liked.

Finally, his year was over and Tony was free to live as he pleased. He was still working at the bookies, earning a regular wage, but he was bored; he missed all the excitement of his past life.

Surely, thought Tony, there must be more to life than this. Is this what I'm going to do for the rest of my days: live with Elle, work at the bookies and take out the odd girlfriend now and again? He felt as though he had no purpose any more.

Tony didn't want a relationship; he wasn't ready to settle down like Jake had. As soon as the women he saw started talking about 'us' and 'we', that was when he started thinking about moving on. Even the prospect of finding a new girlfriend didn't seem to excite him; he needed to get himself sorted out first, the women would come later.

He was reminded that he wasn't the only one with difficulties when Jake came to see him at Elle's. He looked upset and Tony could tell he'd been crying. He presumed he'd had an argument with Sharon.

'What's up, Jake?' he said. 'Wife giving you a hard time? You've only been married a few months, what's so bad?'

'I'm sterile, Tony, we can't have children and it's my fault.' He heaved a sob, then added, 'I've told Sharon to move on, find someone to have kids with.'

Tony couldn't believe his ears. 'You told Sharon to leave you? Why the hell would you do that?'

'Are you deaf? I just said, I can't ever give her children. We've been trying to start a family, but nothing happened, so I went to the doctor to get myself checked out. It seems that time I had mumps... you remember?' Jake broke down in tears.

Tony put his arms around him and held him. He remembered Jake having mumps. They had both got it, but Tony had escaped with swollen glands and a high temperature, whereas Jake had to go into hospital for a couple of weeks, his case was so severe. The doctor had warned Jake at the time that it could cause sterility and that only time would tell, but that had meant nothing to him, then. He'd forgotten all about it, until now. And here it was, like a bolt from the blue.

'Is that really a reason for her to leave you? I thought she loved you. There are other avenues, you know. Look at Elle; she has two sons she never gave birth to. Come on, Jake.' An idea occurred to him. 'I'll donate some sperm, if you like.'

'No, you bloody well won't.' Jake dried his eyes and looked at Tony with disgust. How could Tony talk of having sex with Sharon at a time like this? 'Leave her alone, you randy old sod, she's still my wife, you know.' He paused, then added, 'For now, anyway.'

Tony shook his head. 'No, no, Jake, not like that. God's sake! I mean them donation things you hear about on the television. Give me some credit, I'm not such a low-life that I'd talk about sleeping with your wife.'

Jake sighed. 'No, I'm sorry, Tony, that was a stupid thing to say, of course you wouldn't. Anyway, it's up to Sharon now, I've given her the choice. It has to be her choice. Christ, I just feel like shit.' Then he started crying again.

Jake moved back into Elle's house. Sharon had said it wasn't necessary, but Jake had insisted she had time and space to think.

'I could help, Elle,' said Tony.

He and Elle were having a cup of coffee in the kitchen, while Jake was at work, and had been discussing how to reconcile Jake and Sharon.

She put down her mug and shook her head. 'No, you can't, Tony. I know you offered sperm donation, Jake told me, but don't you see? You can't do that.'

'Why not?' said Tony. To him, it seemed like the obvious solution.

'Because then their baby would be your baby... it's too close to home. The little one could look like you. Jake would be the dad, but you would always be the father.' She wrapped her hands around her mug of coffee. 'And what about the child? In time, he or she might learn that you're their father, which would complicate things further. Don't you see? It could open a whole can of worms.'

Tony had never thought of it like that, he had only wanted to help Jake. Elle was right, though, they had to leave Jake and Sharon alone to sort themselves out.

Finally, a couple of weeks later, there was a knock at the door. Elle opened it to see Sharon standing there. She looked tired and drawn. 'Is he in, Elle?' she said. 'I need to see him.'

'Yes, he is, Sharon, he's upstairs.'

Sharon looked so serious that Elle feared the worst. Maybe having a baby was so important to Sharon that she wouldn't even consider adoption, or even fostering.

'Do you want a coffee or something?'

Sharon shook her head, then shouted, 'Jake!' Her voice carried through the hallway and up the stairs. 'If you think I don't love you and that I'm that shallow, don't bother coming home!'

Elle felt relief wash over her. Sharon gave her a smile, then turned and walked away.

There was Jake's answer: Sharon loved him, no matter what, and yes, there were other avenues to go down.

Jake happily packed his bags and went home. At least, he reasoned with himself, I gave Sharon the choice. It was a big thing, being able to start a family, and it saddened him to think he couldn't give her any children and make their home complete.

They would talk about other options, but Sharon had decided that, before they approached any adoption agencies, they should look like respectable, responsible parents.

She wanted them to have their own home, and be in a better financial position. Sharon and Jake both knew it could take years, but they decided to put it on hold for now, until they were in a better position financially.

* * *

Things settled down for a while, but one evening the peace of Elle's was disturbed by a frantic knocking at the door. Tony answered to find Eddie standing there. His face was flushed, he was out of breath and he looked as though he had run all the way to Elle's house, although Tony knew he hadn't – his car was parked outside.

'Hi, Eddie, what's up?' he said.

Eddie looked uneasy, which wasn't like him – he was an easygoing friendly guy, who usually spent all his time and money down the bookies, where Tony worked. Sometimes he won, more often, he lost, but he didn't care either way, it was all good fun.

'Tony, mate,' he said, 'the bossman wants to see you. He's sent me specially to fetch you.'

Tony stared at Eddie; it had been over two years since he had seen the bossman. 'Why?' he said. 'Why does he want to see me? Why now?'

Eddie gave an open-handed gesture. 'I just do as I'm told.'

'Look, I'm sorry, mate, but you know what I mean. The guy hates me. I've served time for him, wasn't the sentence long enough for him?' Tony shook his head. 'I'm well out of it. No.'

Elle, who was busying herself in the kitchen, had heard the conversation and decided this was her cue to leave them to talk while she went to do some shopping. She knew Tony and Eddie would want to be alone. She wasn't happy that this bossman's name had popped up again, after all this time, but then again she wasn't happy seeing Tony so unhappy, either.

'I'll not be long, Tony,' she said, as she headed out of the door.

Elle knew that although Tony still spent a lot of time with Jake, Jake had Sharon, and he had to put her first. Tony felt like a gooseberry at times, when they were playing happy families.

And, even though Elle had heard Tony telling Eddie he wasn't interested and his answer was no, as she left the house, she had seen that sparkle in his eye again. Maybe this, whatever it was, would lift his spirits and maybe, just maybe, Tony had learnt a valuable lesson in life – not to trust this bossman, or his wife again.

Later that evening, Tony went around to see Jake and told him what Eddie had said. He wanted his opinion.

Jake was forthright and made his feelings clear. 'Stay clear, Tony,' he said, 'wasn't two years enough for that bastard? He doesn't love his wife that much, we both know that, but he's vindictive. Is this vendetta going to carry on forever? Stay away, no good will come of it.'

Jake didn't want to see Tony get drawn in by all that again; he'd been through enough because of that man. Sharon, who was listening to the conversation, had her own piece to say.

'Does Eddie not know what it is, Tony? Can't you find out more from him? Surely, he must hear the odd whisper.'

Tony looked at her, stunned; she was right. So why hadn't Eddie told him?

'She's right, you know,' said Jake, echoing what Tony was thinking. 'Even if he doesn't know all the ins and outs, he has to know something.' Tony and Jake both looked at each other and laughed; that was the obvious thing to think, and they hadn't thought of it.

After a week of hanging around the bookies and trying to talk Tony into seeing the bossman, Eddie gave up and coughed up some more information.

'I don't know what the deal is, but there's talk of some big stuff going on. It's all hush-hush, but the bossman must be desperate, because he's told me to fetch you and offer you 500 pounds for two hours' work, maximum.'

Now, Tony was curious... what was so important that he'd been sent for, again, and with such a large sum of money on offer?

'I'll think about it,' he said, 'I'll let you know tomorrow.'

'Come on, Tony, mate,' Eddie said. 'He's sent me to fetch you, and I can't go back without you, not again.'

'Let some other fool do his dirty work for him, Eddie. Why does it have to be me? He has enough people on the payroll. No, let some other fool do it.'

'Like me, you mean?' said Eddie.

Tony hadn't meant to put Eddie down like that, but he wasn't going to make any decision without speaking to Jake first.

'Well, I can't,' said Eddie. 'I might work for him, but I don't speak Italian and he needs someone who does.'

'Tomorrow, Eddie. I have to talk to Jake first. If it's that important, he can wait another day. I'm not asking how high when he says jump.'

* * *

Tuesdays were Elle's bingo nights, so, tonight, for Tony, it was Sharon's casserole.

Sharon knew Jake and Tony were inseparable, and just accepted it. You married one, you married both, it was as simple as that. Jake never kept any secrets from her, and she knew of Tony's reputation, but he was a loveable rogue; no wonder the girls liked him so much.

Jake laughed when Tony told him that Eddie had been round again, and there was 500 pounds on offer.

'Tony, it doesn't take two hours to beat a man up, let alone kill him. What big stuff is that old man involved in? He's not in the big league, we both know that. What's he up to, and why does he want you so badly?'

'Eddie said something about speaking Italian, but I don't know any more than that.'

Sharon, Jake and Tony all sat at the table eating their dinner, talking it over. Sharon was no cook; she was pretty, clever and funny, but definitely no cook. Tony looked across the table at Jake, who was also trying his best to swallow the casserole without insulting his wife.

'There's only one way to find out, Tony,' said Sharon. 'I can tell that you're curious, and to be honest, so am I. What is it you've got that he wants so desperately? He's not paying you 500 pounds to keep his wife happy.' She raised her fork to her mouth, then put it down again. 'God, this is awful, isn't it?' Then she burst out laughing.

'Yes!' Tony and Jake both echoed her sentiment together, and put down their own forks.

'Well, on your own head be it, Tony, but whatever it is, I'm with you. Okay?' said Jake.

Tony felt embarrassed. He didn't want to drag Jake into the situation, he was just using him as a sounding board.

'No, you've got Sharon to think of, forget it,' he said.

'We're brothers, I'm with you all the way. Brothers, remember?'

Jake's loyalty never failed to surprise Tony. Jake was better than a brother and Sharon was a good understanding sister.

Jake grinned at his wife. 'Now, come on, let's go out and pick up some fish and chips!'

* * *

Tony told Eddie to arrange a meeting with the bossman; he wanted to know more before he committed himself. This would solve the mystery and help him make up his mind.

Going back to the old club felt strange, like being in a parallel world. It hadn't changed much; it was still a dump, it smelt of damp and the paint was peeling off the walls. The junkies and the lowlifes still came to party, which was a shame, given its location.

Memo to self, thought Tony, remember to wipe your feet on the way out!

Tony walked into the back room and saw that the bossman still used an old table as a desk. What big stuff did he have going on? Jake had been right: nobody would do a big business deal with him. Tony also knew, now, that he was a police informer, so what was he getting out of all this?

'Antony, my lad, come in and sit down. You're looking well.' It was like nothing had changed; the bossman was smiling at him and acting like an old friend.

Tony remained standing. 'It's Tony, now,' he said.

The bossman gave him a stern glare. 'Whatever,' he said, and he waved his arm in the air, suddenly carefree. 'You look all grown up now, "Tony".' The bossman emphasised his name. 'Out with the boy, in with the man, eh?'

Tony couldn't help his sarcasm. 'That's what prison does for you,' he said. He still didn't sit down.

There was a silence in the room and the bossman stopped what he was about to say and stared at Tony from across the table. He sat back in his chair and nodded. Okay, there were things left unsaid.

'One day, Tony, when you are married, you will want revenge if some young kid who works for you is having sex with your missus and treating you as a joke, probably laughing behind your back.'

'That won't happen, because I won't marry a woman that would sleep around with her husband's employees,' Tony retorted in a flash. He really didn't care what he said. After all, the man had been desperate enough to send for him twice; Tony hadn't gone crawling back to him, begging for his old job back.

'All water under the bridge now, Tony, eh? No hard feelings and all that, what's done is done.'

No hard feelings? Tony wished Jake was there to hear the man. It occurred to him that the bossman was desperate, because normally he would have told him to get the hell out of there for being sarcastic to him. He always said Tony had a bad attitude and no respect.

'I'm leaving, now. I don't need a lecture, and I have no interest in reminiscing about the good old days.' Tony turned to go; he'd heard enough. He had come, as requested, and he was still no further on in finding out what the bossman wanted.

'Wait, Tony, I know you don't know why I asked you here, and you're probably wondering what it's all about.'

Tony hesitated, then turned back and sat down. Finally, he was going to find out the truth behind this meeting.

'There's a job I'm partly involved in. You're Italian, right?' The bossman already knew the answer to that.

'No.' Tony stood up again to leave; he didn't want to be involved in some job. 'I like my freedom too much; I don't want any part of any job that you're involved in.'

'For God's sake, Tony, sit down,' shouted the bossman. He knew getting Tony onside again wouldn't be easy; he knew he was stubborn and bad-tempered, but he wanted his help.

'As I said...' The bossman took a breath and started again. 'You're Italian, right? You know all the slang words, and not just book learning Italian. I know, because I've heard you and Jake speaking it together.'

Now Tony was curious; why was this man so interested in him being Italian? He was right, of course, he and Jake had often spoken Italian to each other to confuse landlords and other gang members. It was their own protection.

'I want an inside man,' the bossman continued, 'someone who knows the score and can keep his mouth shut. I know you keep yours tightly zipped, Tony, and I respect that. I have been approached about a little business deal, and the men offering the deal are Italian. I want to know what they're saying about me behind my back. I want you to interpret and keep your ears open, that's all.'

Tony was taken aback; he hadn't expected this. 'Don't they speak any English?' he said. He felt it was strange to be approached by someone you couldn't communicate with.

'Of course they do, but like you and Jake always did, they use their own language to speak to each other. I want to know what they're plotting against me.'

'What makes you think you can trust me? Anyway, Joe speaks a little Italian, why don't you get him to help?'

Joe was one of the club bouncers. There had been a time, when Tony and Jake had been speaking – fortunately, for them, about a group of girls – when Joe had interrupted and said he knew what they were talking about and laughed with them.

'Joe's a book learner; he's been on holiday there a few times and picked up a bit of the language, but these guys are going to speak real Italian to each other, slang words and such. You don't speak the Queen's English, do you? But that is how any learner would pronounce things. You're good in business, Tony, at least when women aren't involved. As far as trusting you, I don't, but I'm the boss; I have friends, and I'm not the one just out of prison.'

Tony raised his eyebrow and gave the bossman a wry grin. Despite all the talk of 'no hard feelings', the bossman was still threatening to stitch him up with something. He was prepared to use blackmail and threats. The man, Tony realised, was scared.

Whatever he had got involved in was too big for him, and he was afraid. Tony didn't like the bossman or his threats, but he was interested in this business and what it was all about. The plot thickened.

'Five hundred pounds, right? For two hours, maximum. Where and when? I'll do it.'

The boss nodded; he knew, if nothing else, Tony would take his money. After all, he wouldn't earn much working in a bookies, taking bets on horses all day.

'I'll be in touch,' said the bossman. He picked up his newspaper and started to read it; Tony was dismissed.

* * *

Tony went straight around to Jake's house and told him what had taken place at the meeting.

'That all sounds a bit weird. He must be in it up to his neck with these guys, whoever they are, to make him sweat. I bet he owes them money, or something.'

They both went back to Elle's house, had a few bottles of lager and talked through the night.

Both Jake and Tony agreed; this deal was full of mystery and, as much as they wanted nothing to do with it, curiosity got the better of them. They discussed all the whys and maybes, but still they couldn't figure it out.

'Well, we've just got to wait and see. Eddie still has his ear to the ground, but he's not hearing much; he actually wants information from me,' said Tony.

'I like Eddie,' said Jake, taking another sip from his lager bottle, 'but I wouldn't say anything to him; when he gets drunk, he talks a lot. If the bossman ever asked him if you'd said anything, you know for a fact Eddie would tell him, because he's scared of him.'

'You're the only person I discuss this with, Jake; if you tell Sharon, that's your business, but as far as I'm concerned, I've only told you.'

Tony trusted Sharon, but didn't want to incriminate either her or Elle. Both women knew that something was going on, but at least they could be trusted.

* * *

A few days later, Eddie came knocking at Elle's door again. Fortunately, Tony was home; he had just got in from work.

'The bossman wants you tonight, Tony. He told me to tell you, no messing, he wants you now.'

It was pretty obvious Eddie seemed worried that Tony would change his mind or send him back to the bossman empty-handed.

'Okay, but I need to get ready first. Take the weight off your feet and stop looking so worried, Eddie, for God's sake, you're making me nervous.'

Tony offered Eddie some of Elle's famous shepherd's pie, and his friend tucked in while he showered and changed. There was no way Tony was going to turn up at some important meeting without looking his best.

He wore the best suit and tie that he had, and slicked back his blond hair. He viewed himself in the mirror and smiled to himself. One day, he would be having business meetings, and he would do them a damn sight better than the bossman.

He's so desperate, he's prepared to trust an enemy to help with negotiations... why? he thought. It was a puzzle, but he'd soon know more. He went downstairs.

'Come on, Eddie,' he said, 'you've had your fill, let's go to this meeting.'

Eddie swallowed his last mouthful of food and followed Tony to the car.

The meeting was taking place in one of London's famous hotels. Tony looked on in awe at all the different nationality flags flying outside. He had expected it to be at the club; that was where the boss usually did business, not somewhere like this.

'Told you this was big stuff, didn't I?' Eddie was clearly impressed by the surroundings, too. 'Go on, you go in. He's waiting in the bar. I'll stay with the car.'

'Why?'

Eddie shrugged. 'Just doing what I was told.'

Why isn't Eddie coming in? Tony wondered, as he entered the hotel lobby. Is this a set up? Am I walking into a trap?

He found the bossman waiting for him at the bar, a large whisky in his hand. He didn't offer Tony a drink. Tony looked around and saw Joe was there, as well.

So much for trust. Joe was there to keep an eye on him, to make sure he told the boss everything. Because he spoke a little Italian, Tony realised, he would be able to interpret some things, at least. Joe wasn't fluent by any means, but he could tell the bossman if Tony was lying.

'You ready, Tony?' The bossman put down his glass and walked to the lift. Tony nodded and followed, and Joe fell in behind them.

They travelled up several floors, got out and walked along a corridor. The bossman was just about to knock on a door, when he turned to Tony and pointed his finger in his face. 'No tricks, now; you tell me everything, okay?'

Tony nodded. Inside the room, he looked around and took everything in. He hadn't known that hotel rooms could have large sofas, occasional tables and lamps. It looked like someone's lounge.

In the room were four extremely well-dressed men, three young and one who was a little older. Tony couldn't help but admire their suits; they were jet black, well-tailored and shone like silk. These men had money, and lots of it, by the look of them. What the hell were they doing mixing with a scumbag like the bossman?

The bossman shook hands with the older man, then sprawled all over one of the sofas, making himself at home. Tony and Joe stood behind him, in the same fashion that the other three men stood behind their boss.

'Please, will you have a drink?' said the Italian. 'Some brandy, perhaps.'

The bossman nodded, and one of the younger men poured him a large brandy and placed it on the coffee table.

Tony felt embarrassed because in front of them was an immaculately dressed middle-aged, dark-haired man. His very presence spoke of authority and elegance.

This man clearly looked after his employees, and it seemed he demanded perfection and style.

The bossman was trying to display the same level of authority, but he'd failed miserably. His well-worn black suit, complete with a cigarette ash stain near the breast pocket, made him look cheap, and his once-white shirt was dulled by constant washing. He had made no effort to look the part to meet this man.

Tony felt he had done his best, but he still felt underdressed compared with the other group. At least, he thought to himself, I have enough respect for these men to feel humble before them.

At first Tony didn't realise why he was there, as they were all speaking in English. He looked at Joe quizzically; he looked confused as well.

They were discussing diamonds, uncut ones that were to be picked up. Tony found it interesting.

'I want fifty diamonds, that's my share,' said the bossman.

The Italian man sitting opposite shook his head and held up three fingers, then spoke to one of the men behind him, in Italian.

The bossman turned to Tony, waiting for an answer.

'He said thirty is his best offer,' said Tony. The bossman looked at his Italian counterpart.

No one was saying anything about how they were going to get these diamonds; it seemed to Tony that all those arrangements had been made. This was just the final discussion, about the payment.

The Italian man smiled, and excused himself. He was all flattery to the bossman, and very gracious. He apologised for his poor English and said he hoped the bossman, in his obvious wisdom, could understand him.

Tony felt a little disgusted; why was this well-turned-out man apologising to the bossman?

The Italian then looked at Tony, knowing now that Tony was there to interpret, and spoke to him.

Tony relayed his message to the bossman. 'He says he has been instructed by his boss to offer thirty diamonds, and that's his best offer. Also, you pick up your own diamonds from Amsterdam. They will be left behind and given to an associate. Instructions will follow; they feel it's better that way and there will be no paper trail.'

'Thank God for that,' said the bossman. 'For a moment, there, I thought this greasy Italian was only going to offer three.' The bossman carried on smiling at the Italian; he was treating him like a fool. Tony politely told the Italian that, the bossman was concerned about getting his share. Why couldn't they be dropped off with the rest? Tony was intrigued, he felt there was something under the surface of this meeting he couldn't quite grasp.

The Italian man was all apologies, and kept making mistakes. Tony interpreted, and Joe spoke up now and again, to make his presence known and to earn his money. 'He says, it will be easier that way and your payment will be safe should anything go wrong. Whatever happens you deserve to be paid in full.'

A couple of times, Tony smiled to himself and corrected Joe; he was a decent enough guy, but his Italian was atrocious.

Satisfied and bleary eyed, the bossman grinned like a Cheshire cat as he looked over at Tony. 'Bloody right too. If this plan of his goes tits up I'm not sharing a bloody cell with this lot. Tell him I'll collect my own stash.'

The bossman is a drunken fool, Tony thought to himself. He had no idea when or where he could pick up his diamonds. It all seemed too vague for Tony's liking.

The other three Italian men in the room stood poker-faced, like statues, behind their boss.

The bossman had been kept supplied with brandy throughout the meeting. He gulped back the one he currently had and waited for more hospitality to be offered. Tony noticed the Italian man wasn't drinking. He had a small coffee cup on the table at the side of him, and that was it.

He had apologised to the bossman about not having a drink with him. He had rubbed his stomach and blamed an ulcer.

The bossman nodded and smiled; he was feeling a lot more relaxed and brave, now he had a few large brandies inside him, and knew these Italian men could hardly speak any English.

'All that bloody pasta has given him a bad ulcer,' he muttered to

Tony and Joe, then carried on smiling and nodding at the Italian. 'All those swanky suits don't impress me. I'll show them who's boss. Bloody foreigners, no wonder they need a professional, like me.' He laughed at his own joke. The young Italians kept their poker faces and their boss smiled back.

Tony felt his face burning with anger. The bossman was drunk and insulting, and making a fool of himself.

The bossman agreed to the thirty diamonds, shook hands with the Italian in charge, and left. He walked back to the lift, with Joe and Tony beside him, and once inside, he rubbed the hand he had shook the Italian's hand with down his suit trousers. 'Greasy Italian bastard,' he said.

Tony felt insulted and humiliated; he was a greasy Italian bastard, wasn't he? So that was what this man had always thought about him, the xenophobic bastard! Well, he would soon sort that out.

The bossman reached into his pocket and took out the 500 pounds promised. He was a little drunk, and swaying. 'You did okay, Tony, I'll be in touch,' he said, as he handed it over.

Tony was fuming as he walked back to where Eddie waited with the car. How could that Italian man sit there while the bossman spoke about him like that?

'Well?' said Eddie, when Tony got in the car. 'How did it go?'

'All right, I think.'

'Who was there? What happened?'

'Four Italians. It was just a meeting to finalise payment, I think. Lots of flannel, you know the kind of thing.'

Eddie kept on asking questions all the way back to Elle's. Jake had been right; Eddie was fishing for information. Although it was more like the third degree. Luckily, Tony had learned that silence was golden.

10

A CHANCE ENCOUNTER

Once Eddie had dropped him off, Tony waited until he saw his car turn out of the road, then hailed a passing black cab. He instructed the driver to take him back to the hotel he'd just come from.

When Tony had come up with his plan he had been angry, which had fuelled his bravado. But as he got closer to the room, his courage began to ebb away. He knew he was taking a risk; still, he was there, so he knocked on the door.

One of the younger men opened it and peered at him curiously; he turned to look at his boss, who was still sitting in his chair.

The man, knowing Tony spoke Italian, asked him if he had come back with a message.

Tony replied in Italian. 'No,' he said, 'but I am Italian, too, and that man you're doing business with called you a greasy Italian bastard. I would have liked to have told you earlier, but I didn't want to speak out of turn.'

Tony had blurted out everything he felt, in one breath.

'I know what he said,' the Italian man said, in perfect English. He started smiling at Tony. 'Tell me, do you always show such disloyalty to your employers?' He raised an eyebrow.

Tony blushed. He knew he shouldn't have said anything; he was just being hot-headed. He was out of his depth with this man and he knew it. Whatever he said, this man had his own thoughts about him. Tony pushed his hand through his hair and looked at the man before him.

'He was my boss, once upon a time. He offered me money as a one-off to come and interpret for him, today.' Tony paused, then said, 'May I ask, why did you pretend not to understand him?' Tony couldn't figure out why the man had played the fool.

'Keep your friends close and your enemies closer, that's what I always say, and so does my good friend, Ralph Gold, who put me on to your one-time boss.'

'I'm sorry, sir, I shouldn't have come back. This is none of my business. I just didn't want your boss doing business with a man who doesn't respect him.'

'There is no boss. I am the boss; I make the decisions. So, if not to your one-time boss, who has obviously done you a great wrong in the past, it seems you have a loyalty to the flag. Why is that?'

'I'm Italian; well, half, anyway,' Tony stammered. He felt stupid in front of this man. Embarrassed.

'Please, take a seat,' said the Italian.

Tony sat where the bossman had been sitting, less than an hour before.

'And will you take a whisky?'

'Yes, please,' said Tony, and a glass appeared in front of him almost immediately.

Tony watched the Italian pick up his own whisky glass and drink from it. He couldn't help but smile; he didn't know this man but he felt, somehow, he could trust him.

'What about your ulcer?' said Tony, pointing at the whisky tumbler in the Italian's hand.

'Take a tip from me, never drink when you're discussing business, you make yourself look like a drunken fool.' He cocked his head to one side and looked at Tony, smiling.

Tony put his glass down and thanked him for the drink. 'Sorry, I underestimated you. Again, I shouldn't have come. I just felt I should tell you that the bossman isn't to be trusted. I know, I've been to prison as one of his goodwill gestures. Sorry, and thanks for the drink.'

The Italian held his hand out to Tony and shook it. 'A blond Italian with blue eyes, that's unusual. Thank you for coming back. Honesty is a rare thing in our business. Tell me, what's your name?'

'Tony,' he said.

'Your full name. You say you're Italian, what is your full name?' The man waited for an answer.

'They call me Tony, but my name is Antonias. Antonias Lambrianu.' Tony laughed nervously. 'Is that Italian enough for you?'

The Italian man's head shot up and he looked Tony directly in the eyes. He stared at him for a moment.

'Antonias Lambrianu.' He nodded to himself and looked at one of the other men in the room. He held out his hand again to shake Tony's. 'Nice to meet you, Antonias Lambrianu.'

He took another drink from his glass as he watched Tony leave the room. This really was a strange encounter. It couldn't be, could it?

Tony walked to the lift and got in. It was a strange look the man had given him, almost spooky. Wait till Jake hears all about this, he thought to himself.

Back inside the hotel suite, the Italian man turned to one of his men and waved him forward.

'See that Mr Antonias Lambrianu gets home safely. Do it without being seen. You never know, seeing as there is so much bad blood between himself and that bossman, it wouldn't surprise me if he is having him watched.'

He was right, of course; Eddie had been warned by the bossman to keep an eye on Tony's activities, where he went and who he saw. Thankfully, Tony had left straight away, when he saw Eddie drive off, and so hadn't been followed back to the hotel.

* * *

Tony went straight round to Jake and Sharon's flat. It was late, but he knew they wouldn't mind. Jake probably wouldn't be asleep, anyway, he would be waiting for Tony to get home to tell him what all this cloak and dagger business was about.

'For God's sake, Tony, where have you been?' said Jake, when he opened the door. He had stayed up and waited by the window, looking for him, and he was agitated. He feared something had gone wrong; Tony had said two hours, maximum, and it had been much longer.

'Don't panic, I came as soon as I could. I had some extra business to take care of.'

Jake hugged him; he had never been so relieved to see his brother; he was sure something had happened.

Jake made them both a cup of coffee. 'Well, what was it about?' he said.

'Diamonds. I'm not sure exactly what, but it's something to do with uncut diamonds. The bossman wants thirty as his share, so God knows how many more there are. I don't know any more than that.'

'Who the hell would discuss diamonds with the bossman? He's as cheap as chips.'

'I don't know, I'll tell you about all that in a minute. There was an Italian guy there who was in charge, and he said a guy called Ralph Gold had put him on to the bossman.'

'Shit, Tony, Ralph Gold? That man's into everything, very well-to-do and doesn't suffer fools gladly. Done all kinds of things. He used to supply guns to some Irish terrorist lot, a real mean bastard by all accounts. Supposedly, he's gone all legitimate now. All his friends are important people: judges, lawyers, members of parliament, you name it.'

'Ralph Gold, really? I'll remember that name, it might come in useful one day. Anyway, this Italian guy I was telling you about...' Tony told Jake all about his evening.

Tony spent the night on the sofa at the flat, as it was so late. He hardly slept, though; he was still thinking about that Italian man and how much he admired him. He was in a league of his own and Tony knew he wanted to be like him one day.

11

MIRIAM

Back in Italy, the vineyard operation was now a multi-million-pound business. It supplied all the major supermarkets, restaurants, and professional wine sellers.

Miriam wanted for nothing; she had an excellent team of loyal workers and managers running the business. Fredo had died two years ago. He'd had a massive heart attack one day, and it had all been over so suddenly, they hadn't had a chance to call the ambulance. Since then, she had shared the house with Rosanna, who had first been her maid, then her companion, and now was a dear and trusted friend.

Miriam had everything she needed and more, but money couldn't buy family. There were days she felt she had everything, and yet had nothing.

For eighteen years she had done her very best to find out some kind of news about Annette and Antonias, but there had been nothing. Annette had covered her tracks well. Private detectives had been hired, against Fredo's wishes as he thought it would seem as though Miriam was hounding them in their new life. But she needed to know if they were both okay. She still felt part of what had happened that night had been her fault.

Time and time again, she had cursed herself for not giving Annette all the money she had wanted. What did it matter now? But Miriam had been stubborn and felt bitter when she had realised Annette had been prepared to sell her own son, for financial gain.

Antonias was her only grandchild and she wasn't prepared to wash her hands of him; he was out there, somewhere. He would be a man now, in his twenties. Since Marias and Fredo were both dead, all of this now belonged to Antonias. Before she died, herself, she wanted to see him one more time.

Each Christmas and birthday, Miriam had bought Antonias a present and put it in his bedroom. It was to give herself hope that one day he might return to where he truly belonged.

In the end, Fredo, had stopped her obsession, there was no point to it.

'If it makes you feel better, Miriam,' he'd said, 'just put the money that you would spend on his presents into a bank account for him. He is all grown up now, what does he want with toys?'

So that was what she had done, because if you didn't have hope, you didn't have anything. Besides, it salved her conscience.

Each day, she would visit the little church she had married Fredo in. It was part of the vineyard, dating back to when it had just been a farm and the workers would visit every Sunday to pray. It was a special place. She always lit a candle and prayed, and asked God to keep Antonias safe, wherever he was.

Time and time again she had cursed herself for not understanding Annette better. She feared she would never have peace of mind.

As Miriam sat in her lounge, resting, she heard a car pull up outside the house. That was very unusual; people normally went to the factory or the offices to discuss business.

Rosanna came running into the lounge; she looked panic-stricken. 'Miriam,' she said, 'there's a large black car outside, and Don Carlos is getting out of it.'

Don Carlos was a well-known Mafia boss, and he didn't do social calls. He owned everything, and everyone. Many people owed him favours. His family had helped them all, one way or another, and owing him was like selling your soul to the devil himself.

Don Carlos was the grandson of their friend, Alfonso, who had lived and worked with Miriam and Fredo many years before. They had given him and his family refuge when they fell on hard times, and then Alfonso had left and gone into some kind of import and export business, with his family. This business was Mafia-orientated.

Alfonso had always insisted that whatever businesses they had taken over or taken a commission from, the vineyard was to be left alone. But now that both Alfonso and Fredo were dead, Miriam feared the agreement was at an end.

'Open the door, Rosanna,' Miriam said. 'Show him full respect, and bring in some coffee. Let's find out what he wants... or how much.'

Rosanna was flustered, but hid it when she opened the door to Don Carlos. He was a handsome young man, around thirty years old, and he and his family had a reputation beyond belief. Normally, he went everywhere with his armed bodyguards at his side, so she was a little surprised to see him standing alone. The men had remained in the car.

Rosanna curtsied. 'Don Carlos, you are most welcome. Please, will you come in?'

'Yes, thank you,' he said, and he crossed the threshold.

'If you will come with me, please, I will let Mrs Lambrianu know you are here.'

He nodded, and Rosanna led the way to the lounge. She tapped on the door, then opened it.

'Mrs Lambrianu, Don Carlos is here to see you.' Rosanna curtsied again and left the room to make the coffee.

'Please, come in, Don Carlos,' Miriam said. 'This is a rare occasion. Take a seat, make yourself at home.' Miriam was on her guard. This man hadn't wasted his time coming to see an old woman for nothing; what did he want?

'Thank you,' said Don Carlos. He set down the briefcase he carried and took a seat in an armchair. He was aware of the effect his visit was likely to have, and wanted to put Miriam at her ease. 'Do not distress yourself, Mrs Lambrianu. May I be so bold as to call you Miriam?'

Miriam nodded. Don Carlos could be as charming as he was cold and calculating.

He smiled at her. 'The vineyard is doing very well, I hear. It has a good reputation, and makes a lot of money. That's good, I'm glad you are prospering.'

So, thought Miriam to herself, this is about the vineyard. I wonder how much money he wants not to blow it up?

'Thank you, Don Carlos. Is that what brings you here?'

As an old lady, and an old friend of his grandfather, she felt could speak her mind and cut through all the charming form.

'My grandfather set great store by your family, Mir' always told us of the great debt he owed your husband.' his head slightly. 'I was saddened to hear of Mr Lamb' My condolences.'

'Thank you.'

'You may have heard my grandfather is also dead.'

Miriam nodded. 'I was sorry to hear of it.'

Miriam knew that Alfonso had been shot with a machine gun, many times, during one of his escapades. Apparently, he was so full of holes he couldn't have an open casket, as was the tradition at an Italian Catholic funeral.

There was a tap at the door and Rosanna came in, carrying a tray on which stood their best silver coffee pot and finest cups, in honour of their visitor. Don Carlos had been about to speak, but he held his tongue while Rosanna poured the coffee. She put a plate of homemade biscotti on the table, alongside the coffee things, then left the room.

'Many times,' said Don Carlos, as the door closed behind Rosanna, 'my grandfather said he wanted to pay back the debt he owed your husband. He spoke of you both often. Your very kind and gracious husband would never accept money from him, nor, I believe, any favours. He had told my grandfather they were family, and families help each other.'

'That's correct,' said Miriam. She sipped her coffee. She was getting tired of all this reminiscing about the past, she wished he would get to the point.

'Maybe now I can repay this debt, so that I know my grandfather can truly rest in peace.'

'I don't want your money, Don Carlos.' Miriam shook her head. 'As you said yourself, your grandfather was a good friend – family, even. I don't need your money, I have money of my own.' She waved her hand around the room to prove her point.

'I know, Miriam, I can see that. Your late husband's "secret ipe" is famous and known all over the world.' He nodded at her smiled. 'There are some things money can't buy, though, aren't ?'

Miriam looked at him quizzically. What was this about? What was it that money couldn't buy?

'I can see you're tired, and I apologise for keeping you in suspense for so long.' Don Carlos sat back in his seat. 'There has long been talk about how you have tried to find your daughter-in-law and your grandson.'

'It has been a sadness, to me, that they were never traced.'

'Well....' He sat forward, his eyes locked on Miriam's. 'I have found your grandson, Miriam. I have met Antonias Lambrianu, and I know where he is living.'

The words didn't sink into Miriam's brain at first. Could it be true? she thought. Has Don Carlos met Antonias? She had constantly prayed to God for news of Antonias, but now the news was coming from the very devil himself!

'I know it's been a long time since you saw him, but describe him to me. What features did he have?'

'He was a very small boy when I last saw him, Don Carlos.' Miriam wiped away a tear; she hoped this wasn't some kind of trick. 'His most striking features were his blond hair and blue eyes.' She stood up and walked over to a table on which stood an assortment of fancy frames containing family photographs. She selected one and took it to Don Carlos.

Don Carlos looked at the picture in the frame and nodded. The resemblance was undeniable, the young man who had gone out of his way to warn him that his own boss was going to double-cross him, who had risked his life for him, was the small boy in the picture.

'In that case, Miriam, I have definitely found your grandson. Obviously, I had to check; blond Italians are a rarity, indeed. There is a new problem now, however.' He looked down at the floor and smiled.

Miriam wiped her eyes. 'What is it? Is Antonias ill, Don Carlos? Please tell me, I've waited so many years for news of him.'

'Fear not, he is well, I assure you. I was just thinking to myself how the world is a circle. You see, I have paid my grandfather's debt, but I am now indebted to your grandson. He tried his best to warn me of great danger, and risked his own life doing it, should he have been found out.'

'Forgive me, Don Carlos, but how did you meet Antonias? And what do you mean, he risked his life for you?'

Don Carlos looked at the ceiling, as though trying to gather his thoughts; he was actually deciding how much to tell her.

'We are family, yes? And you know the Italian way, we look after each other, you have proved that. Antonias has made his way in the world as best he can, but he is involved with some, let's say, unsavoury characters.' Don Carlos paused; Miriam waited for him to continue. 'At the moment, a diamond exchange is being negotiated. I'm not sure how involved he is, but he is involved, as am I.' Don Carlos reached into his briefcase and took out a large folder, which he handed to Miriam. 'Antonias is a clever young man, which is remarkable, given his upbringing.'

Miriam took the folder from him. 'What is this, Don Carlos?'

'Before I came to see you, I wanted to check my facts. You are a great lady, and I didn't want to raise false hopes and upset you. I'm afraid Antonias was raised in foster care, after a very difficult early childhood. All the facts are in there but, be warned, it does not make for very nice reading. His address and location are in the back of the folder.' Don Carlos stood up to leave.

He reached out and took Miriam's hand, kissed the back of it, then smiled at her. He hoped, now, that both she and his grandfather would find peace.

Don Carlos or not, Miriam went forward and put her arms around him and hugged him.

'Thank you, Don Carlos. How can I truly say thank you? This is no insult to your grandfather's debt, I just want to express my gratitude for the kindness you have shown to an old woman.'

Don Carlos knew she wanted to give him a gift; she was an old Italian woman, and it was the way.

'I hear you have some very good claret wines in your stores, Miriam, very good wine to go with a good meal.'

Miriam nodded, then went to the door and opened it. 'Rosanna!' she shouted. 'Get the men to put as many boxes of the finest claret as will fit into Don Carlos's car.' She returned to her guest.

'God bless you, Don Carlos.' Miriam hugged him again. Now Don Carlos was grateful he had been wise enough not to bring any of his men in with him. He felt like a small child, in her embrace.

'Good luck in your reconciliation, Miriam, I wish you well.' He turned to leave. He smiled to himself as he headed to the door, thinking how sorry he felt for Antonias. If Miriam had hugged him like that for news of the boy, what would she do when she finally met her grandson? God help him!

Miriam wiped away her tears. She looked out of the window, watching Don Carlos climb into his car. She could see the factory workers still putting boxes of her very best, expensive claret wine into the large vehicle. It was a small price to pay for the news he had brought.

'Rosanna, Rosanna!' she shouted, again.

'Yes?' said Rosanna, as she trotted into the hall.

'Pack the cases, and book us both a flight. We are going to England.'

Miriam bent down to the table and picked up the folder Don Carlos had given her. All these pages were filled with her grandson's life. Everything she had always wanted to know about Antonias was there. She couldn't help but cry, as she sat down and opened it.

Don Carlos had been right; this had been no life for her beautiful grandson. She started to cry again, feeling the pain and anguish he must have felt at times, thinking no one cared about him.

Don Carlos had said that Antonias looked well enough, and she knew he wouldn't lie to her about something like that. What did he look like now? He would be a grown man; the last time she had seen him he was a small child. It was finally time to meet him again.

12

FAMILY TIES

Miriam didn't know what to expect when she arrived in London. She had read every word of the files in the folder Don Carlos had given her and they told a pitiful, heart-breaking story.

She wasn't sure of the best way to contact Antonias, and she didn't expect a warm family reunion, when she did. Why would he care? He didn't know who she was, or what had happened to make his mother run away. Now she had been given this opportunity, she had to admit to herself she was nervous – a little frightened, even – but also excited.

Rosanna had rented the penthouse suite in a large hotel in the centre of London, and she had made the rooms look as much like home as possible. Miriam had insisted many family photos went with them. That way, she felt she could at least prove who she was and show the young man his father and grandfather.

* * *

'Tony, there's a courier at the door, he's asking for you. There's a package you need to sign for,' Elle shouted up the stairs.

Tony was in his bedroom, getting ready for work. A courier with a package for him? He hadn't ordered anything. He ran down the stairs to see what it was. The motorbike courier stood at the door. He held out an envelope, and a receipt pad, for Tony to sign.

Tony's first thought was that maybe it was something from the bossman, but no – surely, he would just send Eddie around, as usual. He thanked the courier and walked into the lounge, with Elle hot on his heels.

Tony ripped open the envelope and found an invitation card inside. It was white, with gold embossed writing on the front. He looked at the card, and then at Elle, who was excited, even though it wasn't for her. He thought there must have been some mistake; nobody sent him posh invitation cards.

He opened it and was surprised to see that the writing inside the card was in Italian. Although he had grown up speaking Italian, he hadn't learnt to read or write it until he was a lot older and had made it his business to. When he'd discovered his name, he had also discovered a sense of identity and had wanted to know everything possible about Italy. Elle had bought him maps and dictionaries and was pleased that he had taken an interest in what was his birth right.

The card held an invitation to tea at a flashy hotel the next evening. Tony figured it must be from the Italian guy he had met at the hotel. He wasn't too surprised that this man knew his address; he seemed to know everything.

After work, that evening, he went to show Jake the card. He seemed very impressed, and handed it across the table to show Sharon.

'I bet it's from that Italian guy I told you about, do you remember? Maybe he wants me to do some work for him.' Tony talked enthusiastically about how the men that worked for the Italian were well-dressed and looked smart, and how maybe he could look like that. Tomorrow couldn't come fast enough.

Jake had asked if Tony wanted him to go with him, or at least wait outside. What if this Italian had told the bossman Tony had informed on him? It could be a trap, he could end up being shot or something.

Tony assured him all was well. For some strange reason, he trusted the Italian; he didn't know why, but he felt he was a man of his word.

* * *

The next day, Tony arrived at the hotel in his best suit and tie, and the freshly ironed shirt Elle had prepared for him. He was excited, and he was also very impressed. He was to go to the penthouse suite.

The lift seemed to take forever to reach the top, but when he finally arrived, Tony knocked on the door, expecting one of the men who had been with the Italian to answer it, but instead it was a woman he didn't recognise. She opened the door and smiled at him, then turned and said, 'Mr Antonias is here, Miriam.' She opened the door wider, for him to step in.

His brows furrowed; he was puzzled by this. Instead of the Italian man he was expecting, he saw an old woman, sitting in a chair. In front of her was a large coffee table, filled with all kinds of sandwiches and cakes.

Miriam felt sick inside with anticipation; the young man standing in the doorway was her grandson. She had still mentally pictured him as the little boy who had lived with her, but here he was, an adult man. He had Annette's blonde hair, and her eyes. 'Blue as the Mediterranean Sea,' Fredo used to say to her.

She could see he was uncomfortable with the situation, as he didn't know what was going on. It was time to put him out of his misery. She stood up to greet him.

'Come in, Antonias, my boy, come, and sit down.' Miriam could not help but admire this tall, handsome young man.

Tony walked forward; he was looking around the room, expecting someone else to come out of one of the doors. He felt ill at ease; the situation was strange.

'Don't be nervous, Antonias; please, sit.' Miriam indicated one of the large armchairs in the room.

'Who are you?' Tony said. He wanted to be respectful because of her age, but there had obviously been some kind of mistake. And yet, she seemed to know him. How?

Again, Miriam pointed to the chair, and he had no choice but to sit down opposite her. 'I'm your Italian grandmother, Antonias.' The introduction was short and sweet, and not what Miriam had anticipated.

Many was the time she had played this scenario out in her mind and imagined what she would say, but now she was lost for words. She saw the shocked look he gave her; his face had paled. Miriam indicated to Rosanna to pour some coffee.

'My grandmother,' Tony repeated. 'Since when? I don't have a grandmother, I don't have anyone but Jake and Elle. If this is some kind of weird joke, you can go to hell, old lady.' He stood up to leave.

Miriam had to think quickly; she had read the file about him being fostered by Elle, a kind woman who had taken him in and looked after him. She also knew a little about Jake, who had also been fostered by the same woman.

'I'm sorry to hear about Annette's death,' said Miriam. She thought the mention of his mother might just make him think again about leaving. Not a lot of people would know about her.

Tony turned. His face was red; Miriam could see she had touched a nerve and he was angry.

'How do you know Annette? Who the hell are you, old lady? I don't need this,' he shouted.

'Annette was your mother, Antonias; she was my daughter-in-law. Look.' Miriam showed him the framed photographs she had brought with her. She was glad she had them, because the meeting wasn't going as well as she would have liked.

Tony looked at the photos; they were definitely of his mother. In one, she stood alongside a man, and a small boy, with blond hair. He wanted to be sick; he could feel the bile rising in his throat. He had put his mother to the back of his mind all these years, and now it seemed she had come back from the dead to haunt him.

He looked at the photo again. The man standing with his mother looked familiar; it was the same man his mother had a photo of in the locket she left him.

Tony put his hand to his mouth, and looked at Rosanna. It was obvious he was going to vomit. Rosanna pointed to the bathroom door and Tony hurried inside.

The two women waited, not speaking, for Tony to return. When he eventually did, he went and sat down opposite Miriam. He felt more composed now.

'Don Carlos told me where to find you,' she said. 'I believe you met him a while ago. He recognised your name at once. Thankfully, everyone knows I have been searching for you for eighteen years and so he came to tell me he had found you.' To prove her point and make him believe her, she carried on, knowing she was on dangerous ground. 'I believe you had a meeting to discuss something about diamonds.'

Tony raised his head and stared at her; she could see he was trying to think of something to say.

'Who's Don Carlos?' he asked after a pause. Tony didn't know who she was talking about, and yet she knew about the diamonds.

'Don Carlos, the Mafia boss. He says he met you, and you warned him about something. Is that not so, Antonias?' Now Miriam was confused, that was what Don Carlos had told her.

Tony realised he had never asked the Italian man his name. Mafia boss? It all sounded a bit farfetched, but why would this old lady make up something like that? To impress him?

'So,' said Tony, trying to gather his thoughts, 'where have you been all these years? Why turn up now, when I'm old enough to look after myself? I needed you once and you weren't there. I've looked after myself, all these years. I don't need you, and this meeting is finished.'

'Please, Antonias, give me a few moments more. I'm an old woman, I'd like some memories of you to take to the grave with me. I've searched for you for years. I contacted your mother's brother, Ben. I sent a letter to your mother and money for the flight home, but she disappeared. No one heard from her again. Maybe you can fill me in on those empty years, and I can fill you in on mine.'

She was pleading. She didn't want their meeting to end like this; she could see he didn't want to talk about his past, so she would help him. She took out the folder and handed it to him.

'Don Carlos managed to get this file from the authorities on you, Antonias. Because of this I know some things, but others, I do not. Please, can we not sit and talk for a little while longer? I have come a long way to meet you, at last.'

Everything she was saying was going around and around in Tony's head. He picked up the folder; he wanted to know what she already knew about him. He saw it had once said 'Antony Perry' on the front, and that had been crossed out and changed to 'Lambrianu'.

It seemed this old woman knew a great deal about him; there was no hiding place. He nodded to her and sat down again.

'Why are you here? What do you want from me, after all these years?' he asked. He felt winded, like he had been punched in the stomach. He felt weak and vulnerable in front of this woman; she knew more about his origins than he did.

'As I say, I have searched for you, Antonias, I have prayed for news of you. Your mother took you in the night, when I was in bed. I never saw you again.'

Miriam could see Tony was thinking, as though she had opened a box containing some long-lost memory.

'You live on a farm with grapes,' Tony said slowly, as though some recollection was slowly working its way back through the fog in his brain.

Miriam nodded. 'A vineyard. I suppose a little boy would remember the grapes.'

'What do I call you?' asked Tony. 'Grandmother' seemed too familiar, considering he didn't know her.

'Call me Miriam, if you wish. I understand all this is quite a shock for you, as it is for me, and I don't want to pressure you into anything. I am just so pleased I have got to see you one last time.'

Miriam couldn't hold it back any longer, she burst into tears; all her prayers had been answered, at last. She didn't expect this young man to trust her, why should he? But maybe they could sit and talk for a while, then if he never wanted to see her again, she would accept it graciously.

'Tell me why my mother left in the night, as you say. Where's my father? Does he know you're here?'

Miriam indicated for Rosanna to pour more coffee, and she also told her to get Tony a large brandy.

'Your father was killed in a tragic accident, before your mother left. Let me just say one thing before I fill you in on all the details.

Your mother is dead now and all her mistakes died with her. I will not speak ill of the dead, may she rest in peace.' She made the sign of the cross on her chest.

Miriam was glad he was giving her this chance to speak; she needed her own absolution, to make her own confession of things that were said and done between her and Annette. At long last, she could get it all off her chest.

She wiped her eyes with a tissue from the box that Rosanna had given her, took a sip of her coffee and started to tell Antonias everything she could. She thought he deserved her honesty, otherwise he would never trust her. As harsh as the bitter truth was, she would tell him everything – if not for his sake, then for her own.

They ended up spending all afternoon together. They had tea together, and talked about each other's lives. Tony felt embarrassed telling Miriam some of the things he had done, and how he had lived, but as it seemed she already knew a lot, he felt there was no point in hiding anything.

On hearing the truth, he couldn't understand why his mother hadn't just left him at the vineyard and got on with her own life. It all seemed so selfish, but he had already come to terms many years ago with the fact that she had been selfish regarding him many times in the past.

Eventually, Tony felt it was time to leave. He had heard enough and had a lot to think about.

'You have never said, Antonias, are you married? Do you have a family?' Miriam asked.

'Definitely not, Miriam, to both. From what I've learnt about women, including my mother, I doubt I ever will.' He laughed out loud.

That made her smile; he had a warm, loving laugh, and it reminded her of her son and his father. He was a young man sowing his wild oats.

'Before you go, Antonias, I want you to have this.' Miriam opened her handbag, took out a bank book, and handed it to him.

Tony opened it and looked inside. He saw his name and a string of entries. He looked at Miriam and then at the book again. There was over a million pounds in the account.

'I don't want your money, Miriam. We've met and we've talked, that's enough. Here.' He tried to hand the bank book back to her.

'No,' she said, firmly. 'It's not charity or a bribe, Antonias, it's yours. For many years I filled your bedroom with toys and gifts for Christmases and birthdays. After a period of time, your grandfather, Fredo, suggested I put the money into this account, instead. This is every penny I would have spent on you. This is your Christmas and birthday presents. Please, take it, do what you want with it.'

'You filled my bedroom with toys?' Again, Tony was shocked. He hadn't known what a child's toy was for years. He hadn't really celebrated Christmas or his birthday properly until he had gone to live with Elle.

'Your bedroom is still there, just as you left it. Maybe you'll come to Italy one day and see the vineyard and the house for yourself. After all, it's yours now.'

Tony just nodded; he didn't know what to say. He took the bank book; he felt it would be an insult to this woman if he didn't. She had apparently thought of him every birthday and Christmas, and bought him a present or put money in his account. Every Christmas he had spent on the streets, freezing and starving, there had been someone out there, thinking about him.

'Are you in trouble, Antonias? Don Carlos mentioned those diamonds we spoke about earlier.'

'It's nothing, Miriam. Don't worry about it,' he said, not wanting to discuss it.

'I'm an old woman, and as strange as it may sound to a young man like you, I have a fancy. Fredo, your grandfather, used to buy me a box of chocolate truffles at Christmastime. Each night, I would have one, with my hot milk. To make them last longer, I used to rub the bottom of the chocolate so that it melted and then I would lick the melted chocolate off. I found if you rubbed the bottom of the truffles, with their odd shape, the chocolate would harden again, and each night it looked like a new box. Look, I will show you. It is a little indulgence of mine.'

Miriam took an oddly shaped chocolate truffle from the new box she had at the side of her chair. She gently licked the bottom, and very gently rubbed it with her finger. The chocolate on the bottom of the chocolate started to melt, then she stroked her finger across it and watched it harden again.

'You see, Antonias?' She was smiling at him. 'Many years ago, they used to put small pennies in them for the children as a Christmas treat. Obviously, no one does that any more, in case they choke.' Tony thought she seemed really pleased with herself, showing him her trick.

Tony gave her a wry smile; he thought the whole thing was disgusting. With all her money, she tried making a box of chocolates last longer by licking them. Yuk! He stood up to leave.

Miriam stood, too, and went to hug him, and he hugged her back. It felt good to know he had roots, even though he felt cheated by his mother for his lost childhood.

Miriam had been very fair; she had not blamed his mother for anything. She had just told him the story as she knew it and left him to make his own mind up.

Tony got into the lift and waited while it went down all the floors to the reception area of the hotel. Once outside, he breathed in the fresh air, then walked around the corner to a side alley, where no one could see him, and burst out crying.

He couldn't stop the tears from falling down his face. It felt more like grieving.

All his nightmares had returned. All the memories of being in the dark squat or on the streets, hungry and cold, being left on his own for days at a time, came flooding back to him.

He even remembered the times when he'd had to inject heroin into his mother, because her hands were shaking so badly she needed his help to shoot up 'mummy's medicine'. He felt real pain for the very first time. He had always shielded himself from pain, but this was agony; he felt sick in the stomach.

When he arrived back at Elle's house, he went straight upstairs and shut the bedroom door. He didn't want to talk to anyone, and he wanted to have a shower before Elle would see his eyes were red and puffy from crying.

'Tony! Tony, come on downstairs and have a cup of tea. Tell me about your fancy meeting at the hotel,' Elle shouted.

'I'll be down later,' he shouted, from behind the closed bedroom door.

Elle knew something was wrong; she had known Tony long enough to know that he hid his feelings very well. There was only one person he would talk to and that was Jake.

Elle closed the lounge door so that she couldn't be overheard by Tony, then telephoned Jake.

'I don't know what's wrong,' she said. 'I thought he would have come back all excited, telling me all his news, but he hasn't. He's in his bedroom. Please come, Jake, he'll talk to you.'

Elle didn't know whether she was doing the right thing, but sooner or later, she would find out. Elle made a cup of tea and waited.

Within half an hour, Jake walked in. 'Where is he?' he said. 'What's wrong?'

Elle shrugged her shoulders and just pointed to the ceiling.

Jake knocked on Tony's bedroom door and then walked in. He saw Tony lying flat on his back on his bed, staring into space. He didn't smile, as he usually did when he saw Jake. Something was definitely wrong.

Jake sat on the edge of the bed and waited. Tony took a big breath then let out a deep sigh; he knew Jake had come because of Elle.

'It seems I have an Italian grandmother, visiting England and staying at that fancy hotel,' he said. He didn't look at Jake; he was staring at the bedroom ceiling.

Jake paused. He hadn't known what to expect from this meeting, but in his wildest dreams he had never imagined this. Tony had a grandmother? Jake wasn't stupid, he knew people had grandparents, but nothing had ever been mentioned about Tony having any. He'd assumed they were dead, like his own.

'What's she like?' Given the circumstances, Jake felt it was better to be casual about it.

'Old, Italian, rich. Says she's been searching for me for eighteen years. That Italian guy I told you about is some kind of Mafia boss, he's called Don Carlos or something. She said he recognised my name and went to see her, to tell her he knew where I was. That's the long and short of it.'

Even Jake found it all hard to take in; no wonder Tony was upset and confused by it all.

'When you say rich, what do you mean?' Jake caught the bank book when Tony took it out and threw it at him.

Jake looked inside and saw the large amount of money that was in the account.

'Jesus Christ, Tony, you're a millionaire! How is she so rich? What does she do?'

'She owns Lambrianu Vineyard; they make wine, quite popular wine, by all accounts. She said the money was what she had put away every Christmas and birthday I wasn't there, but I don't want it.' Tony let out another sigh. He was a troubled man; all this was like some horror movie, a bolt from the blue.

He had been lying on his bed before Jake had arrived, thinking about what Miriam had told him. With every fibre in his body, he had tried to remember something from his past. Instead of nice memories, all he had done was awaken flashbacks to a certain thing he had tried his hardest to bury deep down inside him. He had been a small boy... how could he remember?

'Right, mate, first things first. We're going to go down to a local wine shop or supermarket and ask if they sell Lambrianu wine. Your grandmother's done her detective work, now we're going to do ours. Come on, get your coat, you can tell me the rest later.'

Tony hadn't thought of that. Jake was right; they should go and see if this Lambrianu Vineyard was real. Tony stood up, swept his hair back and picked up his jacket, then looked into the mirror.

'I'm going to wash my face first, got something in my eye,' he said, then walked out of the bedroom.

Jake could tell he had been crying, his eyes were still a little puffy and his face was red. He accepted Tony's excuse. Poor bastard; he had lived on the streets and in bad times had eaten out of bins, and all the time, according to this old lady, he had money to burn.

'Okay, I'm ready,' Tony said, popping his head around the bedroom door a few minutes later, and they both left on their own search for the truth.

They didn't have to wait long for their answer. Jake drove them to a branch of a large well-known chain of supermarkets. He headed for the aisle that sold all the wines, Tony following in his wake.

To save him searching, Jake spotted one of the employees of the supermarket, stocking the shelves.

'Excuse me,' he said, 'I'm looking for a bottle of wine. Lambrianu, I think it's called, it's Italian.'

Jake thought it best if he sounded vague, then if there wasn't any such thing, he didn't look like a fool.

'Lambrianu wines,' said the employee, staring at them both as if they were stupid. 'They are over there in the next aisle, white on the left, red on the right, but we don't sell the clarets, you would have to go to a wine merchant for them. I'll show you.'

The young man led the way and very helpfully showed them the wines. Jake and Tony looked at each other, then they looked at the shelves the employee was pointing at. They couldn't believe their eyes. They both stared, open-mouthed. The shelves were full of bottles of wine, all bearing Tony's name.

How many times had they walked around this store and never noticed the name 'Lambrianu' on the labels? They thanked the man, and Jake bought a bottle to take home and try.

'Bloody hell, Tony, I can't believe it. I'm not going to lie to you, I'm shocked, I don't know what to say.'

'I know the feeling.'

'What are you going to do with the money? It's yours, your grandmother wants you to have it.'

'Don't call her that. I call her "Miriam", that's her name. I don't know what to do.' Tony wasn't yet ready to accept that he had a grandmother; for now, it was easier for him to think of her by her name.

Elle made them a cup of tea when they got back and, with a little pushing from Jake, Tony told her what had taken place that afternoon. She was astounded; there had been nothing in his file about family members looking for him.

'Why weren't they ever traced, on your behalf?' she said.

'Because the family didn't know where I was, Elle, and the authorities didn't know who I was. Simple.'

Elle put her hand over his. 'When you say it like that, it is simple. I don't want to interfere, love, this is your business and you have to deal with it, but I'm sure all of this has come as a great shock to her, too.' Elle paused and looked at Tony. 'Miriam,' she said.

'I'm sure you're right. I don't know why she's dragged it all up. It would have been better left well alone, in the past, where it belongs.' Tony looked sad and was sombre in his mood.

'No,' said Elle. 'By the sounds of it, Miriam has searched for you for many years. Even you admit there was no way to trace you, with no fixed abode and an assumed identity. You need to know your roots. You have to face your demons.'

'Yes,' said Jake, nudging Tony in the ribs, trying to make light of it. 'When I used to get bullied at school, you said I had to face them and stand up to them, even when they still hit me. That was what you said. So, take your own advice, eh?'

Tony smiled at him; he'd felt like he would never smile again, but Jake had achieved the unthinkable.

'You know what?' Tony said, looking at them both. 'Know what I'm going to do with all that money?'

'Oh, God,' joked Jake, 'he's going to buy his own little harem so he doesn't have to leave his bedroom.'

'Why don't you set yourself up in the garage business, Tony? You always were a good mechanic,' said Elle. She felt this money would be put to good use if he invested it in his future. A fresh start.

Tony was laughing again, especially at Jake's suggestion. Not a bad idea, he supposed. 'No. Us three are family, you're the only family I've ever known, and many was the time, Elle, you could have sent me back to that kids' home, but you didn't. You always pleaded my case and stood up for me. You, Jake, have always been at my side, my brother, my business partner.'

'Tony,' said Elle, 'we don't want your thanks. I was never going to send you back, and you know that. I love you, I love you both.'

She was stressing the fact that she didn't want his gratitude. He might have driven her crazy on numerous occasions, but she would never give up on him.

'Jake, you and Sharon are going to buy a house with your share and fill it with all the best gadgets you can find, and you, Elle, you're always visiting that friend of yours, Minnie, and coming back telling us both how much you've enjoyed being at the seaside.'

'You're not buying me a house, Tony, that's your money, fair and square,' said Jake, looking shocked.

'We all share it as a family or not at all. I have Miriam's address, I'll post it back to her. If you do accept your share, Jake, there is just one condition I have to make.' Now Tony was smiling again.

'I don't have a share in this, Tony, this is your inheritance...' Jake stopped halfway through his sentence. 'Hang on, what condition?' What condition could Tony possibly have? What did he mean?

Tony seemed like his old self again, now he had talked it through with the two people he trusted most in the world.

'You buy Sharon a bloody cookbook!' They all burst out laughing. Everyone agreed Sharon's cooking was awful.

'I'll go with that, mate, I'm being slowly poisoned to death. Half the time, even she won't eat it!'

'Elle, we're going to buy you a little bungalow by the sea, near Minnie. That way, you can play all the bingo you like. Jake, you start looking for houses with Sharon. I'm going to get my own apartment, so I can have some privacy.' He smiled at Elle and winked at Jake.

They both knew what he meant. Somewhere to take his lady friends!

* * *

Tony heard refusal after refusal, over the next couple of days, until he was fed up. Elle was constantly thanking him for his offer, but refusing to take it. It was his money, and he should enjoy it.

Sharon was pleased when Jake had told her what Tony had said. She couldn't believe it.

'He wants to buy you a house, Jake, why not take it? What's the problem?'

'The problem is, Shaz, it feels like he's buying me off. Thanking me for our friendship. How can I ever pay him back? People don't just buy houses for people. Forget it.'

'No, Jake, Tony's not buying you off. He knows if the boot was on the other foot, you would do exactly the same for him. As for your friendship, you're not just friends because he has money now, and is buying you a house. You were his friend as a child, when he was in prison, and now when he's in turmoil. Think about it... Tony doesn't show his feelings, maybe this is one way he thinks he can.'

Perhaps Sharon was right. Jake didn't want to insult Tony by turning him down, but he also didn't want him thinking he only wanted him for his money. He didn't care if he had money or not. He was Tony, his brother, who he loved.

'He said I should buy you a cookbook,' said Jake, laughing at Sharon.

She leaned over and lightly slapped the back of his head. 'Bloody cheek,' she said. 'And wait till I see him, he's going to get the same.' They both laughed.

Jake went round to Elle's; he wanted to talk it all through with Tony, again, just in case he had changed his mind.

'Jake, mate, we're going out later when Elle gets back from the shops, so don't make any plans.' Tony could hardly sit still.

'What are you so excited about?' said Jake.

'I've got an appointment with the estate agent for them bungalows in Southend-on-Sea. She can't refuse me, now. She doesn't know yet, so we'll just say we're driving her up to meet Minnie, okay?'

'Oh, okay.'

'By the way, this is for you.' Tony handed a piece of paper to Jake. 'Do what you like with it.'

Jake looked down at the slip of paper he held. It was a banker's cheque, made out in Jake's name, for 250,000 pounds.

Jake was speechless. He stood up, put his arms around Tony and hugged him. 'Thanks, brother,' he managed, and that was all that needed to be said.

13

THE HEIST

It had been the heist of the century! It was all over the news – everyone was talking about it wherever you went, in pubs, offices, factories and shops. The television news was full of reports, theories and interviews with police top brass regarding the great jewel robbery that had taken place in Amsterdam.

Everyone knew that Amsterdam was one of the largest diamond exporters in the world and now they had been robbed of millions and millions of pounds worth of diamonds and other jewels. Not one gun had been used, not one person threatened. The vaults had all been broken into when no one was there. It had been a brilliantly masterminded robbery. Some thought it was an inside job, others admired the skill of the thieves and speculated about how it had been achieved.

Members of parliament were outraged and already talking about how, when these men were caught, they would be facing at least twenty years in prison.

Tony and Jake took in the news headlines, then looked at each other. Diamonds? That was what Tony had heard the Italian and the bossman discussing. Surely, the bossman hadn't had either the brains or the guts to pull off something like that.

New Scotland Yard were working with the police in Amsterdam and had set up their own incident room, in England. They all felt there was an English connection. In fact, the police knew fine well there was, there had been talk about something big going down for a while and now they knew what it was.

All police leave was cancelled. The chief superintendent who was leading the case wanted his best officers on this, night and day. Police were swarming the streets of London, visiting their trusted informers, hoping for information about who might be involved. They visited every known jeweller in the area that they knew dealt in black market goods. No stone was left unturned.

Tony and Jake had no real idea about who had been involved in the heist itself, but they had their suspicions. There were some notorious East End burglars that were known for big jobs like that.

The police were waiting for the diamonds to start flooding the market; they reckoned whoever had stolen them needed to get rid of them quickly. Jewellers were closed down because they couldn't or wouldn't give any useful information, but the police knew them well for all of their dodgy dealings. It was chaos.

The usual well-known suspects were taken in for questioning. Eventually, the police had dredged up a few leads and arrested one man, who it turned out had been a getaway driver. He, not wanting to shoulder the blame on his own, had pointed the finger at one of his associates.

Even that small success was a relief to the police, they had been left red-faced by this embarrassing burglary. Still, at least they could tell people they were getting somewhere, now.

The chief superintendent knew he needed to come up with something more, and fast, to satisfy his superiors. His neck was on the line.

* * *

Eddie came around to Elle's one night; he was a regular visitor, so Tony thought nothing of it, until he told him that the bossman wanted to see him again.

Tony telephoned Jake. They both had some idea what this might be about, and both of them decided to go and meet with him, together. If nothing else, they were curious.

It had been a month since the heist. More men had been arrested after the first two, but although the police had caught some, both in England and in Amsterdam, they knew they hadn't caught the ringleaders.

Tony and Jake followed behind Eddie in their car to go and meet the bossman. It seemed Eddie was the bossman's number one, these days. He always seemed to be doing his bidding.

Tony noticed, yet again, that the club hadn't changed; if anything, it looked even worse than when he'd last saw it.

The old, once-feared bossman, was surrounded by all his usual bodyguards and Tony had to admit that he envied him a little, despite his own recent good fortune. The bossman had everything, but Tony knew he could do so much more with the cheap, empty club that his boss used more for his own recreation than he did to make money. It was full of overweight, cheap prostitutes. And potential. And it was the potential that Tony hated to see wasted.

The room was filled with cigarette smoke and the ceiling was yellow and nicotine-stained. This man has no class, Tony thought to himself. He wore half-decent suits, but he had no class. He was just a fat old man in a half-decent suit, dirtied by cigarette ash.

The bossman waved everyone but Eddie, Tony and Jake out of the room.

When just the four of them remained, he looked at Tony and Jake and said, 'I need you two boys to collect a parcel for me. No questions asked. Do you think you're up to it? Are you both more than a couple of well-known leg breakers?'

Tony looked at Jake; even though this man wanted something from them, he still didn't have the decency to speak to them respectfully. He was still insulting them.

Bearing in mind the diamond heist and the meeting he had attended, Tony had some idea what this parcel was likely to be: the thirty diamonds the bossman had discussed with the Italian.

'I feel you're the one man I can trust with this, Tony. You know about the little chat I had with that greasy Italian, that's why I sent for you. I presumed you would bring him with you.' He looked at Jake with distaste. 'Will you do it?'

'I'll think about it,' said Tony. 'Can I let you know tomorrow, when we've talked it over?'

The bossman opened his mouth to protest, but Tony cut him off.

'This is a big risk, high stakes. Surely you don't expect an answer right now? There's a lot to think about, starting with how much you're prepared to pay.'

'All expenses, plus 2,000 pounds each.' The bossman felt that was a good enough offer for these two.

Tony and Jake left and went back to the car; Jake was already angry, and shaking his head.

'No way, Tony, he's setting us up. No, he's setting you up. He wants us to be mules, carrying his merchandise through customs for him. He's fucking joking. Two thousand for twenty years inside; does he think we're stupid? Let him collect his own parcel. Better still, let him send Eddie, he seems to be his number one arse-licker at the moment.'

They talked it over nonstop, but as much as Jake opposed the idea, he could see Tony was thinking about it.

'Are you crazy, Tony? Those guys who did that job are looking at twenty years. No, we get caught and we're done for. You can't be considering this.'

'Let's go and see Elle, she's still in the middle of packing up her stuff ready for when she moves,' said Tony.

Jake couldn't believe Tony was changing the subject. That usually meant he'd made his mind up. Jake knew, as much as he didn't want to believe it, that for some bizarre reason Tony was going to pick up these diamonds and hand them over to the bossman.

'Okay, mate, you win. Whatever you decide to do, I'm with you, and no arguments. Okay?'

'That's your choice. You're a married man, you have your wife to think of. Me, I have no one depending on me. Think hard before you make the decision, I don't want you or Sharon on my conscience.'

Jake was right; Tony had made up his mind to do it, though God only knew why. After all, he didn't need the money.

Sharon was fussing around, buying things for their new house. The sale would go through quickly, as there was no mortgage to be processed.

Elle was busy packing up her life in boxes. She had lived in that same house for most of her days. It was full of memories – she had fostered many children, some of whom she still kept in touch with.

The new bungalow Tony had bought her was beautiful. It was in a new complex and everything in it was brand new, too. She hadn't wanted to take his money – she reckoned he would need it someday – but he was adamant, and she felt it was easier to agree.

If nothing else, she thought, should he ever need financial help, he can always use the house as collateral. It's an investment for him.

* * *

Jake went around the bookies where Tony was still working. Eddie was hanging around, as usual. He was addicted to gambling; not a day passed without him betting on some three-legged donkey or other. Jake didn't like Eddie much. He appreciated Eddie and Tony had history, but Jake had always kept him at arm's length. Maybe he was a little jealous; Eddie had been in Tony's life long before he had.

'I've been to see the bossman,' said Tony to Jake, while they were alone in the car. 'I'm going to Amsterdam. That sleaze is testing me, and yes, probably going to set me up. He's given me two plane tickets to Amsterdam, but I'd rather go alone, take my chances.'

Looking at the dashboard, Jake sighed. This was stupid, it was as though Tony was pressing a self-destruct button.

'Well, I don't know about you, Tony, but I could do with a break to get away from the women in our lives discussing wallpaper and house moves. Let's do it.' Jake held up his hand and gave Tony a high five.

* * *

They arrived in Amsterdam early and only planned to be there a few hours. They went straight to the address they had been given. It was a large house, surrounded by offices.

Tony had decided not to take his gun, mainly because he knew he wouldn't get through customs with it. When they walked into the house, they were slammed against the wall, palms downs, feet apart, and searched by the men that were waiting for them.

Once they had been patted down and the men were satisfied that they were clean – no weapons, no wires – they were shown into another room.

A man sat at a desk. Before him was a briefcase, and he calmly pressed in the combination.

'Sorry about the search,' he said. 'No offence, boys, but you can't be too careful. There are a lot of thieves about.' He spoke with a Dutch accent and laughed at his own joke.

Tony and Jake said nothing. The atmosphere was tense; something wasn't right.

The Dutchman took a small velvet bag out of his briefcase and put it on the table. 'Count them.'

'No, your word is as good as your bond, we have to trust each other, after all,' said Tony. He picked up the velvet bag and put it in his pocket. He could see the surprised look on the Dutchman's face.

'Are you sure you won't count them?' he said again.

Tony looked at Jake; now they knew something was definitely wrong. Why was this man insisting they counted the gems? Tony handed the bag back to the Dutchman.

'You count them; I don't want you thinking I've got sticky fingers. Count them out to me, then we can both be sure.'

The Dutchman's smile left his face; he wasn't happy, but he was prepared to go along with it. He loosened the drawstring top of the small velvet bag and tipped it up.

Thirty uncut diamonds poured out of the bag and on to a soft, velveteen cloth. The Dutchman picked them up one by one and counted them back into the bag, watching Tony and Jake's faces as he did so. Then he handed the bag back over to Tony.

'Don't lose them, boys,' the Dutchman said, then he nodded to one of the other men in the room to show them both out.

No sooner had they left than the Dutchman took a glass of whisky from one of the other men in the room. A second glass was placed on the desk he sat at.

The bossman walked out of a side door and sat opposite the Dutchman, picked up the drink, and gulped it down.

'It's a shame you didn't get his fingerprints on them,' said the bossman. 'Still, they should keep the police happy and off our backs. This whole thing has got out of hand. The police need a name.'

'So why did you also come to Amsterdam Mr Jenkins?' the Dutchman asked politely.

'I came because I wasn't sure I could trust that bastard. He's an arrogant sod, who needs taking down a peg or two. If he succeeds, then I have my diamonds, if not I will be satisfied that he has gone to prison for a long time and I will get a pat on the back from the authorities. Shit!' said the bossman. 'I might even get a knighthood.' Laughing at his own joke, he left the office.

The bossman had decided that, if Tony succeeded, that was all well and good, and if he got caught, it would be Tony and Jake going to prison and not him. As a gesture of goodwill, Ralph Gold, who had introduced the bossman and the Italian, had also given him 50,000 pounds in cash to do with as he pleased.

* * *

'That fat bastard bossman has just sold us down the river to save his own neck, Jake,' said Tony. 'Couldn't you smell his cheap tobacco smoke, coming from the next room? He was there and he was desperate for us to put our fingerprints on those diamonds.'

They were walking down a high street towards a taxi rank. 'So, Tony,' said Jake, 'what do we do? He's going to look great, isn't he? He's going to give his friends at the police station the information they want, and he's got two mugs, meaning us, to take all the blame. Now what?'

They got into a taxi and were driven down the high street towards the airport. Tony was looking out of the car window on one side, Jake was looking out of the other. Not a word was spoken, especially in front of the taxi driver.

'Excuse me, can you stop here, please?' said Tony, suddenly.

The driver pulled in.

'What's going on?' said Jake.

'Wait here, I'll be back in a minute.'

Jake watched as Tony got out of the taxi and walked across the street and into a large shop. The sign said 'chocolatier'.

Inside, Tony saw the shop was filled with all kinds of exotic chocolates, none of them the kind you could buy from the local supermarket. This store only sold handmade, exclusive chocolates – very expensive ones.

'Do you sell those oddly shaped chocolate truffles?' he asked the sales assistant. 'I'm not sure what they're called, but they're very special.'

An idea had crossed his mind; he didn't know if it would work, but, given the circumstances, he was prepared to try anything.

'Yes, sir,' said the man behind the counter, in perfect English. 'A very good choice. Would you like to try one, to see if they are to your liking?'

This really was a specialist shop. How many stores do you go in where they are prepared for you to eat their chocolates before you buy them?

'I'm sure they'll be fine, thank you.'

'What size box would you like, sir?'

'What size do they come in?'

'We have two sizes: twenty truffles or forty truffles.'

'I'll take a box of forty, please,' said Tony. 'And could you wrap them? They're for my grandmother.'

'Very good, sir.' The man selected a box and started wrapping it up. He finished by adding a large red bow.

'How much do I owe you?'

'That will be five hundred euros, please, sir,' said the salesman.

'I'm sorry, how much?'

'Five hundred euros, sir.'

'Five hundred euros for a box of chocolates? Tony had never heard of anything so ridiculous. No wonder his grandmother made them last a long time!

He paid the man and went back to the taxi.

'For God's sake, Tony, we're up to our eyes in shit, and you're buying chocolates. Are you completely mad?'

'They're for Miriam,' Tony said.

When they got to the airport, they saw that it was swarming with police. Some were armed.

'I need the toilet,' said Tony. He saw a sign for the public toilets and went in. Jake followed.

'If you think I'm swallowing them, Tony, you are seriously mistaken. And you can't flush them down the toilet, they'll sink to the bottom and stay there.'

Tony pushed Jake into a cubicle with him and shut the door. He carefully undid the ribbon the salesman had wrapped around the chocolates and removed the paper gently, so as not to tear it.

A thought had occurred to him. Perhaps Miriam wasn't as bonkers as he thought. She had mentioned to him that people used to hide coins in the truffles... maybe they could hide the diamonds inside them.

He took one out, while Jake watched him quizzically, and licked the bottom, as he'd been shown. He rubbed his finger across it and the chocolate melted. He took a diamond out of the velvet bag and carefully pressed it into the bottom of the truffle, then rubbed his finger across it again, and watched as the chocolate set and hardened. Miriam had been right; once the chocolate had set again, it looked like it had never been touched.

He handed one to Jake and told him to do the same thing he

had done. They did this with all thirty diamonds. This was a careful, slow process, but it would be worth it, if it saved them twenty years of their lives behind bars.

When they had finished, Tony slipped the large bow back over the box, as the sales assistant had done in the shop. Jake opened the toilet cubicle door and, as he stepped out, he saw a man coming in to use the facilities. The man gave Jake an odd look when he saw Tony following him out of the cubicle.

'You do realise,' said Jake, smiling, 'that guy thinks we've been up to no good in there, together.'

'Bound to,' said Tony, 'anyone can see you fancy me.'

'Not as much as you fancy yourself,' said Jake.

They grinned at each other.

Tony wasn't sure what to do next. He looked around the airport; he felt he was being watched. They walked up to the air hostess at the reception desk and handed over their tickets. It came as no surprise when they were stopped.

They were taken into a back room and, despite their protests, both searched. The box of chocolates was unwrapped and checked to see if it contained anything that it shouldn't. When that all came up empty, a doctor came in to carry out a strip search. They were both told to bend over while they were searched internally.

It was horrendous, as well as humiliating. Both men complained loudly and demanded to know what it was all about. They knew they had to protest, and protest loudly.

The airport police explained to them that they were perfectly within their rights to stop and search whomever they liked.

An investigating officer came into the room; all Tony and Jake were wearing were surgical gowns.

'Would you gentleman like us to telephone a lawyer? Would you like some legal representation?' he asked, in his Dutch-accented English.

'I'll want a lawyer soon, when I sue you for all of this humiliation,' shouted Tony. 'Why do you think I need one now? What are you looking for – is it drugs or something? We've got nothing illegal either on us or in us, you've seen that for yourself!'

He knew he had to keep up his indignant protestations. They had to sound real.

Later, they were both being interrogated in separate rooms about why they had visited Amsterdam.

'Are you saying nobody is allowed to visit this place?' said Tony. 'Why else would young men visit one of the most notorious red-light districts in the world, but to have some fun? Jake, the guy you've got in the other room, is married, he's not going to mess around on his own doorstep, is he? We came for some Dutch fun, that's all. It's not a crime, is it?'

'Did you enjoy our hospitality, Mr Lambrianu?' the officer asked.

'I've had better,' Tony answered. He saw the officer look down at the table, where the unwrapped box of chocolates sat.

'Ah', said the officer, 'I see you like our famous chocolate truffles. It's a long way to come for those, even though they are magnificent.'

'They're for my grandmother, it's her birthday, soon,' said Tony. Now he was worried.

The officer removed the lid. Tony felt his palms sweating. This was it; he knew now he had been caught. He was trying to avoid the eyes of the officer and so looked down at the table before him. This was the time to show his poker face.

'They are my favourites, the rough-edged truffles, although on my wages I cannot afford them very often. They are, indeed, a treat. You must love your grandmother very much.'

The officer took one of the truffles out of the box, raised it to his mouth and bit it in half.

Tony froze; he hadn't expected that. The man was just trying to get under his skin, but one crunch on one of those diamonds and this farce would be over. He felt his stomach do a somersault.

The officer was relishing the luxurious chocolate and even went so far as to lick his fingers. Tony showed no reaction.

'I am sure your grandmother will not notice one is missing,' the officer said, sarcastically. He put the lid back on the box and pushed it towards Tony.

Tony decided not to make a fuss; he just nodded at the officer. His throat was so dry, he doubted he could speak, anyway.

The calculating officer had listened carefully and taken note of everything Tony said. Now, he turned to another officer. They whispered to each other, and then left the room.

Tony was anxious and nervous; he was trying to hold his nerve, but he felt this investigating officer could see straight through him. He hoped Jake was okay.

Six long hours later, they were told they could get dressed and leave.

Tony and Jake had both asked what it was all about; surely, they didn't put all their tourists through this? However, they were given no explanation, just told they could leave.

They were escorted to their plane by security, and at long last they were in the air, flying away from Amsterdam.

Neither of them spoke during the flight; they didn't know whether there were any police on the plane listening to their conversation. It wasn't a long flight, but it seemed to take forever. Finally, they landed in England. Home and free!

As they were leaving the airport, Tony spotted a Post Office. He walked in, selected a large padded envelope and slipped the box of chocolate truffles inside. He needed to get rid of them, fast. He fished the piece of paper Miriam had given him, with her address on, out of his wallet, and wrote it on the envelope. Just a few minutes later, the truffles were in a cart, along with other parcels destined for Italy.

From the airport, they went directly to Jake's house, where they could talk in private. Sharon was out and they had the house to themselves.

They were exhausted; the whole incident had been mentally draining. When Tony told Jake the investigating officer had eaten one of the truffles, he saw his eyes open wide, and his jaw dropped.

'If he's eaten one, that is going to be the most expensive shit in the world,' said Jake.

'Don't forget, there were forty chocolates in that box. If he'd have crunched hard down on one of those diamonds, he would have broken his teeth. All the diamonds have to be still in the box.'

'What about your grandmother?' said Jake. 'What if she eats one? It could kill her.'

'She'll be fine,' said Tony, feeling confident. 'She doesn't eat them, does she? She licks them.'

Tony had a feeling his grandmother would know when the truffles arrived, what was in them. She had mentioned his meeting, and had asked about diamonds, then she had gone on and on about how people used to hide things in those chocolate truffles. She was cleverer than she looked.

Miriam had told him what to do, and how to hide them. It had been up to him to understand and to act.

Now was the time for a very large whisky each, Jake decided; they needed it. They both agreed, the police had been tipped off and were waiting for them.

'Thank God for your granny and her bloody chocolate fetishes. Let's face it, that was quick thinking from you. You and your granny have saved us.' Jake took a drink. 'But now what? Surely that two-faced bastard bossman will want his diamonds, and we don't have them.'

'Let him sweat. He'll already know by now that we're home safe and nothing was found. He probably had us followed, anyway, once we picked up the diamonds and left for the airport.'

'Thank goodness Shaz is an understanding wife and knows about all of this.' Jake looked at Tony. 'Well, some of it, anyway. They said you told them that we were hanging around Amsterdam for the red-light district. Thanks, Tony.'

'Sharon's no fool, she'll understand. Why else would a couple of young guys go to Amsterdam for a few hours? I could see their point.'

'I only told her a bit about it, Tony.' Jake looked worried. 'She deserved to know something in case it all went wrong, and we were arrested.' He shot Tony an apologetic look. He didn't want his brother thinking he had betrayed him.

'Don't be silly, Jake, she's family. You were right to let her know something, because those guys were going to lock us up and throw away the key. It was better that she heard it from you, first.'

They had another drink, and discussed their day. When Sharon came home, she seemed surprised to see them.

'You made it home then, you two. Everything okay?' She had been worried all day, and had thought that Jake might at least telephone, to put her mind at rest.

'Of course we did. With that cool-headed sod by my side, it seems we're invincible,' Jake said, trying to make light of it.

14

HIDDEN DEPTHS

The chief security officer at a certain big London hotel had been informed by the security men who watched the monitors, daily, that the CCTV system was not working properly. The problem was sporadic and didn't always affect all monitors, but on at least some, from time to time, the image was blurred, or there was no image at all. One day, it had been the CCTV cameras watching the reception area, and on another it was the outside monitors – even the cameras that covered the staff entrance hadn't worked. The system was faulty. The belief was that something was wrong with the wiring.

The chief security officer had reported the problem to the manager of the hotel, and he had telephoned the engineers, to call them in to repair the system.

In the end, the manager had insisted that the CCTV company should rewire the whole security system, from scratch. The prestigious hotel had some very wealthy visitors, and they needed to feel that they and their valuables were safe.

It was during this period of confusion that Don Carlos had visited the hotel for his very short stay. Don Carlos knew the chief security officer and had not only paid him handsomely to switch off cameras and interfere with the CCTV feed, as necessary, but to alternate the problem cameras, making it look like a fault in the wiring. He had made sure he had never been recorded either going into or coming out of the hotel.

So, although the bossman claimed he had met an Italian at the hotel, there was no evidence of it. The police he gave the information to checked the hotel register; the hotel suite he claimed to have been in had been rented by an Englishman, a well-known politician, who had stayed there with his wife. The hotel had hosted a Masonic Ladies' Evening in the function room, that night, and the politician and his wife had attended, then stayed over.

It was while the politician and his wife had been at the function that Don Carlos used the suite for the meeting with the bossman. The event and the original booking were legitimate, and the politician did not like the police checking up on him. He told them he was going to make a complaint to their superiors.

The police were angry when they realised that their informer, the bossman, was double-crossing them; they knew he was most definitely involved in the diamond heist, but they had no hard evidence. Each time they questioned him, he told them the same story about meeting an Italian, although he couldn't tell them the man's name or give any other details about him. As far as the bossman knew, this Italian was negotiating on behalf of his own boss. The one name the bossman did know – Ralph Gold – was not one he would ever dare to divulge.

The police checked all the CCTV footage and found nothing useful. Of course, as well as there being no sign of the Italian and his associates, there was no evidence that the bossman had been at the hotel, either.

The manager told the police about the problem with the system, which had started around a week before this meeting had supposedly taken place. He explained that the whole system had been affected over a period of time; not just the cameras covering that floor on that night, so he felt it was unlikely anything had been tampered with deliberately. The engineers also confirmed that they had been called out regularly to check the security system and had had to refit a whole new one. The police agreed that nothing untoward had taken place.

The trail was cold and the police were angry; an awful lot of their time had been wasted checking out the bossman's story and each time nothing had been proved. It just made them look foolish. Their superiors wanted the crime solved; they wanted a name, and fast.

The press had a field day with the story about how New Scotland Yard were investigating a well-known politician for staying at one of London's most famous hotels with his wife. It was obviously a wild goose chase, but it made good reading.

In an attempt to save face, the police went to see the bossman again, and told him to come up with some names, or he, himself, would be put in the frame.

The bossman was at his club with Eddie, who was panicking. He knew the job had been too big for him, but greed had got the better of him. Now Eddie was frightened and he didn't know what to do to get the police off his back.

'It's a shame, boss,' said Eddie. 'The only Italian I know who was there that night is Tony Lambrianu.' Eddie looked at the bossman with a smirk on his face.

The bossman glanced up at Eddie and knew that the man was prepared to sacrifice his friend to save his own neck.

'Make the call, Eddie, tell them the Italian they are looking for is Tony Lambrianu.' At last, he had a name to give to the police. Tony didn't match the description he had given them, but that could be sorted out easily enough and it would help him ingratiate himself with them again, and maybe they would leave his other businesses alone; after all, that had been their agreement for years.

Eddie made the call and the police got warrants to search Tony's new apartment and Jake and Elle's houses. The police rummaged through drawers, opening up cushions and lifting up flooring. They left a trail of mess behind them.

Elle's beautiful new bungalow and Sharon's house had been trashed by the police, and they had found nothing. Tony and Jake were taken in for questioning, and their stories were identical to what they had told the investigating officer in Amsterdam.

Jake had begged the police not to tell his wife, Sharon, that he had been in Amsterdam with Tony having a little 'adult fun', as she wouldn't understand. Of course, he knew they would tell her, just out of spite, and they did.

Sharon had gone berserk in front of the police and had thrown Jake out, claiming she never wanted to see him again. She even threatened divorce. Sharon played her part brilliantly; she was so convincing even Jake started to believe her.

The initial excitement felt by the English and Dutch police at being tipped off about Tony and Jake quickly fizzled out. Once again, their investigation had hit a dead end.

The detectives' main suspect was now the bossman; he had given them false leads all the way through the investigation. They had picked up a few unimportant men involved in the robbery, but it was taking too long and the pressure was on from above.

All the police the bossman had once been friends with and given information to now disowned him. They didn't want to be associated with him any more.

The police decided if they couldn't get him one way, they would get him another. They went through all of his accounts from the club and any little side-lines he was involved with, including drugs and prostitution. The bossman would soon be looking at his day in court.

* * *

An invitation for a free meal at an Italian restaurant was put through Tony's letter box. Another restaurant promotion; he threw it on the worktop.

There was still pressure on all of them. Tony felt guilty that Elle's new bungalow had already been tarnished. She said she didn't mind, but it didn't ease the guilt. Poor Elle; she always got dragged into his troubles, and she always shrugged it off. He was so lucky to have her.

Jake was living at Tony's place for a bit. He and Sharon had agreed that it was best to leave it a while before they were reconciled. That meant the police left Sharon alone. Sharon was a good woman; she not only stood by Jake, she stood by Tony, as well.

Jake was making a coffee in Tony's apartment when he spotted the invitation from the restaurant. 'What's this, mate?' he said.

Tony shrugged. 'Some promotion for a restaurant, buy one get one free, I think. Why?'

Jake read the invitation. 'If that's the case, how come it's got your name on it? Do you usually get menus through the door with your name on?' He looked up at Tony.

Tony looked at the invitation again. On the face of it, it was just another restaurant leaflet promoting their offers. He took a closer look; it did have his name on it. It had been posted to him, personally. Who would post him an invitation to a restaurant he had never even heard of?

'Only one way to find out; why don't we go tonight?' said Jake. 'Free food, if nothing else.'

'I don't know. What if it's got something to do with the police?'

There were all kinds of things going on. Tony wasn't sure what was going to happen next. He wasn't sure what had happened to the diamonds; Miriam had never contacted him, or even thanked him for the chocolate truffles – minus one.

'Since when did the police give out free meal invitations? Come on, Tony, you're getting paranoid now. I'm going to work. We'll meet at the restaurant about six, okay?' Jake put down his coffee cup and left. Tony sat on a chair, holding the restaurant invitation; it was a real puzzle.

It was on his mind all day, and in the end, he agreed with Jake. It was better to go and find out who had sent the invitation, rather than sit around wondering.

Jake was already there when Tony got to the restaurant. It was a fairly standard Italian trattoria – small round tables with red and white checked cloths and candles in the centre. The staff were friendly and efficient, and they were soon seated and tucking in to plates of spaghetti.

'Pretty busy, isn't it?' said Jake, looking round. The place was buzzing and there were people sitting at the bar having a drink while they waited for a table to become free. They had expected whoever sent the invitation to come over or ask for Tony, but they had finished their food and still no one had approached them. Apart from the excellent food, it had been a wasted evening. They called over the waiter and asked for the bill.

'Time to go, mate, this was all a waste of time.' Tony put some cash down on the table and smiled at the waiter.

'On the house, Mr Lambrianu, no charge. Did you enjoy the wine?' the waiter said, in accented English.

Jake and Tony looked at each other curiously, then turned back to the waiter. How did this waiter know Tony's name?

'Mr Lambrianu! Mr Lambrianu!' A man dressed in chef's whites was shouting over to him from the back of the restaurant.

Tony and Jake were stunned. They had never been there before, why the hell was the chef shouting to Tony? It was all weird, including the fact that the waiter wouldn't let them pay the bill.

The chef hurried over; he was holding a bottle of wine. 'You enjoy your own wine so much, you should take a bottle home. Here, take this one.' The chef pushed the bottle into Tony's chest. 'Don't forget to decant it, it will still have sediment from the grape. Remember: open, decant, breathe, drink. Enjoy, my boy.'

The large fat, Italian chef put his arms around Tony's shoulders and hugged him, then kissed him on both cheeks.

Tony was blushing, and doing his best to push the chef away without being insulting. He looked across at Jake and could see that cheeky smile spreading across his face.

'Thank you,' was all Tony could say. He smiled at the chef, and started to walk away.

'You speak Italian, Mr Lambrianu?' said the chef.

Tony turned back, and thanked him in Italian.

'Good,' said the chef. '*I migliori saluti, nonna.*' With that, he waved Tony off.

'What the hell was that all about?' asked Jake. 'Are you telling me that invitation was from your grandmother?'

'Seems like it. You know what he said, don't you?' asked Tony.

Jake nodded. 'Best regards, grandmother. But why would she bring you here to tell you that?'

They went home. It had been a very strange evening, especially with the chef carrying on like he had.

Jake opened the bottle of wine. 'It's free, we might as well drink it,' Jake said. He was mimicking the large, fat chef, and putting on a bad Italian accent. He started pouring it out.

'Wait,' said Tony, also mimicking the chef, '*mamma mia*, Jake, you must decant it first.'

They had both already had too much to drink, but they couldn't stop laughing at the way the chef had instructed them to drink the wine. It felt good to have something to laugh about, for once.

Jake handed a glass of wine to Tony, and took a sip himself.

'Not bad; you lot produce a nice bottle of wine, I have to say,' he said. They worked their way through the wine, and when they were coming to the end of it, and Jake was pouring the last of it into the glasses, he heard a 'chink' from the bottle.

'What was that?' Jake stopped pouring and looked at Tony. Tony sat up from his lounging position on the sofa, and watched Jake tip the wine bottle upside down and hit the bottom. A thick grape sediment came pouring out, and with it came thirty diamonds.

Their jaws dropped as they watched all the diamonds slide into the half-empty glass. They grinned, then stood up and hugged each other.

'Nice one, Grandma,' shouted Jake, punching his arm in the air.

Miriam had received the chocolate truffles and, when she opened them, saw immediately that one was missing. She had broken one in half and found nothing, so she tried another one, and saw the sparkling stone buried inside the chocolate. One by one, she had opened them all. Thank goodness Antonias had listened to an old woman ranting on.

She had waited until her next shipment of wine was going to England and instructed that a small black dot was to be put on the label of one of the vineyard's special clarets. She had instructed a case of free wine be sent to a restaurant owner she knew in England, on the condition that he gave her grandson, the blond Italian, a free meal and this very special bottle of wine. That was how she had done it.

* * *

Tony and Jake walked into the club and through to the bossman's office. The bossman looked up; he was surprised to see Tony, and even more surprised when Tony laid down thirty uncut diamonds before him.

Tony and Jake watched the bossman examine the gems. He picked one up and let it roll around in the palm of his hand. 'Beautiful,' he said, watching it sparkle in the light. He was licking his lips in greedy anticipation of their worth.

He pushed two diamonds each towards Tony and Jake, and took the lion's share for himself. He put his diamonds into a small container and locked it in his safe.

Tony and Jake left. Their business was now concluded.

Tony walked around the corner to a public telephone box. He rang the police and asked for the investigating officer in charge of the diamond robbery. Once he said he had information, he was put straight through.

Using a fake accent, Tony told the detective where to find the diamonds, and put the telephone down.

He and Jake went in to a small café, opposite the club, and ordered two coffees, then they sat in a window seat and waited.

The police started to arrive very soon after the call was made, their cars lining the street outside the club. An unmarked Jaguar pulled up and they saw the detective leading the case get out. Other police were surrounding the club and running inside.

'I didn't believe you when you said you were considering handing the diamonds over to the bossman. It's some move Tony.'

Tony took a sip of his coffee as he watched the proceedings. 'That was the deal Jake. And I always keep my promise.' Tony smiled as they settled back in their seats.

Inside the club, the police started searching the office. The bossman couldn't believe what was happening; he was shouting at them to get out. He realised Tony had set him up, and he knew that the police knew the diamonds were in the safe.

The detective from New Scotland Yard walked through the bossman's office door. He was smirking; he had got his man and his reputation was intact. His superiors and the press would be satisfied.

'Open the safe,' he said, and waited for the bossman to produce the keys. His hands were shaking so much he couldn't hold them properly. The detective motioned for one of the police officers to take the keys from him and open the safe. They all watched as the officer took out the container holding the twenty-six diamonds.

Tony and Jake watched as the bossman was brought out of the club in handcuffs, and put into the back of one of the police cars. It was over.

* * *

In a large mansion house, near Berkshire, Ralph Gold sat watching the news reports with his wife, Julie. They were in the lounge and the maid was pouring them champagne.

Apparently, the police had had a really good day. The bossman had given them the names of all the men he knew were involved, and they had all been arrested.

He was blaming everyone but himself, and yet the other men on the job were totally ignorant of the facts. They had trusted the bossman, but now, one by one, he had given their names to the police in an attempt to reduce his own sentence.

The case was closed, apart from the missing diamonds. The police had recovered twenty-six, but many more had been stolen. They were eager to know where the rest were, but the bossman insisted he didn't know. The police thought it was only a matter of time before the diamonds turned up. The main thing was, they had the gang.

Apparently, on the day the robbery had taken place, the thieves, as instructed, had collected a small red velvet bag, which had been in a safe on its own. Their instructions had been clear and they were to hand it over to a courier waiting for them on a motorbike in a specified place. Then they had flown back to London from Amsterdam with the rest of the stolen goods. They had all been nervous as they went through customs, but they weren't stopped. Once out of the airport, they had gone to their planned hide out.

A young well-dressed blonde woman with a Liverpool accent was waiting for them when they got there. She had taken the lion's share of the diamonds and other jewellery from the heist off the thieves and put 50,000 pounds on the table, in a tatty old suitcase. As agreed, the bossman had been instructed to pick his own diamonds up from Amsterdam.

Ralph Gold and Don Carlos had pre-arranged the sale of their stolen diamonds and other jewellery before the robbery and Julie Gold, who had picked them up from the gang, had passed them directly on to an Arabian man whose yacht was moored at the marina in Canary Wharf.

'Cheers, Julie.' Ralph Gold raised his glass to his wife, and smiled. This had been a job well done.

When Don Carlos had first approached Ralph Gold about the diamonds, they had needed a fall guy, someone to organise things in London, using their own contacts, who neither knew nor had met either Ralph Gold or Don Carlos.

Both Ralph and Julie Gold agreed that the bossman, as he liked to be known, would be only too eager to be involved in something so big. He was flattered that Ralph Gold had even heard of him.

The bossman was unambitious; he had stayed in the same position for years, employing young men to threaten the landlords of local pubs for what was, in Ralph's view, not a lot of money. He drank too much and wouldn't be able to stop himself boasting about being more superior than he was, to impress people. He was just what they needed.

Don Carlos and Ralph Gold had made 20,000,000 pounds out of the whole deal and they hadn't got their hands dirty.

'Do you know anything about this Tony Lambrianu, who was put in the frame, Julie?' asked Ralph.

'Not a lot, but I'll find out what I can. He seems ambitious, and Don Carlos thinks he can be trusted.'

Tony took out the two uncut diamonds the bossman had given him; he held them in his hand and watched them sparkle. The bossman had been right; they were beautiful.

'I don't know about you, Tony, but I need a holiday,' said Jake. 'I need to get away from here for a while after everything we've been through; it's been hell.'

Tony nodded. 'You're right, I think we could all do with a break after all this.'

'Any suggestions? Personally, I need some sun. Let's get away from this rain and go and relax for a while.'

Tony continued looking at the diamonds in his hand. Vengeance was sweet, indeed. The bossman had been more than prepared to let Tony take all the blame and serve twenty to thirty years in prison. He wondered just how long the bossman would survive, inside, once word got out that he had been a police informer and he had put all his associates in the robbery behind bars. Not long, he guessed.

'What about Italy?' said Tony. Maybe it was time to face his demons, to see the vineyard and visit Miriam. She had covered his back well; a visit from him was the very least she should expect.

'Yeah, I'd be up for that.'

'I have something I need to do first, and then we'll go. Say, about two weeks?' He looked at Jake for approval and saw him nod his head.

* * *

Tony had got to know a pawnbroker, Solomon Cohen, while working for the bossman. Everyone knew he was a fence for stolen goods. He had started out as a jeweller, however, and still had some skill in that regard.

Tony went to see him and was ushered through to the back room. The man sat at a small table, with a cup and saucer at his elbow. He was looking at some silverware through a magnifying glass, using the light from a little desk lamp to help him check the hallmark.

Solomon was a small, balding man, with round rimless glasses. He looked up when Tony walked in, and put down the magnifying glass and the silverware.

'What can I do for you?' he said.

Tony handed him the two diamonds and saw Solomon's face light up. He sat back in his wooden chair, waiting for Tony to speak.

'I want these made into a pair of stud earrings, can you do that?'

The man nodded. 'Yes, I can do that.'

'Don't try and rip me off with your zircon, mind, or I'll slit your weasel throat.' Tony handed Solomon 1,000 pounds. 'This is for your trouble.'

The look in Solomon's eye meant he knew exactly where Tony had got them, but he couldn't help marvelling at the beautiful, uncut diamonds.

Solomon was calm as he examined the stones. 'Very nice,' he said. He looked at Tony. 'There's a newspaper on the chair behind you. Pass it here.'

Tony did as he was told.

'Now, look.' Solomon put the diamond on the paper.

'What am I looking at?'

'You see the print on the paper?'

'No, not through the stone.'

'Good.' He opened a drawer and took out a gem. He held it up for Tony to see. 'This is glass,' he said. 'Looks the same, yes?'

'Yes,' said Tony.

Solomon put it on the newspaper.

'Don't mix them up!' said Tony.

'Look,' said Solomon.

'I can see the print through the glass stone.'

'But not through the diamond. You see?'

Tony nodded; he'd be able to tell if the stones were switched.

'You would easily know if I tried to double-cross you, Tony; you can check when you come back. In a week?' Tony nodded and left, satisfied that he could trust Solomon to do a good job.

When Jake found out what Tony had done, he thought he was crazy.

'Don't tell me you fancy some woman enough to give her real diamonds! They can be traced, you know.'

'Yes, I know. And they're not just for some woman I'm trying to impress. None of the women I know are worth real diamonds.'

A week later, Tony went back to see Solomon, as arranged. Tony waited while Solomon put the 'closed' sign up at his shop, and followed him into the back room.

Solomon held out a box containing two gold stud earrings, each with a diamond mounted in the middle. He looked very pleased with himself.

'Put them on the newspaper,' Solomon said.

Tony did; they were diamonds.

'These are beautiful,' Tony said, as he admired the earrings. 'You've done an excellent job.'

'Mr Tony,' said Solomon, 'we both know those diamonds are priceless, but they are also worthless, aren't they?'

Tony knew he was right. Who on earth would want to buy them? They were far too hot. You would have to wait a couple of decades to put them on the market without them being recognised.

'Here,' said Tony, 'I want you to do something else with this one.' He handed over another uncut diamond that Jake had given him. 'No tricks, now; this is the last of them, got it?' Tony gave Solomon his instructions, and handed over another 1,000 pounds.

It wasn't a lot of money, considering if he was found with them, Solomon would go to prison, but Solomon felt the cash was easier than trying to sell the diamonds. They weren't worth the trouble.

'It's not often I get to work with such beauty, Mr Tony, and I doubt I ever will again.' Solomon clasped the diamond in his hand. 'It is a pleasure to get the chance to show my skill as a jeweller. Give me a couple of days.'

* * *

Back in Italy, Miriam received a parcel. When she opened it, she found a small box containing a pair of diamond stud earrings. She held the box to her chest and looked up at the heavens.

'Thank you, Antonias,' she said. She took out the earrings she was wearing and put the new ones in at once. It wasn't the diamonds she liked so much, it was the sender, and the gesture. Maybe now, they could put the past behind them.

* * *

Don Carlos was handed a parcel as he sat at his large desk. It was a wooden cigar box, full of his favourite Cuban cigars. He opened the box and noticed in the middle of all the large, fat cigars, one of them was missing the paper hallmark band. Don Carlos picked it up and looked at it.

Replacing the cigar band was a man's gold signet ring, and in the middle of it, was a beautifully shaped diamond.

Don Carlos sat back in his chair and smiled. He knew exactly who it was from, especially as it bore a UK postmark. He put the thick, gold ring on his middle finger and admired it. So, this young Antonias Lambrianu had taste. He found himself smiling as he sat back in his chair and looked at the ring.

15

HOMEWARD BOUND

Tony, Jake, Sharon and Elle had all booked their flights to Italy. This was to be an adventure. None of them had ever been on a holiday abroad, before. Passports had to be sorted for the women, and Elle and Sharon had done their shopping.

This was what they all needed, after the turmoil there'd been in their life, lately.

Elle was a little concerned; she wondered how Tony would feel to be back in his homeland after so many years. It had to be done, though, he couldn't run forever.

They had found a resort not far from the vineyard and booked into a hotel. Instantly, from the moment they stepped off the plane, the mood seemed more relaxed. The sun was hot and bright, and eased their tense muscles.

The fine hotel hosted two swimming pools, and fantastic food. What more could they ask for? They swam, ate and relaxed on sun-loungers, soaking up the sun. It was pure bliss. It was also a honey-moon for Sharon and Jake.

It was Elle who eventually brought up the subject. 'Tony, love, we leave in a few days. Don't you think you should go and see Miriam?'

Tony was pensive; he had thought the same thing every morning he had got up, yet each day he had put it off.

'We could all go together, if you like.' Tony kept his sunglasses on; he didn't want Elle to see that he was a little nervous, or embarrassed.

'That's a lovely idea, I'll go and tell the others.' Elle left straight away to tell them. She thought it was best to strike while the iron was hot, and before Tony changed his mind. She knew he had been avoiding the issue.

The vineyard wasn't hard to find; everyone knew it. It wasn't just some old farm that grew grapes. They had hired a car for the day and when they saw it from a distance, they were amazed. It was a huge operation, rows of vines as far as the eye could see, surrounded by factories, and populated by hundreds of workers.

When they arrived, there were lorries parked outside of the factories, some unloading materials for wine-making, others being stacked with boxes of wines.

'Wow!' said Jake. 'I never expected anything like this. It's mind-blowing.' Jake was just a kid from London who had never ventured much further than that. Places like this were inconceivable.

They had all stopped talking and were just looking around at the scene before them.

Tony shouted out to some workers loading the lorries, 'Where's the house? We're looking for Miriam Lambrianu.' He noticed the confused look on their faces and shouted out to them again, this time in Italian.

He saw them smile and point to the far side of the site, away from all the factories and the vineyard.

They drove for what seemed like a couple of miles, and then

they saw it: a large house with a long driveway leading up to the door. It was enormous, the biggest house they had ever seen.

They parked at the front, then looked at one another nervously, wondering which one of them was going to use the great big iron knocker on the wooden door.

Elle felt she should take the lead. Jake was still turning around and around, pointing things out to Sharon and looking at all of the goings on near the factories, and Tony still sat in the car, looking dazed. Elle felt he looked like he wanted to drive off. She was just about to knock when the door opened.

'Mr Antonias, come in. Please, all of you, come in. Miriam saw your car from the window. You are all most welcome.' Rosanna, smiling, beckoned them inside.

Miriam sat in her chair, waiting. She wanted to savour this moment. At long last, her grandson had come home. This was a memorable day.

Rosanna showed them all into the lounge, where Miriam waited. She, too, was nervous. It had been a long time since Antonias was in her lounge. She stood up and greeted Antonias and his friends. She understood why he had come mob-handed, it must all be very strange for him. He was lurking at the back, hidden behind Jake and Sharon. He looked like he was trying to go unnoticed.

It was almost lunchtime; Miriam instructed Rosanna to make coffee and prepare some food, then she walked forward. 'Antonias, my beautiful grandson. Welcome home.' She held out her arms to him and hugged him, as tears flowed down her face.

The tension was broken. They took seats and made their introductions.

Rosanna was quickly back and she brought in far more food than was necessary. She broke any awkward silences by chattering away about the vineyard and how she would arrange for some of the workmen to give them a tour.

She was a typical Italian woman. She wandered around, making herself busy, while chattering away to anyone who would listen.

Tony noticed Miriam was wearing the diamond stud earrings that he had sent her. When she saw that he was looking, she raised a finger to her ear and touched one, and smiled. Not a word was spoken between them.

'I hope you will all be staying for a few days,' Miriam said. She paused, and watched them all look at Tony; he said nothing.

'Well, maybe you will all indulge an old woman and at least stay for dinner, now that Rosanna has slain the fatted calf?'

Tony nodded his head, and they all agreed that they would love to stay for the evening.

Tony stood and began looking at all the photographs that were in Miriam's lounge. The mantelpiece was full of silver photo frames, containing images of his mother, father and himself. Some were of Miriam and a man, who he presumed was his grandfather. He wished he could remember his time in Italy and his Italian family better.

That evening, they all enjoyed the amazing meal prepared by Rosanna and the cook. The talking was easy, the mood relaxed. Miriam sometimes slipped up and spoke in Italian, and was impressed when Jake answered her. Antonias had taught his brother well.

It was starting to get dark and everyone was beginning to feel the effects of the wine Rosanna had been serving all evening.

'You have to stay the night, all of you; the roads are dark and you are not familiar with them,' said Rosanna, who had joined them at the table to eat and be merry. 'Plus, you have been drinking. You cannot drive, you must stay.'

Elle looked at Miriam from across the table and gave her a secret smile. She knew she had planned this with Rosanna. Tony and Jake both had to agree to stay the night; they had been so carried away with tasting the different wines that they had forgotten they were driving.

They all talked till late and then Miriam said she was going to retire for the night. She kissed each, in turn, on the cheek.

The rest of the party decided that they, too, were ready for bed. Rosanna showed them all upstairs to their bedrooms; again, she had been clever. All the beds were made up for them, and the rooms had been aired.

Tony stopped suddenly at the top of the stairs and stared. He didn't know why it was, but there was a bedroom door at the far end of the landing and he couldn't take his eyes off it. There was something vaguely familiar about it, like some flashback of memory.

'What's in there, Rosanna?' He pointed to the door.

Rosanna flushed red; she didn't know what to say, so ignored Tony's question and carried on showing the others to their rooms.

Tony grabbed her by the arm. 'Rosanna, what's in there?' he asked again. He stared directly into her face, waiting for an answer.

'Tony, stop it, you'll hurt her,' said Elle. This was a strange situation. They all looked at Tony, confused.

Miriam came out of her bedroom and saw Tony holding Rosanna's arm.

'Show Antonias his bedroom, Rosanna,' she said calmly.

Rosanna did as she was told. She walked to the door, turned the handle and opened it slowly. She switched on the light, then stood back, to allow Tony to walk in. They all waited on the landing as Tony walked forward and entered the bedroom.

The room had barely been touched since the night he had left it. Tony walked in and looked around. It all seemed familiar, like something from a dream. He noticed in the far corner, near the wardrobes, were boxes of once gaily wrapped presents, all with his name on the labels.

Tony looked at the wall above the small bed; there was a crisp, brown piece of paper pinned to it, and it was a child's drawing.

He suddenly couldn't breathe; his lungs wouldn't fill with air. Miriam had kept his room exactly as he had left it. It held all the memories of his childhood.

Miriam stood in the doorway, watching him. She hadn't wanted him to see it, not yet, anyway. The room had been her way of keeping Antonias alive, and not just a memory.

Tony sat on the dusty bed, and cried.

Jake walked forward. He could see the pain in Tony's face, and it hurt him, not knowing how to ease it.

'Rosanna, you can clear this room, now. Antonias is alive and well; he is no longer a memory to us,' said Miriam. She turned and walked back into her bedroom; there was nothing more to say.

Jake put his arm around Tony. 'Come on, mate, it's been a long day, time for bed.'

Tony dried his eyes, and put his arms around Jake. It had been a hard day, and Tony had a lot to think about, but that could all wait. For now he needed to sleep.

* * *

They ended up staying with Miriam for a few days.

Miriam took Tony to the little church on the vineyard, and showed him how to take Mass and thank God for his safety.

They were all given a tour around the vineyard, and Tony couldn't believe his eyes. It was truly a lovely homecoming.

On the day they were all due to leave, Don Carlos came to visit. He asked if Miriam would like to show her guests some areas of the vineyard they might not have yet seen.

Miriam knew this was his way of asking everyone to leave except Antonias; they all understood and made their excuses.

Jake would have liked to stay with Tony, but he was enthralled by the vineyard. Besides, he knew Tony would tell him everything later, anyway.

Don Carlos had another man with him this time, though Tony didn't think he looked like a member of the mob; he looked quite plain, in comparison.

After sitting down and asking if Tony was enjoying his stay in Italy, Don Carlos got to the point.

'There's a fly in the ointment, Antonias. I need to make a man disappear, if you get my meaning.' Don Carlos waited for Tony to indicate that he understood.

There was a pause, and Tony nodded.

'It makes no difference whatsoever to me how or when this man disappears, but I thought you might like to do it, given the circumstances.'

Tony was astounded; this man that he thought he could trust was asking him to kill someone.

'I'm not a murderer, Don Carlos, as well you know. Why are you asking me to kill a man I don't know?' He spoke with respect, keeping his voice low. This was not a man to be crossed.

Don Carlos nodded his head. He looked at the other man who he had brought with him, then back at Tony. 'That is the point, Antonias, you do know this man. It seems that your good friend, Eddie, is the one who betrayed you. Granted, he was possibly under threat, but he was the one who gave your name to the police rather than protect you, as a friend should.'

Don Carlos waited for Tony's reaction; maybe he already knew it had been Eddie who had made the telephone call to the police, giving Tony's name.

Instantly Don Carlos saw the look of disbelief on Tony's face. He carried on.

'He has laughed and drank with you, my friend; he has sat at the same table as your family and eaten with you all, watching, day after day, as their houses were searched and torn apart.'

Eddie? His good friend Eddie had betrayed him? Don Carlos must be mistaken; they had been good friends for many years, and Eddie wouldn't do that.

Seeing Tony's confused look of disbelief, Don Carlos put his hand out to the other man in the room. The man opened his briefcase, took out an old-fashioned tape recorder and handed it to Don Carlos.

Don Carlos put it down on the table before them and pressed the 'play' button, so that Tony could hear for himself.

Tony raised his eyebrows and looked at Don Carlos, then turned to the other man in the room. He recognised Eddie's voice instantly, there was no mistaking it. He listened to the tape.

How on earth Don Carlos had managed to get his hands on the original telephone call made by Eddie amazed Tony, but then again, with this man's connections, nothing surprised him.

Tony felt sick inside when he heard his old friend telling the police that the Italian man involved in the robbery was Tony Lambrianu. His face flushed red, deepened by the blondness of his hair, and he was angry. He couldn't believe his ears and asked Don Carlos to play it again, just to make sure, and then he watched as Don Carlos switched off the machine and handed it back to the other man.

'Did you not know, Antonias, that your friend was also in Amsterdam with his bossman? They set you up. He and your so-called friend watched you and your associate being arrested. Possibly he didn't want the diamonds; after all, what was he going to do with them? No fence in their right mind would touch them given the publicity they had. Putting you in the frame seemed like a good alternative and gave him a lot of brownie points with his friends in the police force. No doubt he would even get a reward, as one was offered for information.' Don Carlos cocked his head to one side and smiled. He knew he was pressing all of the right buttons to get Tony fired up.

Tony stood up; he was fuming. He started pacing the room and punching his fist into the palm of his other hand, while shouting about what he was going to do to Eddie.

Don Carlos knew Tony had a reputation for being quick-tempered and feisty; he waited for him to calm down a little.

'Sit down, Antonias. It seems your friend Eddie is a witness for the defence, and he is going to swear an oath that he drove you to the hotel that night. Now do you see why he needs to disappear?'

'Thank you, Don Carlos, for telling me this. I appreciate it. I will kill him, truly I will, with my bare hands, if necessary. If not for myself, I'll do it for all the pain he's put my family through.'

Don Carlos smiled at the other man in the room, and then he shook his head and waved his finger at Tony.

'No, Antonias, stop thinking about what you will do to this friend of yours and sort out your alibi. Never do a deed like this without careful planning. Never show your feelings, especially anger. It shows weakness and lets other people know what you are thinking.'

As angry and upset as he was, Tony knew this man was right; he had no alibi, and he would be playing right into the hands of the bossman and the police. It would prove to them all he had been involved and that he was as guilty as them. Nothing he could think of would hold up in court; he was at a loss. Eddie was going to get away with it.

Don Carlos stood up; he could see that he had given Tony a lot to think about. 'I've kept you from your friends and grandmother for far too long. But hear me, Antonias, I will let you do your deed, and I will take care of your alibi. Okay?'

'How? And why would you want to do that for me? I hardly

know you.' Tony looked at him warily. Why would a man like this help him out with an alibi?

Don Carlos gave him a knowing smile. 'We are almost family. Ask Miriam, maybe she will fill you in on the details one day. By the way, Antonias, what's your ambition? What is it that you are striving for in life?'

Don Carlos waited. He knew this wasn't all Antonias wanted; he was an ambitious young man.

Tony swept his hands through his hair. Telling Don Carlos what he would like seemed rather pathetic, but he had asked and so he would answer him truthfully.

'I would like to take over the bossman's club one day, Don Carlos. I have always felt it was wasted on him, and with the location and the right management, it could be a goldmine. That's what I would like to do, but there's no way he would let me manage it, or buy it, if I had the money.'

Tony laughed, to lighten the mood. He felt childish telling Don Carlos what he had always thought to himself, each time he had gone into the club.

'That brings me to another matter. Thankfully, you have saved me the trouble of asking you. Your so-called "bossman" doesn't own the club, Ralph Gold does. It has always been used by the firm to launder money. I tell you this as family, Antonias, and I am presuming it will go no further; am I right?'

Tony sat down again, thinking that explained why the bossman had never bothered with the club. Why would you spend all that money on something then leave it to rot, as he had? Now it made sense.

Don Carlos explained that the bossman was the front man for their money laundering, he was the go-between. That was how Ralph Gold knew him, and knew that he was a fool.

Ralph Gold let everyone presume he didn't own it, so if the

money laundering were ever discovered, he would not be to blame. Ralph Gold never got his hands dirty.

It seemed now that Ralph Gold and Don Carlos needed a new manager, someone they could trust. They wanted to know if Antonias would be interested.

Tony looked at him, as he swept back his blond hair and rubbed his chin. Money laundering? No, that was big business. Was he being used as a pawn in their game, the same way the bossman had been?

'No thank you, Don Carlos,' he said. 'Tell Mr Gold I appreciate the offer, but I don't want to be caught for money laundering, either. If and when I accomplish my goal, it will be by my own doing, and legal, but many thanks.'

Don Carlos narrowed his eyes and looked at Tony; this man is no fool, he thought to himself.

'What if Ralph Gold was prepared to sell it to you, and gave you his guarantee that he would?'

Tony's eyes shot up and he looked at Don Carlos; he liked the sound of that. And, in their own way, these men were honourable men. If Ralph Gold said he would sell the club to him, he knew he would.

'How much is he asking? The club is worth nothing on its own. It's a drug dealers' den full of prostitutes; no one in their right mind would want to go there for a night out. But the land it stands on in the West End is very valuable, even I know that.'

'The price is Ralph's decision, but I guarantee you could afford it.' He nodded reassuringly. 'Here.' Don Carlos took a sealed envelope from the man that was with him and showed it to Tony.

'In this envelope is the price Ralph Gold is asking for the club. We both knew you wouldn't want to be the manager of that hole for too long. He is a very reasonable man and a lifelong friend of mine. It's up to you to prove to him that you can be trusted with the laundering and that he would be a fool to sell it to anyone else. It's yours for the taking if that is what you want. If you keep it run down and worthless, then he will sell it off, but, I feel as this is your ambition you will show him that you are a club owner and a businessman.' Don Carlos laughed and put his arm around Tony's shoulders.

The word club owner rang in Tony's ears. This was his security. Don Carlos was telling him in a roundabout way that Ralph Gold would sell him the club, on the condition that he would make a go of it. Mentally, Tony was already making plans for it. He would show this Ralph Gold just how ambitious and serious he was about the deal.

'Mr Gold and I still need to conclude some business there.' Don Carlos looked into the air while he was thinking. 'Manage it for, let us say, one year, and then, if you're still interested in buying the club, you can have the opportunity. Sign the back of the sealed envelope, Antonias, so that, if and when the time comes it will prove to you that it has never been opened.' He indicated the other man. 'This is Mr Mathews, a trusted lawyer of mine. If you agree, it will go into his safe until you are ready to read it.'

Tony was already thinking it over; this was the opportunity he had been waiting for. It had its risks, but didn't all business? How much did Ralph Gold want for the club? Tony's mind was working overtime.

'In the meantime, Don Carlos, could I do whatever I liked with the club? Could I make it my own?'

'Do what you want with it – your bossman did. We just need a base for a while. If you think you can make money out of it, then do so. That's not our concern, what is yours is yours.'

'How long do I have to think about it?' said Tony. 'And how do I let you know my answer?'

'Ah, Antonias, showing your feelings again.' Don Carlos waved a finger at him. 'I can see that you're interested in the offer. I will be in touch, after you have done your deed. Go to the Italian restaurant you visited at your grandmother's invitation the day before you settle your score with Eddie, okay?'

Tony took a pen from Mr Mathews, the lawyer, and signed his name over the sealed part of the envelope; he was surprised when Don Carlos did exactly the same thing.

In its own crooked way, this deal seemed legitimate. Don Carlos wouldn't put his name in writing if he didn't mean what he said, even Tony knew that.

Their business was at an end; they shook hands, and Don Carlos left. When they were back in his car, Mr Mathews finally spoke.

'Do you think he will do it, Don Carlos? He seemed very hesitant.'

'He will do it; he's an ambitious young man. Yes, he will definitely do it.' Don Carlos laughed out loud.

16

MISTAKEN IDENTITY

Back home, in the living room of Jake and Sharon's new house, Tony told them what Eddie had done, and how he had heard it with his own ears, via Don Carlos's recording. He also told them about the business proposal made by Don Carlos.

'I told you, but you wouldn't believe me. I told you that Eddie was a lowlife all along, but you wouldn't listen, would you?' said Jake. He was smug and feeling triumphant in his judgement.

'I really don't need you telling me "I told you so",' said Tony.

'You're not really thinking about killing Eddie, are you?' said Jake. 'How the hell are you going to do it? It's a ridiculous idea!'

'I don't know, Jake, but once I've done it, I have to go to that Italian restaurant again. I'm seriously beginning to think that restaurant is the Mafia headquarters.'

'You're taking a huge risk. What makes you think this Don guy can give you an alibi? You might be thinking about killing Eddie, but you're putting your life in that Don Carlos's hands.' Jake sighed. 'Oh well, whatever you do, I'm by your side, in for a penny and all that.'

'No, I'm doing this alone and no arguments, because I don't

know what the alibi is. And, as far as I'm aware, it's an alibi for one, not two. Anyway, what do you think about managing the club?'

'Not a lot, it's a rathole. Not exactly a prize payment for killing someone, is it?'

'It could be, Jake, it could be, and Don Carlos has said I can do whatever I like with it.' Tony picked up his coffee cup and raised it to Jake's, to celebrate.

'This is your venture, I'm not gate-crashing it. You manage the club, it's your trophy.'

Tony was hurt and insulted by Jake's words; he stared at him in amazement.

'Hang on, what about always being at my side? You'll help me kill someone but you won't run a club with me – why?'

'I know nothing about clubs, apart from drinking in them. Come to think of it, neither do you.'

Tony smiled and gave Jake a cheeky wink. 'No, Jake, but you do know an awful lot about bookkeeping, and that's a start. Personally, I just think I add the glamour.' Now he was laughing at Jake, but he was right – both Sharon and Jake were good with money. That was a start, and the most important thing if they were going to make money.

First things first, though, he had to work out how and when to get rid of Eddie. Tony had an idea; why not start by taking him for a nice Italian meal, at a local Italian restaurant?

* * *

Tony went to the bookies, as normal, and waited. He knew it wouldn't be long before Eddie turned up; betting was his life.

'Hi, Tony, how was your holiday?' Eddie said, when he came in. He was all smiles and friendly, as usual, without a care in the world.

It made Tony's blood boil, but he remembered what Don Carlos had told him about not showing his feelings, so he kept his emotions under control and played the same deceitful game as Eddie.

Tony told Eddie all about the hotel and the sightseeing he had done. He skipped the part about seeing Miriam.

'Guess what? Have I got big news for you.' Eddie was spilling over with excitement, just desperate to boast about his good fortune. 'I'm going to take over the club, while the bossman is otherwise engaged. It's all mine now, Tony. You can have your old job back, if you like; that's you and Jake that is.'

He was so full of his own importance, it made Tony smile.

So, the bossman was taking Eddie for a fool, as well. It wasn't the bossman's decision to make; after all, he didn't own it, but he was giving that impression out, which is what the owners wanted.

Tony gave Eddie a big heartfelt congratulations. He made sure to sound very impressed and grateful to be offered his old job back.

'Thanks, Eddie, maybe some time later. I'm done with all that for now, and Jake won't get involved, now that he's married. If I change my mind, I'll let you know.'

Eddie sat at the side of the counter, looking very pleased with himself and oozing with authority. Suddenly a thought occurred to Tony. This was his chance to get Eddie to the restaurant. The invitation wouldn't be out of the blue; it would be to celebrate Eddie's good fortune.

'I tell you what, Eddie, as a celebration, and as you're one of my best mates, why don't I buy you a meal? I'll get Jake to come, as well, then we can all three of us have a good catch up.'

Eddie's eyes lit up. He felt Tony knew his place and was trying to ingratiate himself with the new boss of the club; after all he was the 'bossman' now.

'Sure thing, Tony, give me the address and I'll see you there.'

Tony did, and Eddie almost skipped out of the bookies, even though he had just backed another loser.

What was it Don Carlos had said?

Keep your friends close and your enemies closer. Tony had to agree with him; how true that saying was.

When Jake and Tony arrived at the restaurant, Eddie was already there, sitting at the bar waiting for them. He waved to attract their attention and they joined him for a drink.

Tony said hello to the waiter who had served them last time, but he just gave a pleasant smile, as he would to any customer. Things are different in the restaurant this time, thought Tony. What a difference a couple of weeks makes. After the big friendly farewell they'd had from the chef and the waiter last time, they were now all but ignored.

They were soon shown to a table, and ordered from the menu.

During dinner, Eddie was full of himself; neither Jake nor Tony seemed to be able to get a word in. He talked with his mouth full, telling them both about how he was the boss now and how he was going to get rid of all the guys he didn't like and who wouldn't respect him.

As much as it pained him, Tony smiled and even encouraged Eddie to tell him his plans. Tony could see Jake was bored, but gave him the nod to join in and congratulate him. Jake was as pleasant as he could be, knowing this so-called friend was now showing his true colours.

Behind the laughter and the drinks, Tony watched Eddie. He was seeing him through different eyes. He could have killed him on the spot, he hated him so much.

After dinner, a waitress came over and put the bill in the middle of the table.

'You don't look well, sir, was your meal okay?' said the waitress to Tony.

Tony assured her he was fine and both Eddie and Jake looked at her strangely. That was an odd thing to say to someone who had just eaten in their restaurant.

'My father always says, whenever he is not well, he does what he has to do first thing in the morning and then he goes home and stays there all day and rests. He doesn't step outside the front door for twenty-four hours and then he always feels better.' She was smiling, as though she had given good advice.

Tony nodded and paid the bill. He looked at Jake and then at Eddie. This place was getting stranger by the minute. Who cared what her father did?

'Silly cow,' said Eddie, as she left the table with the money on a plate. 'Nice arse, though. Are all Italian women like her, Tony?'

Eddie had had too much to drink and was being offensive. He was so full of his own importance, he thought he could pass judgement on anyone or say anything he liked and it was okay. He was full of arrogance.

Tony and Jake dropped Eddie off in the taxi first. They said their farewell and agreed to meet up again, soon.

'So,' said Jake, 'what the hell was all that about? Since when were waitresses doctors?'

'I don't know, but I feel as though we should take her father's advice. I have to do what I have to do early in the morning and then stay indoors for the rest of the day. It might be a load of rubbish, but I felt she was saying it for my benefit, don't you?'

Jake nodded at him. 'Either that or you looked as sick of Eddie as I was.'

When Tony got back to his apartment, he was still thinking over what the waitress had said. There was a knock at his door and he opened it to see it was one of the neighbours, an elderly gentleman. He never mixed with his neighbours, he just kept himself to himself.

'I'm sorry to disturb you so late in the day, but I have something for you and I have to go out early tomorrow. I thought better now than then.' He handed a parcel to Tony. 'The postman asked me to take it in for you.'

'That's very kind of you, thank you.'

'I'm going away for a few days to stay with my daughter,' he said. 'That's why I had to come now.' He smiled. 'I've taken lots of parcels in for people, over the years. I've lived here for a long time, you know. Heavens, I've seen some changes!'

Tony smiled and thanked him again; he was trying to get rid of the old man as politely as possible so he could see what was in the parcel, but the man was in the mood to chat. Finally, the neighbour went, by which time Tony had felt like strangling him just to shut him up.

He opened the parcel; inside, he found a few pieces of metal, and then it dawned on him what he was looking at. He took out the metal parts and started putting them together. It was a gun with a silencer.

There was no message, and the postmark was the United States of America. This was the weapon he was to kill Eddie with.

Tony could hardly sleep that night. He sat up for most of it, trying to think through his plan of action carefully. At last, it was morning.

Tony dressed very plainly, in an old T-shirt and jeans. He wore a baseball cap to cover his unmistakable blond hair. He put the gun inside his coat pocket and caught the bus to the club.

He knew Eddie would be there, even at that time of the morning. He had already boasted to Tony and Jake that he was staying there, now that he was in charge.

Tony let himself in through the back door. Typical, he thought to himself, nobody even thought to lock it. All kinds of people doing their deals were free to come and go as they liked.

Tony looked around the place with a satisfied grin. When the place was his he would have CCTV, so that no one would be able to creep up on him without being noticed.

Tony checked to see if there was anyone around. The place seemed empty, but he could hear a voice.

He thought about hiding, but then thought better of it. Why would anyone think it so strange that Tony had come to see Eddie? Maybe he did want his old job back.

He walked towards what used to be the bossman's office; that was when he realised Eddie was on the telephone. That was the voice he could hear.

Tony stood in the doorway. When Eddie saw him, he waved him in; he still had that friendly smile on his face.

He was wearing the same shirt and trousers that he had worn the night before, when they had gone for the meal. It was obvious he had stayed up all night, drinking with his friends.

Eddie was sitting back in the chair, with his crossed legs on the desk, while talking on the telephone. Tony watched this new display of Eddie in charge. Eddie was a different man; God only knew what the other men who had worked for the bossman thought of him and his new-found power. Tony could only imagine. He was a joke, an upstart, and he didn't have a clue how to run a business.

Tony waited patiently while Eddie ignored him and continued talking on the telephone. He couldn't believe his ears; it was early in the morning and yet, from what he could gather from the telephone call, Eddie was already gambling on the horses.

'Well, Tony,' Eddie said, when he put the phone down, 'I knew you'd change your mind about coming back to work for me. When do you want to start?' Eddie seemed very smug and pleased with himself that Tony had gone cap in hand to ask for his old job back. The great Tony Lambrianu, begging for a job!

Tony didn't delay matters with small talk; he had a job to do and he had to do it fast. He didn't know if anyone would be coming in soon, or if Eddie had been entertaining one of the prostitutes upstairs. Any minute now someone could walk in and his moment would be lost.

Tony shut the door, then turned to face Eddie again. He took the gun with the silencer on it out of his jacket pocket, and pointed it at Eddie.

Eddie paled. He took his legs off the desk and would have stood up, if he had thought they would support him. He felt weak as a newborn foal.

'Tony, mate, what the hell are you doing? We're friends, for God's sake. What's all this about?'

'I know what you did, Eddie. You rang the police and gave them my name. You betrayed me for that fat old man.'

Eddie would have shouted out, but there was no one to shout to. He opened his mouth to try and worm his way out of it, to blame the bossman or anyone else he could think of, but he didn't get the chance.

'Bye, Eddie.' Tony pressed the trigger on the gun and fired a bullet straight into Eddie's head.

Tony looked at Eddie, slumped in the chair, with just one hole in his head. Good, thought Tony. He would never betray anyone ever again, especially not him.

Tony quickly rang Jake to put his mind at rest. 'All done,' he said, and put the telephone down.

Now it was time to leave as quickly and as quietly as possible. Now was definitely not the time to be seen.

Tony was thinking about what the waitress had said, and so he caught the train and went straight to Elle's seaside bungalow. That way, he could definitely keep a low profile; even if someone checked his flat, he wouldn't be there.

Elle knew something was wrong. Since when did Tony offer to help her tidy up and finish the rest of the unpacking? Well, she thought to herself, he'll work out whatever he has on his mind, he always does.

* * *

At lunchtime the next day, Tony decided it was time to go home. It had been nice spending time with Elle again, having dinner and sharing small talk.

No sooner had he turned up at his apartment than the police were at his door. Tony's heart sank. It was two uniformed officers, and they asked if they could come in. That was strange; he had expected them to put the handcuffs on and take him away.

'We'd like to ask you some questions about Eddie Rawlings,' they said. They both sat down and one took out his notepad.

'What about him?' asked Tony. He was putting on a brave face, keeping his nerve, but inside he was shaking like a leaf.

'He's been shot dead. He was found yesterday, in his office – or, rather, in Charlie Jenkins' office.'

'Charlie Jenkins? Who is he?' asked Tony. 'And what's all this about Eddie?'

He hoped he looked genuine enough; possibly the fact that he didn't know who Charlie Jenkins was would make it look more believable.

'Charlie Jenkins,' said the officer, 'is the real name of the so called "bossman"; didn't you know that?'

Tony shook his head. He had never thought to ask the bossman his name, and no one he knew had used it when talking to him.

'Look,' said Tony, deciding that now was the time to say his piece, 'if you think I've hurt Eddie in any way, you're definitely wrong. It was only the other night we went out for a meal together, him, me and Jake. You can check, if you like.' Tony felt the best form of defence was attack.

'No one is accusing you, Mr Lambrianu, we know exactly where you were, and we know you went out for a meal with Eddie. What we want to know is, can you shed any light on any enemies he may have had?'

What did they mean, they knew where he was? He had covered his tracks well by going to Elle's, he hadn't set foot outside of her house all day. What did they mean?

'Eddie Rawlings was killed between eight in the morning and twelve, noon. We know that because he spoke to his regular gambling bookies and backed some horses around eight and he was found around noon; what happened in between, we don't know.'

They were being genuine. They weren't there to arrest him, they just wanted to know if Eddie had mentioned anything to him and Jake about being threatened, or if he was scared of anyone. He knew the police would already know how he had met Eddie and how long they had been friends, maybe it was time to play on their heartstrings.

Tony put on a sad face and acted distressed on hearing the news about Eddie. 'God, that's awful,' he said. 'Eddie was one of my oldest friends.' He was wringing his hands and showing concern, and reminiscing to the police about how he and Eddie had been in a children's home together.

'What do you mean, by the way, you know where I was?' he asked. That part confused him. Had they been watching him at Elle's?

'Fortunately for you, Mr Lambrianu, the manager of the prestigious store you were drunk and disorderly in doesn't want to take things any further, considering you paid the bill for all of the breakages you caused. The manager, customers, and of course, the security camera footage, can all confirm where you were. It must have been quite a night.'

The police stood up to leave and thanked him for his time. They said if he could think of anything, or anyone, that Eddie had mentioned, to let them know.

Tony shut the door behind them and breathed a sigh of relief. He thought he should warn Jake, because they were bound to go and see him, as well. He picked up the phone.

'Jake, something really weird is going on,' he said, when Jake answered. He went on to tell him what the police had said and then put the telephone down.

Tony needed to go to the shop the police had mentioned. He was drunk and disorderly? What the hell did they mean?

* * *

Tony walked through the door of the famous department store and was instantly met by security guards. They asked him to leave.

'I've come to apologise to the manager,' said Tony. He didn't know what he was talking about, but he was prepared to try and bluff his way in.

The security guards nodded to each other, and told him to follow them. They took him to the manager's office. When the manager saw Tony he didn't look very happy to see him at all.

Thinking about what the police had said about being drunk,

Tony thought he would appeal to the manager's better nature. 'I was very drunk, sir,' he said, showing the man full respect and humility. 'I can't remember very much, but I apologise sincerely, and if I owe you anything, obviously I'll pay for any disruption.' Tony smiled his most charming smile. Dear God, Tony thought to himself, this is like standing in front of the head teacher at school.

'As you seem to be at a loss for your behaviour, Mr Lambrianu, then I will show you. I respect that you have come here today to apologise, but you must realise, however much money you intend to spend here, we cannot accept that kind of behaviour. I have my other customers to think about.' The manager looked very stern and unforgiving.

He held out his hand towards a chair, then telephoned security to bring him the recording of Tony in his store.

Tony was intrigued; the manager even knew his name. What the hell was he supposed to have done?

Tony sat, stunned, as he watched the recording. He knew it wasn't him on the screen, but even he was beginning to doubt it.

The recording showed a blond man, Tony's height, wearing sunglasses. He was bumping into everyone in the store, drunkenly apologising. He had leaned on the glass-topped perfume counter and knocked over their expensive display. Then, he had wandered off to the area where the wines were and had helped himself.

People were disgusted as they watched this drunken man making a fool of himself in the shop. When he had been challenged by security, he had shouted at them that the wine was his, because his name was on the label. He was Tony Lambrianu.

That had been when security telephoned up to the manager and asked him to come down.

The manager had asked him discreetly to leave the store, and Tony had thrown an American Express card at him, and told him to help himself. Then he had been escorted out.

The manager switched off the television monitor showing the recording, then opened a small drawer in his desk. 'I believe this is yours, Mr Lambrianu, and here is your receipt for the damages.' The manager passed the American Express card to Tony, and with it, the receipt.

Tony stood up; again, he apologised to the manager profusely, and hung his head in embarrassment.

The manager seemed to accept his apology and thanked him for coming in personally to apologise. He even shook his hand to show there were no hard feelings.

Tony walked out of the shop. He was elated; there was no doubt the man looked very much like him and, as a bonus, he had a credit card with his name on it.

Thankfully, the recording was in black and white. Tony nodded his head and smiled to himself. Don Carlos had done him proud. He had said he would sort out the alibi and he had. It was cast iron!

No wonder he had been told to stay indoors all day; after all, he couldn't be in two places at once, could he?

Tony couldn't wait to get home to tell Jake all about it, although he was glad he had gone alone to kill Eddie. Jake had his own alibi; he'd been at work. He had been seen by everyone there, so he, too, was in the clear.

While he was at Jake's house telling him the news, the police came. Two of them were the detectives in charge of the case and one was a uniformed officer. They introduced themselves and showed their warrant cards. They didn't seem too surprised that Tony was there, but this time they wanted to talk to Jake.

'We need to know your whereabouts, Mr Sinclair. I'm sure Mr Lambrianu has told you all about the murder we're investigating,' one of the detectives said.

'There's no need to point the finger at me, officer. Tony tells me that Eddie was killed in the morning. I was at work all day, you can check.'

'We know where you were, Mr Sinclair, we checked before we came here. We just want you to confirm everything, as a matter of procedure.'

Jake went step-by-step through what he had done that day and they seemed satisfied.

There was no forensic evidence, and for the moment the police were thinking that maybe Eddie had got a little bit greedy with one of the drug dealers that hung around the place.

They wanted to know if Jake and Tony knew any of their names, or where they could find them, as it seemed they had all disappeared.

'Nobody uses their own names,' said Tony. 'Everyone seems to have some kind of nickname or something. After all these years, I didn't know the bossman was called Charlie Jenkins, so why would we know a drug dealer's real name?'

The police knew this made sense, but they were grasping at straws. There was nothing to go on to lead them to Eddie's murderer.

The police told Tony and Jake that the bossman was Eddie's biological father, and Eddie had found him after all those years in care. Tony and Jake were astounded. Eddie had never mentioned that.

The police could see their surprise was genuine by the way they looked at each other and stared at them. Even though he had just heard what they said, Tony was finding it hard to comprehend.

'Are you telling us that the bossman was Eddie's father, really?' Tony asked, amazed.

The uniformed police officer nodded. 'Eddie was illegitimate, of course. His mother couldn't keep him, as he was born out of wedlock and her family disapproved.' He closed his notebook. 'Will you want to know about the funeral?'

'Well, yes, of course, he was our good friend. We'd like to pay our respects.' Like hell, we would, thought Tony, but he knew he had to see this through to the end.

'Oh, by the way,' said the policeman, 'Eddie left a letter in the safe. We'd like to call it a will, but it's not official. It seems Eddie stated in writing that you, Mr Lambrianu, were to take over the running of the club, if anything should ever happen to him.' They waited for Tony's reaction. They had thought that if he knew this, then that would have been a reason to kill him. They were fishing.

Tony burst out laughing. 'I didn't even know Eddie could write. When did he say this?' Again, Tony's surprise proved his innocence to them. It was obvious to them that he didn't know anything about it.

'Well, he could, and it was written on the same night that you both went for a meal with him. That is why the detectives working on the case think he may have told you that night if something was bothering him.' Again, the police waited, but they could see they were wasting their time. They stood up to leave and said they would inform them both of any funeral arrangements.

Tony put his fingers to his lips to indicate to Jake to say nothing until they had gone.

Jake and Tony both looked out of the window and watched the police drive away. Jake was the first to speak.

'Who put that letter in the safe, Tony? Because you can bet your life on it that Eddie didn't put it there.'

Tony shook his head; he was standing up and his arms were folded, then he swept his hands through his hair. 'Whoever did it, Jake, did it when we were at the restaurant and they knew for sure that Eddie wasn't there. Hell, this is better than a military operation; scary when you think about it.'

They sat down and were silent for a moment, both at a loss for words.

'Well, at least that's solved one problem. With everyone thinking the bossman was Eddie's father and that he owned the club, that now makes you the official manager of that rathole, as bequeathed by Eddie. That's a bloody joke in itself. Did anyone tell Ralph Gold that?' said Jake and they both burst out laughing.

17

OUT WITH THE OLD

Tony had been getting bored. Following the murder of Eddie Rawlings, he and Jake had kept their heads down and carried on with life as normal, so as not to bring any attention to themselves. If they were being watched by the police, there was absolutely nothing for them to see.

'So,' said Jake, 'how long do we wait before taking over the club? How long is it going to be before the police have finished with it?'

'As long as it takes. Who cares? In the meantime, you and I have business to attend to.'

By the smug grin on Tony's face, Jake knew he had a plan, and what was more, it was going to be dangerous. Jake sighed. He reckoned it must be bad, as only two things got Tony excited: money and women.

'Okay, fill me in. I know you've been thinking about something, so let's hear it.' He sat back in the armchair, crossed his legs and waited for Tony to speak.

'Don't you see, Jake? All those people the bossman and Eddie collected protection money from aren't paying a penny to anyone.'

Jake had never even considered that. He reckoned those days

were behind them and he had presumed Tony just wanted to take over the club. He realised he'd also been wrong about the things that got Tony excited – there were actually three things. Fighting; that appealed to Tony's nature, too.

'Someone will have already stepped in and taken it over,' Jake said.

'Well, if they have already been visited by some mob, it's up to us to make them change their minds. It's a free-for-all; we have to claim our turf.'

'What can we do, just you and me? The others will have gangs, with knives and guns. What the hell are we supposed to do?'

Tony was smiling and rubbing his hands together. He looked like a kid on Christmas Eve. 'Well, I, for one, don't intend to pay anyone to protect our club. We're going to need every penny if we're going to put that place in order, so we'll get some knives and guns as well.' He laughed; he couldn't wait to get started.

Jake watched as Tony got a pen and some paper and started writing down the names of all the pubs, clubs and snooker halls they had visited on the bossman's behalf.

'Look here,' he said to Jake, 'is there anywhere I've missed?'

'Tony, you're crazy, mate, we can't do this on our own. We'll get ourselves killed.'

'Watch me.' He looked up at Jake and held his gaze. 'Are we brothers, or what? We can do this, Jake, and then the world really will be our oyster.'

Jake knew he had to discuss this with Sharon. After all, she was his wife, and she put up with a lot, from both himself and Tony. She deserved to know Tony's plans.

When Sharon arrived home, her suspicions were already alerted by the fact that Jake had laid the table for two and her favourite Indian takeaway was keeping warm in the oven.

'What's all this, then? It's not my birthday and I know you

haven't been with another woman, so it has to have something to do with Tony. Am I right?'

She leaned over to kiss Jake; she could read him like a book. She loved him and that was all that mattered.

Jake started putting the food on the table. 'Am I so like a pane of glass to you, Shaz? You've seen straight through me. Here, have a glass of wine. We need to talk.'

Jake felt guilty. They hadn't spent a lot of time together recently, and he made a silent promise to himself that he would make more of an effort in the future.

While they ate, he told Sharon all about the club and how Tony was to take it over and clean it up. He looked at her smiling, trusting face over the candle he had placed in the middle of the table. The candlelight seemed to make her face glow, and her eyes shone brightly.

'Tony thinks we could take over the protection racket that the bossman and Eddie used to have in the East End. I know it sounds crazy, but I see his point, and Tony doesn't intend to pay anyone to protect the club.'

'Well, I knew you were both cooking up something. I presume, by all of this, Tony has walked clear of the police again?'

Sharon didn't know all of the details of what had happened. She knew something was going on, and eventually Jake would tell her, but this sounded dangerous. The kind of men that wanted protection money weren't easily going to hand everything over to Tony and Jake. There would be a fight, and not just involving fists.

She also knew Jake wouldn't want her to worry, so for now, at least, it was time to put on a brave face.

'You have to stand with Tony, he's expecting it. He must have some plan cooked up in that brain of his. We both know he likes taking risks, but he wouldn't let you take the brunt of his foolishness.'

'Have I told you, Sharon, just how much I love you,' whispered Jake. He felt a lump in his throat. In her own way she was giving him her blessing, for whatever the future held.

'Not nearly as often as you should, Jake, my love, but don't apologise for standing by Tony. Love means never having to say you're sorry, or so they say. Come on.'

Sharon blew the candle out, then held out her hand to Jake. No words were spoken. This was their moment.

They went upstairs together, and Sharon made love to Jake as though it was the very last time; after all, it might be, she thought to herself.

* * *

The next morning, Jake lay in bed, staring up at the ceiling, thinking about Tony's crazy scheme. Tony had never let him down before, but Jake felt he was being a little blind and overconfident with regard to the protection racket. In the grand scheme of things, they were outnumbered.

He glanced across at Sharon, who was sleeping soundly, her long blonde hair draped over the pillow. Jake reached out and stroked it; he hadn't meant to wake her, but she opened her eyes.

Jake had always felt that he had been very lucky to have Sharon as his wife. He had always felt he was punching above his weight. She was a beautiful, sexy woman, who had chosen him, for whatever reason.

'Sorry, I didn't mean to wake you, love, go back to sleep.' Jake withdrew his hand.

'Don't stop, it's nice.' She smiled up at him. 'Come here, and show me you love me some more.'

Sharon reached out and pulled him towards her; she kissed him gently and put her arms around him.

* * *

Tony had hardly slept. He had been awake for most of the night, working out how he was going to make his plan work. He knew it wouldn't be easy, but it could be worthwhile in the end. First things first; he had to find out who, if anyone, had taken over the collections from the pubs.

Tony met up with Jake later that day, having purposely waited until Sharon had gone to work before he put in an appearance. He knew he had taken up a lot of Jake's time recently, and felt guilty about that. Sharon was his wife, and of course she should always come first, but just now, Tony needed him. If everything worked out as he hoped, they could all earn a lot of money.

They went to pub after pub, and then eventually to the Crown – one of the most popular, and the most profitable.

Again, as had happened in the previous pubs, the landlord recognised them from when they'd been collecting for the bossman.

Mick, the landlord of the Crown, was a friendly, bubbly man. He was taking glasses out of the washer and wiping them with a tea towel, before placing them on the shelves.

Mick liked Jake, but his blood ran cold when he saw Tony. He knew they were always together, like some crime-fighting duo, but Jake seemed to see reason, whereas all Tony saw was red.

'I know why you're here, lads,' he said, 'but someone has already beaten you to it.'

Tony leaned on the bar, his arms folded. He looked at Jake, and then back at Mick.

'What do you know we're here for, Mick? Just making a friendly visit, that's all.'

'I'm guessing you want something, though.'

'Well, you're right about there being something I want. I want to know who has taken over the protection in this area. Mick, who are you paying?'

'I'm not going to lie to you, lads, everyone probably knows anyway. It's the South London mob. They don't usually come to this side of the river, but I guess they knew we had no one else here, and they would have started a lot of trouble if any of us had refused.' Mick continued polishing glasses, more for something to do, than anything else.

Tony looked at the usually bubbly landlord; he had always been in good spirits. He'd been happily married for many years, and had a family he adored, but Tony sensed that things had changed – or rather, Mick had changed. He didn't seem as carefree as normal. No, Tony thought to himself, Mick isn't paying protection to keep the troublemakers out – the troublemakers are firmly in and have him bent over a barrel.

The only protection he had been offered was from threats to his livelihood and his family, threats made by the very people that were swindling him, to keep them safe, not his business. No wonder Mick had lost his sparkle.

Tony held out his hand to shake Mick's. 'If you don't ask, Mick, you don't get, am I right?' Tony smiled at Mick. He felt he had enough to cope with; the poor man was drowning and he had no way out.

Mick looked at Jake and then at Tony; he was a little wary of refusing Tony and holding out his hand to shake it. He wasn't sure if this was one of Tony's tricks. He would probably break his arm or his hand, given the chance, but still, it was better to be on the right side of the devil. After all, Mick didn't know if Tony was working with the South London mob.

Mick shook Tony's hand and watched him as he gave his most charming smile, his face full of concern. That wasn't the Tony he knew. Everyone knew Tony was a loose cannon, a man who some would describe as being a bit of a psychopath. There was something dark behind that smooth exterior and charming smile.

Tony gave Jake the nod to leave and waved goodbye to Mick, then they went back to the car and got in.

'What the hell was all that about, Tony? Is that all we've trailed around London for, to shake hands and have a chat?' Jake was surprised at Tony's reaction; he had never known him to walk away from anything and now he was shaking hands and smiling about the South London mob stepping in.

'Respect breeds respect, Jake, and that's exactly what we want, if we're going to do this right. We're businessmen who offer a service for a price. You have to look at the long term. The South London mob are going to end up cutting their noses off to spite their faces.'

As he drove along the London streets towards the West End, Tony passed the bossman's old club. Soon, he thought to himself, soon you are going to be mine. He stopped in Chinatown, the heart of the West End. He left Jake in the car and went into one of the side shops near one of the many restaurants there.

Jake waited patiently in the car. He had no idea what Tony was scheming, but whatever it was, he knew it was going to be a rough ride.

When Tony came back he threw a large plastic carrier bag in the boot of the car, then opened the driver's door and got in.

'What's in the bag?' asked Jake.

'Our trump card, Jake. Believe me, one more journey and all will be revealed.' Tony was laughing to himself.

'Bloody hell, Tony, you sound like some madman off the television. Where are we going?' Jake was shouting, now.

'Okay, okay, Jake. I didn't tell you earlier, because I knew you would hate the idea. I'm going to arrange a meeting with the South London mob boss. I thought it might be him that had muscled in on this, and I was right. And look at Mick and the others. Not one of them is happy that this mob boss, whoever he is, has taken over their protection.'

Tony's temper was rising, his face was flushed and he, too, was tired; it had been a long, stressful day, but he had needed to do the groundwork first. He needed to know if all of the landlords were content with the takeover, and it was more than obvious they weren't. That was half of his plan sorted.

He wanted to see this mob boss, in all his glory, and to inform him that he intended to take the East End protection over, and more. They could either speak like two businessmen who each owned their own turf, or they could fight like two dogs over a bone.

Tony knew he had to go through with this; if he didn't, not only would he look weak, but he, too, would end up having to pay these people when he had the club. As much as he wanted to clean it up, that would mean it was open to any drug dealer and pimp that the mob boss commanded Tony let in the place. No way was that happening!

They drove over to the south of London. Jake looked around as they passed Elephant and Castle tube station.

'Who are you going to see? Do you know someone who can arrange a meeting with this mob boss?' said Jake.

'I might know someone,' said Tony.

'Might? For God's sake, Tony, you're not in charge yet, we're nobodies and he's someone, with a bloody lot of backup. How are we going to get a meeting with him? We're dead meat!'

Jake now realised that Tony was going to face this boss head on. There was no way they could just walk into his place of residence, which was above a local pub, and demand to see him.

Jake couldn't get through to Tony, no matter how hard he tried. He had never met this mob boss, but he had heard of him and they'd had dealings with his henchmen before. He decided to go along with it; after all, it was in for a penny, in for a pound, wasn't it?

As Jake and Tony walked into a pub, the first thing Jake noticed was a mouse running along the stone floor. The place was dimly lit, and the walls were brown from the nicotine. Customers and anyone else were still allowed to smoke in this pub – to smoke something, at least.

'Over there, just as I thought,' said Tony. He strode over to the far side of the bar. He had hold of Jake's jacket sleeve and pulled him along with him.

'Bennie, how great to see you, after all this time.' Tony shouted a friendly greeting along the bar as he walked over to a middle-aged black man wearing a trilby hat. The sides of his shortly cut afro hair were grey, now, but Tony still recognised him.

Bennie looked up. He stared at Tony and realised he was at a disadvantage. This man obviously knew him, but he was at a loss.

He waved back. 'Hi,' he said. The clean-cut blond man in the suit didn't look like the police, but he definitely didn't look like one of the regulars, either.

'It's me, Antony, Annette's son. Don't you remember me?' Tony smiled innocently at the man. He had known Bennie for many years, especially in his childhood. He had been his mother's dealer.

Bennie's face broke into a broad smile, showing a top row of gold teeth. He held out his arms to Tony.

'Antony, my man, how are you doing?' He held Tony by the shoulders and pushed him back to take a better look at him. 'You're looking good and fancy.'

'You're looking good, yourself, Bennie. I thought you might still drink in here. Can I buy you a drink?'

Tony looked at Jake to order some drinks, and to make sure Bennie got a very large rum, which he figured would help case the way.

With one large gulp, Bennie swallowed the rum, and Tony gestured to Jake to order him another.

'Why you here, Antony? Tell me everything you been doing.' His strong Jamaican accent, especially now he was starting to slur slightly, made it hard for Jake to understand, but Tony seemed to understand him perfectly.

'I sorry to hear about your mother, Antony, my boy. I did pass on all of your messages, I swear.' Bennie made the sign of the cross on his chest.

Tony winced inside; he knew Bennie would have passed on some kind of message to his mother, but she had obviously ignored it. It still hurt when he thought about it, which is why he had put it into a little box at the back of his brain and left it there.

'Everything's great, Bennie. This is Jake.' Jake shook hands with Bennie, and also got a hug from the drunken Jamaican. There was yet another large rum on the bar in front of him.

'I hear you're friends with the South London mob boss, Bennie. I don't suppose you could arrange some kind of meeting for me, could you?' This was make or break time. Tony was aware that Bennie knew this boss well; he had been his pusher for many years, and made the man a lot of money.

'Shush, Antony.' Bennie put his finger to his lips and looked around the bar, to see who was listening. 'You got business in the south? Why you want to meet with him?'

Bennie had always boasted how well he knew this guy, and that they were friends. Tony just hoped there was some truth in it, because that was how he was going to get to meet him.

'Bit of business,' Tony said.

Bennie nodded. 'Give me five minutes.' He walked away.

Tony swept his hands through his hair, then picked up his orange juice and turned to face Jake.

'Who the bloody hell is Jaws with the golden smile?' Jake said. 'And you owe me forty pounds for bloody rum, by the way!'

'Well, firstly, Bennie is our passport in, and secondly, you'll get your money back.' Tony glanced over to where Bennie was standing. Bennie was beckoning to him, trying to attract his attention without being noticed. 'Shut up,' he said, 'here we go.'

Tony took a hold of Jake's elbow and the two of them followed Bennie towards a small wooden door marked 'staff only'.

'You got five minutes, Antony, boy,' Bennie said. 'He's a very busy man, but as you're a friend of mine he's willing to see you.'

They passed through the door then walked up a long musty staircase, with a worn carpet and chipped banister. Tony looked at his surroundings carefully; if the stunt he was pulling went wrong, this was the only exit.

The staircase took them into the living quarters of the pub. There were many rooms, but Bennie steered them towards a doorway where a multi-coloured beaded curtain hung.

Bennie put his hand in the curtain and parted it, then nodded to Tony and Jake to enter first.

An obese black man sat at a desk, counting out money and putting it into piles of different denominations.

The man had a shaved head and multiple gold chains around his neck and wrists, and there wasn't a finger without a gold sovereign on it. He didn't look up when they entered, he ignored them and carried on counting his money.

Behind him stood two bodyguards. Tony recognised them as members of the South London mob. Their boss had obviously called them away from whatever they'd been doing to be in on this meeting that Bennie had so hastily arranged. They looked down their noses at Tony and Jake.

Tony ignored them. He walked up to the man at the desk and held out his hand.

'Thank you for giving me a few moments of your time, it's much appreciated,' he said.

From where he was standing, all he could see was the top of the man's head. The man still ignored them. Tony withdrew his hand.

'I just came to let you know,' said Tony, in a calm voice, 'that I'll be taking over the protection racket in the East End, leading all the way to the West End. I inherited the territory from the bossman and Eddie. As always, the south of London is yours, for as far as you want to go. I won't tread on your toes. Thanks for your time; goodbye.'

Bennie's jaw dropped. He hadn't expected to witness this. He looked at Jake, then at Tony, and felt himself sober up a little. He knew he was going to take the full blame for this; after all, he had introduced Tony to the boss.

Tony turned his back on the man and indicated to Jake they were leaving. He made his way to the door slowly, knowing full well he would be called back.

'Wait!' said the man at the desk. His voice was loud and commanding. 'Turn around, boy, I want to see your face.' He had stopped counting his money now. He was eyeing Tony, scrutinising him carefully. He continued looking at Tony, as Tony gave him a charming smile and an enquiring look, as if to ask why he had been stopped from leaving.

The two bodyguards stepped forwards from behind the boss's chair and started to walk towards Tony. The man at the desk raised his hand to stop them and turned towards Bennie.

'What the hell are you doing, Bennie, bringing this clown up here to waste my time? You said it was business.'

Bennie was physically shaking. He knew he was in trouble; he was trying to coax his alcohol-soaked brain to think and come up with an answer to the boss's questions.

'I swear, boss, he said it was business. I thought he might need a little something from you.' Bennie turned and looked at Tony. 'What the hell you doing, Antony boy, coming in here and tricking me like this, and paying no respect to the boss, here?' Bennie looked pleadingly at Tony.

Tony glanced his way, and then at the boss at the desk; he was now staring straight into his face. 'I just came to tell you my plans.' He looked very casual and nonchalant about it all.

'Get out, boy, while you can still walk,' said the boss. 'Take your little friend and get out.'

Although he was doing his best to appear calm, it was obvious to Tony this man was angry. He thought back to Don Carlos's words: 'Never show your feelings.' This South London mob boss was furious; you could see the whites of his eyes, they were open so wide, and his nostrils were flared.

Tony again looked at Jake. They walked back out through the beaded curtain and towards the staircase. When he was halfway down it, Tony shouted, 'I'll be at the Crown, tonight, if you want to discuss terms.' Then he pushed Jake through the doorway, walked quickly through the pub, stepped outside and filled his lungs with air. That had been a tense meeting, and it had taken all his courage to see it through; after all, he had been trapped in an upstairs room, surrounded by danger.

He grinned at Jake. Despite all that, he'd got away with it, again.

Jake sat in the passenger seat of the car and put his head in his hands. He was sweating slightly. He couldn't believe the situation Tony had just put him in. He knew they had been lucky to escape.

It was Jake's turn to be angry. 'Are you deliberately trying to get us killed? You have just seriously pissed that guy off. You do realise, no one knew we were in there apart from a drunken drug dealer, a mob boss and two armed guys ready to cave our heads in.' He gulped. 'We could have vanished without a trace. Sharon would never have known...'

'Calm down, Jake, for God's sake,' said Tony. He was driving away from the pub, heading for more familiar territory. 'While you were cuddling up to your wife last night, I was thinking. Apart from the odd hiccup, I know what I'm doing, believe me.'

Tony didn't want Jake to see that he, too, was a little unnerved by it all. He had done it now, though, and he felt he had given this guy ample warning of his intentions. He had wanted to meet him and get the full measure of him, and now he had. The man, like the bossman had been, was cocky and sloppy. He wasn't prepared to listen to Tony's plans or even to hear him out as to why he thought he could take over the protection in the East End. Instead, he had just thrown him out, like a piece of rubbish.

The next time I have a meeting with that man, Tony thought to himself, closing his ears to Jake, who was still ranting on in the background, he will be more gracious.

Tony did feel a bit guilty about leaving Bennie to face the music alone. Maybe he would go and see him later; no doubt he would still be on the same street corner, peddling his drugs.

* * *

The disgruntled boss started counting his money again, occasionally casting a glance up at the empty doorway through which Tony had left. Talking to no one in particular, and raising an eyebrow, he said, 'Who is that blond boy, anyway? What's his name, again?'

One of his bodyguards walked up to his desk and then shouted out to one of the other rooms, where another group of men were cutting and bagging up the cocaine they were going to sell. A man parted the beaded curtain and came in.

'Undo your shirt,' said the bodyguard who had just called him through, 'undo your shirt, and show the boss that scar of yours.'

The man looked at him. 'Why?'

'An old friend of yours has been visiting.'

The man started unbuttoning his shirt.

'What you doing, man,' shouted the boss. He waved him away with his hand. 'Put your shirt on before someone comes in.'

'Wait, boss,' said the bodyguard, 'he's going to let you know that blond boy's name. That what you want, isn't it?'

The boss rolled his eyes. It seemed no one was listening to him. All he'd asked was who that blond boy was and now he had a coked-up sidekick, who was obviously helping himself to the goods he was meant to be cutting, stripping off in his office. He waited while the man before him took off his shirt, then turned around. The boss looked in horror at the man's scarred back.

'That is that blond boy's name, boss,' said the bodyguard. 'He did that to my brother. He's bloody lucky you were here because I would have shot him dead, otherwise.' He took his gun out from the back of his trouser waistband and kissed it. 'So, he's going to be at the Crown, tonight, is he? Well, he's going to get more than he bargained for, the cocky little bastard.'

The boss looked on in amazement at the name that had been carved into his sidekick's back.

'Are you telling me that you let that cocky upstart do that to you?' the boss said. He was breathing heavily; he remembered the time when the man had nearly bled to death, because of the deep wounds that had been inflicted on him. He looked at the scar bearing the name 'Lambrianu'; it was a horrible sight. He could barely believe that the man who had just stood before him, full of bravado, was capable of this.

'I didn't have no choice, boss, he's crazy. He carved me up well and truly, the little shit! Going to get my own back now. He's going to pay.'

Again, the boss looked at the deep cuts on his soldier's back. This was a sign of somebody who didn't care who knew what he did; he'd signed his name on the man's back and to hell with the consequences. Maybe, just maybe, thought the boss to himself, this is a man to watch out for.

* * *

Tony stopped the car at a burger bar. 'Come on, Jake,' he said, 'let's get a coffee and something to eat.'

Jake got out and slammed the car door as hard as possible, just to get across to Tony how annoyed he was.

When they'd picked up their order and were seated at a table, Jake said, 'Tell me these plans of yours, Tony. I need to know what's going on in that head of yours.'

'Okay, eat your burger, drink your coffee and listen. We are going to cause chaos tonight.' Tony started to laugh. 'Absolute chaos, Jake, and we're not even going to be there. When it's over, watch them all come crawling to us.' Tony filled him in on the rest of his plans. He hadn't wanted to tell Jake everything, because even he wasn't sure if any of his plans would work out, starting with finding Bennie. Now they'd got that far, he felt he could tell him everything.

'You've got to be joking! Are you seriously telling me that you're going to set the East End on fire? This plan is crazier than I thought. No way, Tony, this is going too far.' Jake sat back in his chair, picked up his coffee cup and took a large drink. Tony had been known to have some crazy ideas in the past, but this was completely bonkers – and Jake was right in the middle of it!

* * *

After their meal, Tony drove to the street corner where he knew Bennie would be trading, as usual. He kept the same turf, so that people would know when and where to find him. As Tony and Jake walked up to him, they could see that Bennie had been badly beaten up. His eyes were swollen and turning purple, and there was a cut on his lip that had been bleeding.

'Get away from me, Antony, man, pretending to be my friend and letting me introduce you to the boss, knowing all the time I was going to get into serious trouble. How could you do that?' Bennie turned his back on them. He took out his hip flask and took a sip of rum.

Tony looked at Jake. He felt guilty about what had happened. The mob boss was supposed to be a friend of Bennie's; they had worked together for a long time, dealing drugs. The boss was the supplier and Bennie was the trader. Did friendship count for nothing?

A man walked up to Bennie. Tony and Jake watched as the stranger whispered something to him and pressed some money into his hand, then Bennie reached into his inside pocket and took out a small package, which he gave to the man. The stranger didn't acknowledge Tony and Jake; he could only presume they were there for the same thing.

'Sorry, Bennie,' said Tony. 'Honestly, I didn't think he would do that to you. What happened?'

'You were recognised. When the boss found out you were the man that carved Lee up that day, he went ape. He said he could have been killed, and I just took you in there, like you were a friend.'

The boss had got his men to throw Bennie out into the alley and give him a good kicking, as punishment.

'They kept blaming me and saying that you could have been armed and shot the boss, and it was all my doing.' Bennie wiped a little blood away that had dripped from his lip.

'I'm really sorry, Bennie,' said Jake.

'Be warned, Antony, my man, it isn't just the guys that you saw in there. There were others in the back room, and believe me, what they did to me is nothing compared to what they have planned for you. I heard everything.' He pointed a finger at Tony and took another sip from his hip flask.

'Will they definitely come to the pub tonight, do you think, Bennie?' said Tony.

'Oh, yes, man, they coming, especially that cocaine-loving brother with the patchwork back. He doesn't pay for the goods, either. If I don't give, I look like this. Be warned, you boys are dead meat, especially you, Antony. He can't think straight on all that stuff he takes.'

Tony looked at Jake; this was actually good news. He had left the bait and hoped that curiosity would cause this boss or his men to come to the pub tonight, but now he knew for definite they would be there, for revenge.

Again, they waited while someone tapped Bennie on the shoulder and whispered to him; the exchange was made and the stranger walked away. It was all done very discreetly.

'I'll sort it out for you, Bennie, I promise,' said Tony. He remembered when Bennie had once got him something to eat when he'd been starving on the streets. He looked at his friend's broken, swollen face and regretted his actions. His cockiness had done this; trying to prove himself had got his old friend beaten up.

'I need you to trust me one last time. I promise, I will sort this out, but I need one small favour off you, and it is small, if what you're saying is true.'

Bennie adjusted his hat and, as much as they could, his eyes widened. 'A favour? No way. I want no part in your fight. Sure, he beats me up now and again, but he's a regular supplier. I don't bite the hand that feeds me, boy.'

Tony opened his wallet and took out fifty pounds. 'This is so you're not out of pocket.' He offered the money to Bennie.

Bennie looked at the money in Tony's hand. Money always spoke to Bennie; it was his only language. He smiled his golden smile and said, 'Is that for me?'

Tony nodded.

'Okay, Antony, what is it you want so badly? And how are you going to look after your old friend, Bennie?'

The ice had thawed; Bennie was smiling again. He looked around furtively and took the money out of Tony's hand.

'All I want is for you to give more than the usual amount of cocaine to those guys. We both know they'll have been sniffing it all evening before they turn up at the pub to kill me. Go and give them more of it, as a friendly gesture to say sorry for your stupidity, eh?'

'That it?' Bennie grinned; this was easy money. He would be threatened into handing it over, anyway, so he might as well give it freely and get some cash off Tony, as well.

'Consider it done, Antony, my boy.' Bennie straightened himself up and adjusted his hat and his coat against the night air. 'Be careful, boy, and be lucky.'

Tony nodded at him and looked at Jake. 'Time to go and have some fun. One more hour, Jake, and we're done.'

Tony started to walk back to the car. It had been a long day, and he was stressed and tired, but now he was on a roll. There was no turning back.

Now Jake knew what to expect, he felt more at ease, although all of this seemed to be turning into some sort of horror film. Did everyone but him think this was normal life?

Tony drove the car to the East End and parked up around the

corner from the Crown. He sat in the car and looked around, then saw exactly what he was looking for; the usual crowd of youths were hanging around on the street corner. They were always there, some group of teenagers with nothing to do and nowhere to go. They were the usual troublemakers who scared the neighbourhood.

Tony wound down the car window and shouted to them. 'Hey, guys, you look like you need some fun. Come here.'

The group of teenagers, all wearing black hoodies, looked up when they heard his voice. One took a large draw on his cigarette and blew the smoke out through his nose. He swaggered closer.

'What do you want, mister? Can't you see we're busy?' He put his cigarette back in his mouth and took another drag, then blew the smoke out towards Tony, as though trying to prove he was some hard-faced ringleader, in front of his friends. He was obviously the main man to speak to.

Tony smiled to himself; he liked this boy's arrogance, it reminded him of himself. He got out of the car and got the bag from the boot. It was filled with the things he had purchased earlier, in Chinatown. He handed it over to the boy.

The boy looked inside the bag.

'The big one goes in the Crown; if you have the guts, that is.' Tony was teasing him in front of his friends, knowing there was no way this boy wanted to lose face.

The teenage boy looked at Tony.

Tony took twenty pounds out of his wallet. 'As I say, the big one goes in there, in one hour, or are you chicken?'

'For the record, I'm not chicken, but why in there? Mick's okay, he gives us crisps and stuff.' He gave Tony a stubborn glare. Tony withdrew the hand holding the money and reached for the bag to take it away.

'Never mind, kid, I'll find someone else to play my joke on Mick.

I just thought you might be up to it.' Tony knew it was too tempting for the boy to let it go.

'One hour, you say, mister, and then we can let them all off.'

Tony nodded.

'And just the big one in there, is that right?'

'One hour, and counting.' Tony smiled at the teenager.

The kid smiled back. He had a bag full of enormous fireworks – large rockets, the kind they used for the Chinese New Year display – and this guy wanted him and his mates to have a little fun and let them off. This was going to be the best night they'd had in ages!

'Oh, and for the record, we never had this meeting. After all, I know where to find you.' Tony handed over the twenty pounds, got back into the car, wound up the window, and drove off.

'What a cheeky little sod, eh?' Tony laughed. 'I like him, Jake, I'm sure I can come up with some other things for him and his bored mates to do. Right, let's park here and walk.'

Tony turned into a side street and parked the car, then they both got out and walked back down the street. They disappeared into the darkness of an old alley, opposite the Crown.

'Bloody hell, Tony, it's freezing. Why are we standing in a cold dark alley, watching a pub?' said Jake. He was rubbing his hands together to try and get warm and wrapping his coat around him.

'Apart from the fact that Sharon must be really pleased you're out of the house and not moaning your head off to her, as you are me, we're here to watch those guys turn up. Once we know they're there, we can make ourselves scarce.'

Jake looked up; he couldn't see Tony's face, it was so dark down the alley. When he looked towards the top of it he saw two cars turn up and park, badly, outside the Crown. Five men got out. He recognised one of them who'd been at the pub when Bennie had introduced them to his boss.

Jake and Tony watched them all walk into the pub. They could see the guys were armed, and that they were either very drunk or drugged up. Possibly both. It looked like Bennie had kept his word.

'God help Mick and whoever else is in there, Tony; that lot are off their heads. Have you seen the state of the cars? They're not parked, they've just been stopped in the middle of the road. One of them still has the door open. They're gunning for you, Tony, they want to kill you. Let's get out of here; our work is done.'

'Order a takeaway and get it delivered to your house. We'll be there, soon, and I really don't fancy Sharon's cooking tonight, not after the day we've had.' He nudged Jake in the ribs as they walked back to the car.

Jake burst out laughing. 'You know what, Tony? Neither do I, but don't tell her I said that.'

18

A WELCOME PROPOSITION

It had been a couple of days since that fateful night at the pub, and Tony had heard nothing. He was beginning to wonder whether those teenage kids had kept their word. He'd expected someone would have been in touch by now.

There was some good news: the police came and informed him that their inquiries into Eddie's murder had drawn a blank and they were closing down the investigation. It would stay on record as an open case, but without additional information, it was a dead duck. The club was cleared of all police and Tony was handed the keys and told he could go in and take it over, if that was what he wanted. Even the police looked hesitant at the thought of that.

Tony and Jake headed for the club later that day, intending to take stock and make a start on clearing it out. Tony tore down the police tape that was still on the doors and kicked away the pieces that had been left on the ground.

He put the key in the door, then hesitated and looked at Jake.

'You ready for this?' said Jake.

Tony nodded. 'Yeah, I think so.' He felt an odd mix of excitement and dread – excitement that the place was now his to manage and dread at the thought of what he might find, especially in the small office. The last time he had been in there, he had shot Eddie Rawlings in the head as revenge for betraying him. He knew Eddie's body had been removed, but wondered what might have been left behind.

'Come on then, let's go,' said Jake.

Tony turned the key in the lock and pushed the door open, and he and Jake entered the dark, gloomy, dusty club.

'Oh, Jesus, that's rank!' said Jake. He wafted his hand in front of his face.

'It stinks,' said Tony. The air was stale and fetid, and the buzz of flies could be heard from further inside the building. The police had made their own mess, and there were also plenty of partially full pint glasses on the bar. Patches of mould bloomed on the surfaces.

They looked around the club then turned and looked at each other. 'It's going to be one hell of a job to get this place up and running, mate, it's more of a dump than ever,' said Jake.

Tony nodded; they'd have their work cut out, no doubt about it. 'Come on, let's see the full horror.'

He walked to the back room where he had shot Eddie. It looked exactly the same as the last time he had been there. He looked at the chair Eddie had been sitting in when he killed him and had a flashback to the sight: his shocked expression, the hole in his head. He swallowed; at least there was no blood to clean up. Everything else would be thrown out, with the rest of the rubbish.

Tony felt better having faced his fears. He took off his jacket and hung it on the peg on the back of the door. 'Right, Jake, let's get to work,' he said.

He walked back into the main area of the club, taking in everything that needed doing to the place. There were areas he hadn't been in before, and he went to explore those, next.

'Is that the living quarters up there?' said Jake. They were standing at the bottom of a flight of stairs.

'I suppose so,' said Tony. 'Come on, let's have a look.'

They climbed up the painted wooden stairs, pushed open a door and found they were in a large apartment. It was filthy, which was no surprise, but it was spacious. There were three bedrooms, a big kitchen, a roomy lounge, and a bathroom, and it was right in the middle of the West End.

Jake let out a low whistle. 'This has to be worth a fortune on the property market,' he said.

They opened wardrobes and drawers in the master bedroom and found some of the bossman's clothes – half-decent suits, ruined by the smell of tobacco.

'He must have stayed here when he couldn't be arsed to go home,' said Tony, remembering the bossman's wife and the fling they'd had – and what it had cost him.

'And when he was entertaining his tart,' said Jake. A couple of plates sat on a bedside cabinet. They contained half-eaten sandwiches, and were surrounded by flies. Jake gagged. 'Open the bloody windows before I throw up.'

Tony threw the bedroom window open, and tried shooing the flies out. He opened the windows in the other bedrooms and the lounge, then they went into the kitchen, where French windows led onto a small balcony. Tony parted a dirty net curtain and opened them, then stepped outside. From where he stood on the small balcony he could see all of the theatres surrounding the area.

'The place is a pigsty; it's going to cost a fortune to make it liveable,' said Jake.

'Be worth it, though,' said Tony. He could visualise the apartment as he would have it. As much as Jake was disgusted with the place – and he was right to be, at the moment – it would look stunning after a full refurbishment. How wasted it had been.

'You're making plans, aren't you?' said Jake. He knew the signs.

'We're going to make a fortune, Jake. Admittedly, not as quickly as I would like, but I'm going to sell my apartment and eventually move in here.' Tony stepped back inside.

Jake coughed. He still had his hand over his mouth and nose to try to avoid the worst of the stench. He had an idea; he knew Tony wouldn't be over the moon with it, but he reckoned it was worth suggesting.

'It could take a while to sell your place, then to get the apartment ready. You can live with me and Sharon while you're waiting, but instead of paying bank loan interest rates' – he paused, then plunged on – 'why not ask Miriam to lend you the money until your place is sold? Then you can pay her straight back.'

Tony shook his head. There was no way he was going to do that; he was going to do this on his own.

'No, listen, Tony, I'm not saying ask her to just give you the money, what I'm saying is, ask Miriam for the bridging loan. The interest rates at the bank will be ridiculous and you might need the money for a while. Instead of forking over cash to the bank, you could be investing it in the club. Miriam will only want her capital back. So, you're not going cap in hand, asking for charity, you're going to do it on your own, just without interest.'

Tony thought what Jake said made sense, but he still didn't like the idea of it. He rummaged in a cupboard and found some bin bags. 'Come on,' he said, 'let's get some of this stuff bagged up.'

'If you don't want to ask Miriam, you could use our house as collateral for a loan,' Jake said, as he dropped stale food and maggoty plates into a bin bag.

'Not a chance!' said Tony. 'That's an even worse suggestion than asking Miriam. I bought that house for you; I'm not going to take it back.'

'You wouldn't be, you'd be leveraging an asset.'

'Not my asset to leverage, mate.'

'Okay, well what about Ralph Gold?' The surfaces in the kitchen had been cleared, so they moved into the main bedroom.

'What do you mean?'

'Well, it's his club, why isn't he paying for the refurb?'

'It's my club, well, it will be. Ralph Gold isn't selling yet, but he will I'm sure of it. Don Carlos will see to it. I have savings Jake, you know that. I still have my share from Miriam's money, but for what I want it isn't going to be enough. I want it all Jake.' Tony stressed, 'This is my dream and if I have to sleep with Ralph Gold for this club I bloody will!'

Jake noticed a familiar look in Tony's eyes; they always seemed to change colour with his mood. All Jake could see was a washed out club and a flee pit flat, but Tony saw it all differently. This was his chance to be someone. To make his mark on the world. He would use his savings and anything else he could get his hands on.

Laughing, Jake looked across at Tony. 'Firstly mate, I don't think your Ralph Gold's type. Not from what I hear anyway. You might be blond but, you don't have the tits for it,' he joked, 'but, on a serious note Tony. It's not your club yet, and it may never be, come to that. For now, you're the manager.' Jake started piling the bossman's clothes into a bin bag, avoiding Tony's eyes.

'They're putting us to the test,' said Tony, 'and we, and I emphasise the word, "we", are going to sort it all out. Any money he puts into the place will only add to the price, when I buy it. That is why I want to pay for it. He will also see that I mean business and I'm not going cap in hand to him for him to decorate it the way he wants it.' Biting his bottom lip Tony nodded. 'I tell you what, if he doesn't sell the club to us, then I will make a point of asking for the money we've poured into the place to make it liveable. I think they would pay up, don't you?' Tony wasn't sure himself. He knew he probably sounded foolish to Jake, but Don Carlos seemed like a good man.

'That's fair, but I think you should make that known before you use up every penny you have including anything you might borrow. This place is going to take a fortune to make it into something decent people would want to spend time in. Don't get in over your head,' Jake stressed.

'I want it to have the very best Jake. A place where people are gagging to go to and boast about when they have been to it. This isn't going to be a night club. This is going to be the most infamous nightclub in London. Ours Jake. This is our future.' Tony was almost shouting, as his ambitions and feelings got the better of him.

'Well, then, ask Miriam.' Jake looked at Tony. 'It makes good business sense, and you know it.' He opened another drawer and started to clear it out. 'You and your damn pride.'

Tony made his mind up and nodded at Jake. 'Okay, I'll ask Miriam.'

By the time they'd cleared the detritus, both upstairs and down, and taken all the rubbish bags outside, they'd done as much as they could for the time being. They left the upstairs windows open, just a little, and then left. The place needed airing before they could do anything else to it, and they both decided they knew just the woman who would enjoy the task of turning this hovel into a home: Elle.

* * *

When Tony eventually got home to his own apartment, the first thing did was clean himself up. He felt filthy after spending time in the club. As he showered, he tried to mentally calculate how much he might get for his apartment. He'd decided to make the telephone call to Miriam straight away, and needed to work out what he would ask her for. He hated doing it, but it was worth a try.

When Tony went to the phone, he noticed his answerphone was

flashing. He pressed the button on the machine, and heard the voice of Mick, the landlord from the Crown. With his towel still wrapped around his waist, he put his hands on his hips and smiled smugly to himself, while listening to the message. This was what he had been waiting for.

'Tony, lad, erm, sorry, Mr Lambrianu, would it be convenient for you to come to the Crown, around midday tomorrow? I and some of the other publicans and businessmen in the area would like a word with you, please.'

'Mr Lambrianu': Tony liked that. Things must have gone better than expected, if Mick was calling him 'Mr' and had corrected himself after calling him 'Tony' and 'lad'.

Now, it was time to make the telephone call to Miriam. Jake was right, the interest they would pay on the loan would be wasted money.

Miriam was pleased to hear from him, and asked all about him. Tony was happy about this, because it paved the way for what he wanted to ask her. He told her about the club and what his plans were, but avoided asking for money directly. Instead, he said he would have to ask the bank for a bridging loan until his apartment was sold and that could take a while. He could use his apartment as collateral, until it was sold and then he could pay the loan off. He winced inside as he said it. He swept his hand through his hair, waiting for a response. He was just about to ask outright, when Miriam scolded him and told him not to be such a fool, when she could easily lend him the money.

He realised she knew why he was ringing her and he felt embarrassed; he hardly knew the woman, and here he was asking her for money. He put on a surprised voice, and assured her that wasn't why he had called her. The lie sounded hollow and he knew it.

'Antonias, my boy. You have many friends and people who love you, but I am your family. You should always come to me. If I can be of any help to you, I will be. I will get some money transferred to you immediately.'

Tony felt a lump in his throat, and a tear came to his eye. Yes, she was his family, and this wasn't the first time she had helped him out. He suddenly felt compelled to say something.

'Thank you, Grandma.' It was the first time he hadn't called her 'Miriam', but accepted her for who she was. His family, the only real family he had. He put the telephone down and brushed the tears from his eyes. He was grateful no one had been there to see them.

He composed himself, got dressed, and then rang Jake and told him all about the meeting at the pub tomorrow. He had saved the message on his answerphone for Jake to hear when he came around. Then he told him, that 'Grandma' was going to send him some money to sort the club out.

Jake immediately picked up on the word 'Grandma', but didn't say anything. He was glad that Tony was accepting her at last. Whatever had gone on before with Tony's mother hadn't stopped Miriam searching for her grandson. It warmed him to think maybe, somewhere inside, Tony was finding peace.

The next thing they had to do was speak to Elle. Tony and Jake both went to visit her and, as always, it was like the prodigal sons returning home. Elle fed them and fed them until they were fit to burst, while listening to all their plans.

'The thing is, Elle, we're not so good at organising cleaning and stuff. We wondered if maybe you and some friends or someone could help,' said Jake. He was giving her his boyish grin, and had his arm around her waist.

'I knew you two wanted something.' She ruffled his hair. 'Of course I'll help you, although from what you say, it's going to need an army. Minnie used to do some cleaning for an agency, so maybe she could get some others to help, as well.'

Elle stood in between her 'boys'. They each had an arm around her waist and kissed her on each cheek. 'Thanks, Elle,' they said, in unison.

* * *

The next day, Tony took his time getting ready for the midday meeting at the Crown; he wanted to look the part. If you were going to be the boss, then you had to look like one – unlike the bossman, with his cheap suits covered with cigarette ash.

He checked his tie and then his watch for the hundredth time. He didn't want to appear too eager; he needed to be cool and calm, with an air of authority. He felt like a stiff drink, but apart from the fact that he would be driving, he remembered Don Carlos's words about not drinking when discussing business.

After he picked up Jake, he began to feel better. He parked up and they both sat in the car, around the corner from the pub, and waited until quarter past twelve. Again, Tony didn't want to appear to be too eager. When it was time, they both straightened their ties, cleared their throats and gave each other a high five.

When they got closer to the pub, they were surprised to see that a couple of the windows were boarded up. Tony pushed the door, but it was locked. They shared a look; had they walked into an ambush? Who was behind that closed door waiting for them?

'Let's go, Tony, I don't like it,' said Jake. 'This whole set up doesn't feel right.'

Tony had to agree; something was definitely wrong for the pub to be shut at that time of day. They were about to walk away when they heard the bolts on the other side of the door being moved across and then Mick opened the door.

'I've been looking out for you both,' said Mick. 'I forgot to mention the pub was closed.' He opened the door wide and waited for them both to walk in.

The devastation that greeted them was shocking. The pub was a bombsite. There were bullet holes in the walls and patches of plaster had come off. Another part of the pub looked as though there had been a fire there: the ceiling was blackened and the walls were smoke-damaged. The boarded-up windows cast a dim light over the place, making it eerie to stand in.

They could see Mick and his family had been cleaning up. Despite the devastation, the floor was swept and the wooden chairs were, as per usual, stacked on the tables. Mick walked through the pub and to the stairs to the family home.

'Sorry about all the mess. I've got to leave it as it is until the coppers are finished and the insurance investigators have been and had a look,' he said. 'Obviously, I can't open up when it's in this state.'

Tony and Jake glanced at each other, but said nothing. They followed Mick upstairs to a bright and airy flat. It was a typical family home, with children's shoes scattered on the landing and coats on the banister. Mick walked them through to the large kitchen. Seated around a table, mugs of tea and coffee in hand, was a group of people, mainly publicans they knew from around the area. Mick's wife, Shirley, was also there.

When they saw Mick enter the room with Tony and Jake, the conversation stopped and the men stood up. Again, Jake and Tony cast a furtive glance at each other; this situation was getting stranger and stranger. They were given chairs and invited to sit down at the table. Everyone sat, but no one spoke. The atmosphere was tense and strained.

Tony decided to take the lead. 'So, gentlemen,' he said, 'what can we do for you?'

It seemed Mick had been nominated as spokesperson. 'I don't know where to start, really,' he said. He took his wife's hand. She was not only the tea-maker, she was sitting in on the meeting in her own right, as the landlady of the Crown.

'As you both can see, by the state of the pub, I've had a bit of trouble.' Mick put his hands to his face and they heard him stifle a sob. 'My bloody kids were up here in bed, while that madman was waving a gun around downstairs, shooting the walls and the ceiling,' he said, his voice anguished. He rubbed his face and tried to compose himself.

Jake could see he was distressed and tried to comfort him the best way he could. 'Okay, Mick, take a breath and tell us what happened.' Nothing was said for a long moment, so he looked at the rest of them gathered around the table. 'Are any of you going to help Mick out?'

One by one, all the publicans spoke up, then talked over each other. Once they were in their stride, the story started to unravel and Jake and Tony learned about the gruesome goings on in the pub.

As Jake and Tony already knew, a few of the South London mob had gone into the busy pub. They had ordered many double whiskies, and Mick had given them, not knowing what else to do, although he could see they had already had more than their fair share. They were loud and they were threatening some of the regular customers. It was pretty obvious they had gone there for a fight. They had each, in turn, pushed customers out of the way and tipped up tables, as they searched the pub, including the toilets.

Then, to the horror of Mick and his wife, two of the men had run upstairs, shouting and screaming, and had pushed open the doors of the kids' bedrooms. One had grabbed Mick's wife, Shirley. 'Where's that blond bastard?' he had screamed at her, his face so close and his anger so intense that when he shouted, he was spitting in her face. Crying and struggling to free herself of the hand that gripped her throat, she had sworn she didn't know who he was talking about. The man had pushed her aside and immediately she had run to her children's aid, gathering them to her while the men searched their flat.

Downstairs, Lee, the man intent on killing Tony, had laid out a line of cocaine on the bar and, ignorant of customers watching him, started snorting it up his nostrils. Suddenly, there had been a loud bang and a lot of smoke, followed by more loud bangs and flashes of light. Some young hooligans from the neighbourhood, known troublemakers, had set off a load of fireworks. Some, including a large rocket, were thrown into the pub. The noise had been deafening, causing panic amongst the customers. The smoke from the fireworks seemed to form a large curtain of smoke, almost a fog.

Lee still sat at the bar, sniffing cocaine. He heard the bangs and saw the smoke and instantly took his gun from his jacket pocket and randomly started shooting. In his drunken, drugged up state he had thought the bangs were gunshots.

Jake looked at Tony; he was listening, but found the story hard to stomach, knowing they had both caused this mayhem.

There had been a few casualties. People had fallen and got trodden on while people were rushing towards the doors. A couple of them been shot; they had escaped death, but had flesh wounds. The fireworks that had gone off and seemed to be going on forever continued to cause an even thicker smokescreen; people were coughing and choking, trying to escape.

One of the men that had been upstairs ran down to see what was going on. He pointed his own gun towards the noise of the gunshots in the pub and fired several shots. The shooting stopped and he went over to see who he'd hit. He was shocked to see that he had killed his own brother. Lee was lying lifeless on the floor with a single bullet through his chest, and the floor was covered in blood.

Someone had obviously heard the gunshots and seen the mayhem, and called the police. They arrived in their droves. Having heard there had been gunshots, they had called in the armed police as backup.

When they finally stopped talking, Mick let out a huge sigh. 'Basically, that's it; well, the short version, anyway. You can imagine the rest... police interviews and so on. The gang were all arrested, but being totally off their heads on drugs they were fighting with the coppers, right up until they were handcuffed and thrown into the back of a van. Lee's brother put his gun in his mouth and shot himself.'

As Tony and Jake listened, the blood drained from their faces. They could see everyone else in the room was badly shaken up. It had been worse than even Tony had imagined it might be.

Thank God I wasn't there, he thought to himself. I would have been dead by now if I had been.

Trying hard to remain composed, Tony looked around the room at the people there. 'Obviously, I'm sorry to hear this, Mick, I really am, but I don't understand why you've asked me here today.' Tony and Jake watched them all, in turn, look at each other, confused.

Mick's wife, a forthright woman who'd had enough of all this pussyfooting around, stuck her chin out and pouted. 'Well, if they're not going to say it, I will. You're the blond one they were looking for, aren't you?'

Tony put his hand up to stop her speaking further and stood up. 'Come on, Jake, we're leaving.'

'No! Wait!' Mick's wife sounded panicky. 'I didn't mean that, it's just that it was going to take five of them to take down one of you. And you, of course,' she said, as she looked at Jake apologetically. He just smiled at her. 'Please sit down Mr... erm...' She looked at Mick.

'Mr Lambrianu. This is Tony Lambrianu, love, and this is Jake Sinclair.'

'Please, sit down,' said Shirley. 'I'll put the kettle on and make some tea for us all, then we can talk.' She stood up to busy herself at the kitchen worktop.

Mick's wife may have blurted out what they were all thinking, but you could see by the expressions on all of their faces that they were relieved that someone had said it.

Tony and Jake pulled out their chairs and sat back down again. Emotions were running high.

This was what Tony had fought for, this was one of his dreams. He didn't want to go into the pubs shouting threats at the landlords and demanding money for protection. He had wanted them to ask him, then it would be their choice. Gratitude, loyalty, respect, that was how Tony saw it. There would be no violence, just a civilised business arrangement between the publicans and himself. They were scared and at their wits end; they needed him.

'They'll probably burn our pubs down for refusing to pay them for protection, but what have we got to lose? Look around you, they've already done that, Mr Lambrianu. Mick's out of pocket, this is his livelihood, God knows when he's going to get the pub up and running again. You came around the other day offering protection at a price and stupidly, because we were scared, we turned you away. That South London scum had already been with their threats and we had no choice but to pay them.' The publican slammed his hand down on the table and stood up in despair. 'We're all losing business; nobody wants to come around here for a quiet drink. Can you help us, Mr Lambrianu, or not?' He sounded desperate, but defiant, raising the question to Tony as if it was a challenge.

Tony sat forward and scanned the room, then he looked at Jake and smiled. Looking back at the group of men before them he said, 'Yes, I can, if you want me to, but I don't offer security and protection for nothing.'

Mick's wife put two mugs of steaming tea in front of Tony and Jake, passed them the milk jug and sugar bowl, and smiled.

'We know we have to pay, Mr Lambrianu, that's the name of the game around here, isn't it?' one of the publicans said. 'But, can you offer us the kind of protection that will keep us safe from those people? We pay to keep the bad guys out, we don't pay them to come in and fire guns at our customers.' They all nodded in unison at what he had said.

Tony gave Shirley a charming smile, took a sip of his tea and thanked her for it. He was thinking fast. 'Firstly, Mick, you can't pay me anything with no money coming in. Get some workmen in and get the place decorated for opening. I'll lend you the money until your insurance comes through; no interest. It's in my interests that there's money in your cash register, okay?'

Tony and Jake watched as they all nudged each other, smiling and nodding approvingly at this gesture of good faith. That was what they needed, someone they could ask for help when they needed it.

'The South London mob won't bother you again, I promise you. Leave that to me and Jake. That's our business. You sort out your own businesses, with peace of mind.'

Shirley had tears rolling down her face and couldn't stop thanking them both. She looked as though she was going to hug them, but stopped herself short. She knew the insurance company would take at least a month to pay up – that is, if they were going to pay up at all.

Jake spoke up and asked her how her children were. She dried her eyes and explained to Jake that she had sent her children to her mother's house, until they got themselves sorted out. The youngsters were badly shaken up.

Again, this was showing a touch of humanity and concern for the people they would be doing business with. The people round that table could all see now, Jake was the reasonable one and Tony was the fighter. They all looked pleased and more relaxed. Mick was a well-respected publican; the other businessmen in the area trusted his judgement. They felt he had done the right thing by asking Tony and Jake for help.

The meeting carried on in an informal manner. Each, in turn, discussed their terms of payment. They told Tony and Jake how many other businessmen in the area also wanted to be under their protection, but explained that they couldn't all attend today; they were waiting for Mick to sort out a meeting, first. They all shook hands and Tony told them he would be in touch, then left.

Back in the car, Tony and Jake each let out a deep sigh. They had been keeping their feelings in, as they watched everyone fall apart before their eyes.

'For Christ's sake, Tony, did you expect all that to happen? Poor sods, what a mess they're in.'

Tony ran his hands through his hair and laid his head back on the seat of the car. 'No way did I expect to hear all that. I do feel guilty about Mick's wife and kids, though.' His voice was low, almost a whisper. He straightened himself up, and took a breath. 'Right, Jake, one last hurdle. Let's go and see that mob boss, talk some terms and get the ground rules sorted out.' With that, he started the car and drove off towards South London. Tony worked best on adrenaline. He was now in charge and people were depending on him; all he had to do was prove himself.

* * *

Tony and Jake walked into the pub where the mob boss lived and, now knowing the way, went through the door marked 'staff only' and on up the stairs to his office and living quarters. The boss was shocked; he had heard footsteps and presumed it was one of his own men, but no, it was that blond nuisance and his partner.

Three tall black men walked forward and took guns out of their waistbands. Tony and Jake swallowed hard. Maybe this was a mistake; it was pretty obvious that these guys meant trouble. They looked as if they were going to take great pleasure in beating them both up and possibly killing them. All they needed was the nod of approval from their boss and it would all kick off.

Tony acted as cool as ice and ignored them; even though inside he was shaking, he didn't want to show it.

'I come in peace,' he said, and smiled at the boss. 'I'd like a truce, and I have a proposition for you.' He hoped his words might at least provoke some curiosity in the boss's mind.

The boss looked Tony up and down with a sneer on his face. This man had wandered into his office, without invitation; he had caused a war and two of his men were dead. Three others were remanded in jail, facing a host of charges too long to list. What trouble had this blond upstart come to cause now?

He looked at his three bodyguards, their guns in their hands, just waiting for the 'okay' from him, and then looked back at Tony and Jake. If nothing else, he thought to himself, this man has a lot of guts. It was either that or he had a death wish.

The boss waved his men away. 'Sit down,' he said to Tony and Jake, then he fixed his eyes on Tony. 'You've got five minutes; now, say what's on your mind and get out, before the boys get itchy fingers with those guns.'

Tony and Jake glanced at each other as they took their seats; this was a huge improvement on last time; for a start, they were offered a chair. Fortunately, as Tony hadn't wanted to feel vulnerable and at the mercy of the boss's men when he walked in there again, he had taken his own gun, just in case they had need to shoot their way out. Stupid, he thought to himself, that this boss didn't have his men check us for weapons. He would have had them searched.

His faithful gun made him feel safe and on level ground with these trigger-happy thugs. He remembered fleetingly the night he had picked it up off the ground, when this very same gang had gone to cause trouble at the club he now managed, where he was meeting a woman he'd thought he loved and ended up fighting alongside Eddie Rawlings. A lot had happened since that night.

Now seated and at eye level with the boss, Tony started again. 'As I said, I would like a truce between us. I've heard you've had some trouble, and I've come to assure you it was none of my doing. Now you have the police breathing down your neck and who knows what they'll discover.'

Tony turned his head to the table at the far side of the room, where some men were bagging up cocaine for sale. The boss followed Tony's eyes and then looked back at Tony and Jake, still saying nothing.

'The publicans from the East End have approached me to take over the protection in the area. It seems they've lost faith in your men,' said Tony. He made it sound light-hearted and nonchalant, not threatening or sarcastic. 'I didn't have to tell you that, but I want to start out by being honest with you.' They could both see that the boss was listening; they also knew, following recent events, this boss couldn't possibly think the men involved that night were worth his steady income. Even so, the silence was deafening.

Tony took a deep breath and started again. 'I want the territory in the East End, leading up to the West End. You have the south of London, leading up to wherever. That's none of my business. I have my turf and you have yours. I also know that you don't trust me. That feeling is mutual, I don't trust you, either. The bossman, as was, ripped you off constantly, which was what caused so much bad feeling between you. He was greedy, he wasn't a businessman. You are a businessman and so am I, and we have to start somewhere and build that trust. Don't you agree?' Tony paused, waiting for some kind of acknowledgement, but none came. On the other hand, he thought, we haven't been shot or thrown out yet and he is listening. He threw his hands up in the air and carried on, even though he felt his mouth going dry.

'Of course, you could have those guys put a bullet in my brain, right now, and who would know? Either Jake would shoot you, or you would end up in prison for the next twenty years, considering the police are not happy and know those guys work for you. You're their prime suspect. But where would that get us? There is money for both of us out there, we're not dogs fighting over a bone, we're businessmen. With us both dead, someone else would step in and take over, and we would both end up with nothing.' Tony finished his speech and swallowed; he licked his lips and waited for a response.

He could see the boss was listening; he didn't need any more trouble, either. The police had been all over his place and he'd had to flush a lot of his drugs down the toilet. A lot of money lost, and all for what? Revenge.

The boss sat back in his chair and folded his arms. He had listened to Tony, and to be honest, the last thing he wanted was any more dealings in the East End. The police were watching him and, after what had happened, no one would pay up anyway, and he knew Tony knew that. At last, he spoke.

'That bossman was always trying to swindle me. What makes you so different? And don't mess me about, man, I know it was you behind my men being arrested and killed. You planned it all, although you didn't get your hands dirty.' He nodded and smiled. 'Nice trick. Very clever, in fact. I've been asking around about you, blondie, and your man here. People say you're nuts, *loco*. Why should I listen to you?'

Tony smiled. 'I'm being straight with you now.' This man was serious about business, but obviously didn't trust anyone due to recent circumstances, and he had done his homework about him and Jake. Being called 'nuts' and 'loco' was not exactly a compliment, but it had served its purpose.

The boss cocked his head to one side, and looked at them both. 'South London is all mine, correct?' he asked. Tony nodded. 'I'll give you a three-month trial to prove yourself. I warn you, cross me and I'll put a bullet in your brain, no matter what.'

Tony felt like punching the air with excitement, but he remained calm. That would come later. He stood up, as though to leave, then had a second thought. 'You have the advantage over me,' he said. 'My name is Tony, Tony Lambrianu, and this is my brother, Jake. And your name is?' Tony waited. There was a pregnant pause. Possibly, he thought, this man has been called boss for so long he's forgotten his own name.

Tony and Jake watched as they saw the boss turn around and look at his men, then he turned back to face them. He reached out his hand to shake Tony's. 'They call me Marlon, remember that, Tony. As I said, do not cross me or tread on my toes. Three months is all you have to stay alive; three months, and counting.' Tony and Jake both shook his hand in turn, then left.

Back at the car, Tony was exuberant. He was all smiles and full of chatter, telling Jake about all the plans he had. His face was red with excitement and his blue eyes shone like sapphires.

Jake was laughing, but more in wonderment; he couldn't believe what had just taken place in there. 'You pulled it off, Tony! How the hell did you do it? My God, you have a lot of balls, walking in there like that.'

'*We* pulled it off, Jake.' Tony was emphatic. True, he had done most of the talking, but he couldn't have done it without Jake at his side, giving him confidence. 'Marlon is a businessman, he really doesn't need any more trouble. And when the publicans refused to pay his men, what was he going to do? Kill them all?'

They started to drive away. 'Come on Tony,' said Jake, 'let's drop the car off. I need a large, stiff drink after that and I'm sure you do, too.'

'Too bloody right! We do that and then we get down to business; we have a lot to do.'

Marlon started to count the previous day's takings that had been brought in. His three men approached and stood at the side of his desk, making him look up at them to see what they wanted.

'Are you sure you want to do business with him, boss?' said one of them. 'Why share it when we could have the east and south of London? We could have it all.'

Marlon stood up and slapped the man across the face, angry that his decision was being questioned. 'We're not sharing anything, moron, we'd already lost it. Look at the devastation that man has caused, and he wasn't even there. Yes, he is nuts, and he's dangerous. Now, I may as well trust him, but I'm going to watch him like a hawk, believe me, and you lot are not going to make any trouble. Let's see how it goes first, okay?'

They all nodded. There was a lot of sense in what the boss had said. Tony had just signed his own death warrant, if he crossed Marlon.

Back at Jake's house, he and Tony got out the champagne and popped the cork. Even though they were thoroughly mentally and physically exhausted from the last few days' events, they were laughing, slapping each other on the back and dancing around the room.

They were telling Sharon some of it, even though they saw her disapproving looks, but she was relieved that it all seemed to have gone okay. It had all been one big life-threatening risk but, as long as they could prove themselves to Marlon, everything would be okay. In fact, it would be better than okay; it would be great.

'Are you telling me,' she shouted over their laughter and excitement, 'that you two are now in charge of the protection racket in the East End? For real? Well, if that's the case, Mr Gangland Bosses, you're going to need some men of your own. You can't be everywhere at once, can you?'

Suddenly, in one fell swoop, Sharon had wiped the smiles off their faces. She was right, of course. Tony hadn't thought that far ahead; his only interest was sorting out the business side of things and making a deal with the publicans and the boss. Now realisation was dawning. As much as Sharon had laughed and joked about them being bosses, she was right. They were the bosses of the East End, now, and they couldn't look like amateurs. They needed a firm.

'I wouldn't want any of the same guys that were used by the bossman and Eddie,' Tony said, as the three of them sat around the kitchen table. 'We need new, fresh faces that no one knows.'

'You're right, Tony,' said Sharon. 'All those men know each other; they all took pleasure in ripping each other off, drinking the profits and causing trouble; that's not what you want. You have to look like a legitimate businessman, on the surface, at least. After all, you're soon going to be a club manager, and you haven't even got a drinks licence yet.' Both of them looked at Sharon; they were struck dumb. Bloody hell, she was right.

'I'm not going to get one, I've got a prison record,' said Tony. 'What the hell are we going to do?'

'I can get one,' said Sharon. 'I don't have a police record, nor have I been in prison.' She smiled at them both. 'Well, you two might be the godfathers, but it seems I'm the godmother.' They all burst out laughing.

* * *

Four months after the deal with Marlon had been shook on and, as there had been no complaints from either side, it seemed a mutual respect had begun. Even the police seemed satisfied that whatever deals were being done were all low key.

Tony and Jake had gone back to the Crown one evening and sought out the youth that had thrown the rocket in the pub. They had found him and his gang hanging around, as usual. They were known all around the streets as troublemakers and petty thieves, but Tony had other plans for them.

Again, as before, he had driven up to the corner where they all stood around, wearing their hoodies, making even the bravest people feel vulnerable, and called the ringleader over. Recognising the car, the youth had approached, and Tony wound the window down.

'You're a good guy,' said Tony, 'but I need another favour from you, a regular one, if you want it.'

The youth pulled his hoodie closer around his face, then leaned on the car. 'What's that, then?' he said, showing his usual bravado.

'I want you to be my eyes and ears. You know how to keep your mouth shut and I respect that, but I want these streets clean and I want you and your little friends to stop frightening the neighbourhood. I want you to look after it, for a change.' Tony knew he was challenging the boy, and he liked his spirit.

'How, mister? What do you want me to do, and how much are you paying?'

'You keep me informed of any strangers in the area, and tell me any gossip that may interest me. For that, I'll pay you fifty pounds a week – if you're up to it, of course. If you're no good to me, then you don't get your money.'

'You're that Lambrianu bloke they're all talking about, aren't you?' he said. 'Why do you want me to grass on people when you know everything, anyway?' Again, his tough manner made Tony smile; this teenager reminded him so much of himself.

'Yes, I am Tony Lambrianu, and because people say things in front of children that they wouldn't say in front of adults. Is it a deal, then?'

'Sixty pounds,' said the youth. 'And you won't be sorry, I know everything that goes on around here.'

'Done,' said Tony, and held out his hand to shake the teenager's grubby paw. 'What's your name?'

'Daniel,' said the teenager, 'but people call me Dan. Does that mean I work for you, now, then?'

Tony nodded and handed him a twenty-pound note for the time being, to set the wheels in motion. Obviously, Dan was going to enjoy the esteem of telling everyone he worked for Tony; it had given him a step up the ladder.

As they drove off, Jake turned to Tony, 'You're actually going to trust that little runt and pay him money?'

'I sure am, Jake. He knows these streets and everyone on them, and he'll be valuable. Stupid, though, if I were him I would have asked for a hundred pounds, I was expecting that, and I was prepared to pay it.'

* * *

When Tony's apartment was put up for sale, he moved his own things out and handed the keys over to the estate agent. The last thing he needed was to have to organise his life around property viewings. Initially, he would be staying at Jake and Sharon's house, until his exclusive apartment above the club in the West End was ready.

Jake had been right to suggest asking Miriam for the money to help them get by, because the apartment was taking time to sell and her money had allowed them to begin the refurbishment at the club. Miriam had been more than generous.

Elle was curious. 'Couldn't you have just bought the place at a knock down price Tony? You're spending a king's ransom on this place and it isn't yours.' Seeing the disappointed look on his face, Elle smiled. 'Although you're right, I'm sure they would pay any outstanding bills for refurbishment and as Jake is an accountant, he can keep all of the receipts'.

'They are testing me Elle, and if I lose my money then I do. At least I can say I've tried. In my opinion the only failures in life are the people who don't try.' Kissing her on the cheek, he gave her a cheeky wink.

Tony and Jake, under Elle's guidance, called in a building firm to rip out the guts of the building, bit by bit. Every stick of furniture, and even the doors and windows, had been removed. It had become an empty shell, a blank piece of paper to start afresh on. Some of the builders had renovated the living quarters, while others had taken the club apart. The only instructions he had given the builders and the designers were to make it a very light, modern bachelor apartment, suitable for entertaining.

They instantly knew what he meant – for entertaining females, something Tony just hadn't had time to think about for months. Now things were up and running, it was time for some light entertainment and some fun. The designers, knowing they had free rein and a blank cheque, worked their magic and transformed the place.

Sharon had applied for the necessary licences, and after weeks of investigations and checks, she had been given not only a drinks licence, but an entertainment licence, also. The licensee nameplate above the door read 'Sharon Sinclair'. Everything, finally, was coming up roses.

Tony was still fighting and getting his hands dirty; he wasn't prepared to sit back like the other bosses and let everyone else do his work for him. This way, he could keep in touch with everything, and make himself known to the possible troublemakers. They all soon learnt not to mess him around. Even though he appeared to be a calm, charming boss on the surface, they all saw that under-neath he was still Tony, the well-known leg-breaker, running all the usual protection rackets.

Tony liked the fact that fear awarded great power and both of those things brought wealth. He would never be poor again, scratching around on the streets, searching bins for pieces of left-over pizza and begging money from people passing by.

The work was pouring in, and the money was mounting up. Sharon had been right; they couldn't cope on their own any more, they needed help. They needed to look like a business, but the only people they knew were the same collectors they had hung around with when they were both collecting for the bossman. They had decided they wanted new people, fresh faces, not the same corrupt men they had worked with. The question was, who?

The last few months had been hard going, as they were managing the work at the club and the protection racket on their own, and then, on top of that, Tony had started a money-lending business. The owner of a local off-licence and grocery store wanted to extend the shop into a sort of mini-market. He mentioned that he had been to the bank to see if he could borrow some more money, but had only been offered half of what he'd asked for and needed.

Tony saw this as another opportunity to make money. He offered to lend the owner the 20,000 pounds he needed to extend his shop, but at a very high interest rate, and as collateral, he demanded the deeds to his house. The owner had seen it as a good offer. The shopkeeper had agreed to Tony's terms and, through a solicitor, had made a contract stipulating that once all the money was paid off, the deeds of his house would be returned. Each month, the man paid the amount agreed, plus the interest, and seemed very satisfied, so much so, word spread throughout the neighbourhood.

Before long, Tony was approached again, this time by a local restaurateur who wanted to redecorate. The man was already pleased that his windows were no longer being regularly broken by the neighbourhood gang of kids and nor did they hang around outside, intimidating would-be diners. He wanted to borrow money to do the place up to attract new customers, as the area felt safe again, something they all knew was down to Tony and Jake. The same arrangements were made and the debts were being repaid.

Sharon, who always seemed to think of the practical side of things and pour cold water on their grand schemes, had said they had a flourishing business, but no headquarters or office to do business from. It was time for them to think again.

'Badger,' said Tony one day, as they watched more scaffolding being erected around the club. He slapped his hand against his forehead. 'Why didn't I think of him before?' At last, he had the answer to his problems. Badger would have some contacts, especially the kind they needed for the work they did.

Jake frowned; he knew their workload was stressing them both out, but now he thought Tony was losing his marbles. 'Who the hell is Badger?'

'My old cellmate from prison. You met him once, remember? He's been in and out of prison so many times, he knows everyone. He's bound to know some ex-cons who can't find a job because of their record.'

Jake thought back, and then nodded. 'Yeah, I remember him now, but you can't be serious. They're all thieves and God knows what else, why would we employ those kinds of people?' When Jake saw Tony's stern expression, he wished he'd kept his mouth shut.

Tony raised one eyebrow and looked at Jake, his face serious. 'What, you mean ex-prisoners? Like me?'

'No, Tony, that wasn't what I meant and you know that. All I'm saying is, what makes you sure you could trust those guys?'

Tony took a deep breath before he spoke. He knew Jake didn't mean to put his foot in it, but there it was: the prejudice.

'Because,' Tony said, 'self-opinionated folk like you are not prepared to give those guys a second chance. They all have to report to a probation officer weekly and they are all trying to find jobs. That, Jake, is why they all end up back in prison again, they're living on meagre benefits and the future on the outside looks bleak.'

Jake could see Tony's reasoning and felt guilty about what he had said. He remembered how low and despondent Tony had been when he came out of prison; maybe he had a point. 'If they're on benefits and reporting to probation officers weekly, how are they going to work for us, cash-in-hand?'

'They won't be. It's all going to be above board; they'll be paying taxes and everything. Club bouncers with wage slips. Of course, what we give them cash-in-hand as a bonus is our business.' The more Tony thought about it, the more he liked the idea. Those guys would be grateful; if they messed up, that was their business, but he reckoned most would welcome the opportunity.

Tony contacted Badger and sure enough, he knew of a few good guys that were having a hard time now they were back in the real world. He gave Tony all the information he had about them and where they lived. Prisoners hardly ever spoke about their private life inside prison. It was personal.

Following Badger's leads, they managed to trace some of the men. Some were living in hostels, others were back with their families, living hand-to-mouth. Tony recognised that bored, depressed feeling they all seemed to have. He had felt like that, once, enough that he had worked for the bossman again. One of the men Tony and Jake visited was a mechanic from the garage he had worked in himself.

They used a backroom in one of the pubs to hold proper interviews for the jobs. They both outlined that they would be employed as security guards, for the Sinclair Security Agency, and would be paying tax. Of course, if they proved reliable, there would be bonuses. It was up to them to earn them.

Jake was surprised that they all seemed to jump at the chance with no arguments, they wanted that feeling of independence and a chance to work. In short, a little respectability.

Twelve of them were accepted; their crimes had been petty – nothing sexual and no drugs. One of them, John, had been the driver of a getaway car, and Tony chose him as his personal chauffeur.

At last, Tony's apartment was finished. The designers had telephoned him to come and see if he liked it. Inside the club, work was still ongoing. Wiring was hanging from the ceiling where the electricians were still working and the plasterers were making the walls more presentable. Jake and Tony walked up the new spiral staircase that had been put in place, opened the door and looked inside.

They were amazed, and stood in awe, just looking through the doorway. It was a beautiful, classy apartment, fit for royalty. The designers had really worked their magic and let their imaginations run wild. The kitchen floor was a grey marble. There was a glossy black breakfast bar, with a glitter sheen that sparkled in the shape of an 'L', for 'Lambrianu'. There was a fully fitted kitchen, with every appliance you could think of. There were white horizontal blinds hanging at all the windows. The lounge area had large cream leather sofas standing on dark cherry laminate flooring, and sheepskin rugs. And, at the head of the room, was a large white fireplace with a log burner. It was a totally different place.

The main bedroom made them both laugh out loud – what a

sight to behold. One wall was completely mirrored, making the room look larger. A king-size-plus black velvet bed dominated the room, and there was a full music system installed in the headboard. There was even a mini-bar against the wall.

'Bloody hell, Tony,' said Jake, laughing his head off and looking around the room, 'it looks like a tart's paradise.' They were both laughing, while looking around. This was definitely not the same dump the bossman had lived in, even though it did have its quirky points.

Tony's new workforce were all dressed in black suits and ties, and they were instructed to attend the gymnasium weekly. He didn't want fat, out-of-shape men, who didn't look and couldn't act the part.

His old apartment finally sold and the moment he got the money for it in his bank account, he transferred it all to Miriam. He wanted to look like a man of his word to her, and he vowed to himself that the rest would follow. At long last the designers and decorators were given the green light to work their magic in the club; if they did half as well as they had with his apartment, it would look fantastic.

Tony had his own vision for the club, and he discussed it with Jake and Sharon at their house. He had one selfish desire, and wanted to see what they both thought about it.

'Jake, Sharon, we're equal partners in everything we do, you know that, don't you.' Jake and Sharon both thought that Tony looked embarrassed. He was starting to blush and looking down at the table as he spoke. Sharon took hold of Jake's hand; what could possibly be so important to Tony that it made him look like a schoolboy in front of the headmaster?

They looked at each other. 'For God's sake, Tony, whatever it is, spit it out, will you?' said Sharon.

The air was tense; there was a dramatic pause, as they waited for Tony to speak.

'Well,' he said. He ran his hands through his hair, as though too nervous to say anything else. 'The designers want a name for the club, and as we haven't discussed it yet, I thought...' He coughed to clear his throat, then took a drink. Jake and Sharon both sat on the edges of their seats, waiting.

Tony looked down at the table and, almost in a whisper, he said, '"Lambrianu's", that's what I was thinking.'

Sharon and Jake both took a breath; was that what was causing all of this nervous tension? They squeezed each other's hands and nodded.

'Is that it?' said Jake. 'Is that the big secret idea?' He had been waiting for something far worse than this. 'I like it, Tony, it has a glamorous ring to it. What do you think, Sharon?'

She nodded and smiled. 'Definitely, it sounds classy.'

'What about you two, though?' said Tony. He was biting his bottom lip and still looked nervous.

Jake spoke first. '"Sinclair's" doesn't have the same glamorous ring to it, does it? And you deserve something. Sharon's name is above the door, apparently I own a security firm, so now it's your turn.' They all agreed it was a good name for the club, and then Tony went on to tell them, if they approved, he would like it in fancy pink neon writing. That shocked them both.

'Why pink, Tony? It's not very masculine, for a man of your reputation,' said Sharon.

Tony shook his head. 'I don't want it to be masculine. It's a night-club for men to bring their girlfriends to. It looks different and fancy.'

Jake raised his glass. 'Okay, here's to pink neon "Lambrianu's".' They all put their glasses together to seal the deal.

Tony had his own personal reasons for calling the club 'Lambrianu's'. People knew him, they feared him, but he wanted them all to see he had done well for himself. He wanted everyone who had looked down on him and dismissed him as a common street urchin to know that he was Tony Lambrianu, the man who had the best nightclub in town. He wanted to shout it from the rooftops.

'What if,' said Sharon, 'what if you can't afford to buy the club when the time is up? What happens then?' She was again baldly stating a fact that both Tony and Jake were conscious of, but had chosen to ignore.

Jake gave Sharon an angry glare. 'We'll cross that bridge when we come to it, won't we, Tony.' He didn't want Sharon killing Tony's dream. For once, he was happy. 'Anyway' – Jake laughed, trying to ease the tension – 'Tony has already said he's prepared to sleep with Ralph Gold. How could anyone turn that offer down!' This made them all laugh in turn.

Each day, in between seeing to his usual day-to-day business dealings, Tony popped into the club to see how they were doing. He loved watching this downtrodden dump rise like a phoenix from the ashes. He was like a kid in the run up to Christmas, anxiously waiting for the big day.

His name had already been put above the door by the sign makers and he loved just looking at it, switching it on and seeing the neon burn hot pink in the dark of evening. *Lambrianu's*.

Finally, he got the call to say that everything was ready for his final inspection. Tony grinned; he couldn't wait to see his club.

When he thought back over his life so far, he realised he'd played some very dangerous games, although possibly none so dangerous as facing up to the boss of the South London gang. Killing Eddie Rawlings had been a close second, but he'd got away with murder. Despite having seen hard times, he'd come out triumphant, the undisputed winner. He had money, looks, charm, and powerful allies. He'd achieved his dream and now had the club to manage. In less than a year, it would be his for real – he would own it outright. He refused to believe the deal could fall through. Don Carlos had proved to be a man of his word by organising his alibi and he had also reassured him that he would be able to afford the price Ralph Gold was asking for the club, but he had to prove himself a worthy owner of such a property. Tony felt that was fair, otherwise it was just another millstone around Ralph Gold's neck. And he would probably just sell off the land. Deep down he knew the club was his, which was why he had put his own stamp on it. Start as you mean to go on. With all of his money invested in it, how could Ralph Gold believe he wasn't serious about it? Mentally, he knew these were men to be trusted and Lambrianu's, the hottest nightclub in London, would be his for the taking!

Could life get any better than this? Tony Lambrianu couldn't wait to find out.

ACKNOWLEDGMENTS

Thank you to Sue and Avril for always supporting me. Many thanks to the Boldwood Team and especially Emily Ruston, my editor, for all her hard work and confidence in me.

Lastly, thank you to all of the readers new and old who have supported me through my writing journey.

MORE FROM GILLIAN GODDEN

We hope you enjoyed reading *Dangerous Games*. If you did, please leave a review.

If you'd like to gift a copy, this book is also available as an ebook, digital audio download and audiobook CD.

Sign up to Gillian Godden's mailing list for news, competitions and updates on future books.

http://bit.ly/GillianGoddenNewsletter

Gold Digger, another gripping read from Gillian Godden, is available now.

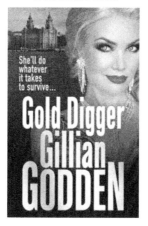

ABOUT THE AUTHOR

Gillian Godden is a Northern-born medical secretary for NHS England. She spent thirty years of her life in the East End of London, hearing stories about the local striptease pubs. Now in Yorkshire, she is an avid reader who lives with her dog, Susie.

Follow Gillian on social media:

 facebook.com/gilliangoddenauthor
twitter.com/GGodden

ABOUT BOLDWOOD BOOKS

Boldwood Books is a fiction publishing company seeking out the best stories from around the world.

Find out more at www.boldwoodbooks.com

Sign up to the Book and Tonic newsletter for news, offers and competitions from Boldwood Books!

http://www.bit.ly/bookandtonic

We'd love to hear from you, follow us on social media:

facebook.com/BookandTonic

twitter.com/BoldwoodBooks

instagram.com/BookandTonic

Printed in Great Britain
by Amazon